MARKED BY CAIN

A.R. ROSE

Editor: Virginia Carey

Proofreader: Nicole Bucciarelli

eBook ISBN: 979-8-9882875-0-6

Paperback ISBN: 979-8-9882875-1-3

OTHER TITLES BY A.R. ROSE

Ridgewood Series
Between the Flames
Wicked Games We Play
Marked By Cain

Standalones
Wreck Me
Only One Night

Twisted Heroes
A Captain So Callous and Cruel
Siren

With a Kiss
Sins of Sorrow
The Sinners
Sins of Bliss

To Amanda & April - my soulmates, my best friends. A little bit of the three of us lives within Rosie. Aplexda forever 🤍

A NOTE FROM A.R. ROSE

Marked By Cain is a contemporary romance novel created for adults. This story depicts dark adult scenes and situations.

Reader discretion is advised. Marked By Cain contains content that may be triggering for some.

Your mental health matters. For a full list of content warnings please visit www.authorarrose.com/content-warnings.

For those of you ready to begin, I hope you enjoy 

CHAPTER ONE

Rosie

Six Years Ago

"I'm not sure what you're not comprehending, Rosie. You either get a fucking job and throw down on a portion of the rent, or you find somewhere else to stay. It's not like you're doing anything else to help us with this fucking house." Brent slammed the dresser drawer shut, smashing the arm of a t-shirt as he did. My boyfriend was such an asshole—so hot and cold about literally everything.

"You can stay here as long as you need, babe."

"Don't worry about rent, babe. Focus on finding a job."

My plan was never to stay here permanently, but I needed more time to get on my feet. I just moved here because of him. We weren't serious enough to move in together, but a fresh start sounded like exactly what I needed, so I figured, why not? I'd get a studio, find a job, screw my boyfriend.

Life would be easy.

Except it wasn't. Finding a job was proving to be a little more difficult than I had initially thought, but it was fine. I just needed to lower my standards of where I was applying.

Once I did, I had three interviews lined up. One of them was bound to hire me. *Hopefully*.

The grocery store would, no doubt. Who got turned away by a grocery store?

It'd been two months, and I didn't want to be in Brent's bed every night any more than he wanted me in it. We had a very... relaxed relationship. And by relaxed I mean, we played the part of boyfriend/girlfriend when we felt like it but weren't so serious that we were discussing solid plans about our future.

And before you go chastising me and thinking, *'but Rosie, you moved for him'*, just remember, I moved for *me*. He just happened to present me with a place to stay and a crutch to lean against as I got settled.

Brent and I were not headed toward Mr. and Mrs., that was for damn sure.

Sounds awful, right? I did love Brent. I just didn't see us growing old together. He was my right now, not my forever. There was a difference.

"Why would I help with the house when I'm not the one who makes the mess? I keep my shit clean. It's really not that hard, Brent. You and your brother should figure out how to do the same."

"You're such a fucking bitch sometimes, you know that, right? I think I've been more than fair to you, Rosie, and I'm done with you and your games."

I rolled my eyes and glanced down at my black-painted

nails in boredom. "Yeah, yeah, Brent. Done with me until tonight, when you beg me to spread my legs."

"I don't beg for shit."

"Keep telling yourself that. I'll keep them closed for a while and we'll see how long you can hold out for."

"You think I won't go elsewhere?"

"Don't care."

"We'll see how much you don't care later when I make your ass sleep on the couch and you have to listen to me pound into someone else through these paper-thin walls."

"Go for it. I'll just crawl into your brother's bed," I spat, my heart skipping a beat at the very thought of it.

See, while I may have met Brent first, it was hard to deny the attraction I had for his brother.

Brent was your classic all-star, preppy, clean-cut, boy-next-door. The type who was the perfect person to bring home to your parents and start making lifelong plans with.

On the outside.

On the *inside*, he could be a real-fucking jerk. Like, want to scratch his eyes out and punch him in the nuts, kind of jerk.

It was baffling how he'd somehow wormed his way inside of my heart.

We'd been together for over a year now, if you don't count the month we were broken up. I *did* care about him. Honestly, what we had worked for us. And when he wasn't being a raging dickwad, Brent was actually very sweet and attentive. We had fun together. High highs. Low lows.

Toxic, I know. What I just described was practically the definition of a walking red flag.

But again, it worked for us. It worked for *now*.

Brent was a few years older than me, and the type of relationship he wanted was one of convenience and fun. It was a relationship I knew I could easily give him, because in return he could give me the sense of stability I craved. I was a little wild, I knew it and owned it, and I needed a person in my life to ground me—balance me out. Most of the time, he gave me that.

It also didn't help that Brent was pretty damn hot. But while he had the boy-next-door vibe, his brother was his polar opposite...the bad boy. Two years younger, rough around the edges, and devastatingly, ruggedly, gorgeous. Even his name was as sinful as he was—*Cain*.

He was covered in tattoos—which really matched my energy—and he didn't give a fuck about anything or anyone.

Actually, the only thing he did give a fuck about was Brent.

And *me*.

Which was a real bitch since I was technically with his brother.

Cain and I just connected better than Brent and I did, though we never crossed *that* line. But man, if you could actually fuck someone with your eyes, there wouldn't be a time or a place he hadn't taken me. Many late nights were spent in each other's company, talking about anything you could imagine. Our guards had come fully down, and I honestly wasn't sure anyone knew me better than he did. So many times I'd thought about telling Brent we were finished. I was hopeful I could leave him and one day move forward and be with Cain.

But Cain was never willing to let it happen.

Because I was his brother's girlfriend, I was off-limits completely. He'd never disrespect his older brother like that—which was wildly disappointing for me. I wasn't a cheater, and I never would be, but if Cain asked me to leave Brent for him, I wouldn't think twice.

Hell, if Cain asked me to leave Brent in general, I probably would.

I cared about Brent, I truly did. I loved him. I just wasn't sure if I was *in love* with him. How could I be when my heart beats for another man? His *brother*.

"You think crawling into my brother's bed is a threat? Cain is loyal to me, Rosie. He'd kick you out on your ass faster than you could blink," Brent spat, dropping onto his bed and crossing his legs at his ankles. He locked his hands beneath his head, his elbows sprawled, looking as relaxed as could be.

"I'm not sure why I bother with you, Brent. But I'm over this bullshit. You asked me to move to this freaking city with you, knowing I wouldn't have a job or a place to live. I'm done. Find yourself some other girl to fuck with." Lucky for me, my suitcase had never been unpacked because the jackass didn't have extra space for my shit in his dresser. All I had to grab was my phone charger and bathroom stuff.

Walking across the hall, I grabbed my makeup and hair care products, cradling them in my arms as I made sure I didn't leave anything behind.

I wasn't positive where I'd go tonight, but I'd figure it out. I always did.

Tossing everything into my suitcase, I zipped it up and

expanded the handle to roll it out. "Last chance to be a gentleman, Brent."

"Nah," he said without looking at me, pulling out his phone.

My eyes narrowed into slits and my head bobbed as I watched him scroll mindlessly as though I wasn't even in the room anymore. Tilting the suitcase, I rolled it behind me as I walked out of his bedroom.

The hallway was dark, the house quiet, as I moved through the small space toward the front door. When I reached for the knob, a deep voice sounded from the shadowed living room beside me.

"Rosie," Cain called. He sat on the couch in the dark, his face illuminated by the soft moonlight flowing in through the window.

"What, Cain?" What was there to even say? His brother was in the next room, probably listening for the sound of the door closing. This wasn't the first time we'd broken up, or the first time Cain had wanted to say something as I walked out the door after a fight with his brother. But like every other time, Cain said nothing and stared at me from his spot on the couch, his eyes blazing with unspoken words. The rigidness of his features told me he had heard mine and Brent's exchange and he hadn't liked what he heard.

Turning my head back to the door, I twisted the knob and walked out.

When it closed behind me, I didn't bother looking back. Instead, I held my head high and walked down the path, using my key fob to pop open the trunk of my car. The sound of small rocks crunching beneath the wheels of my suitcase battled against my heartbeat that echoed in my ears.

I was so frustrated with Brent and how I let him toss me to the side *again*, and how Cain let his brother treat me like shit and didn't speak up, *again*. I guess it wasn't fair of me to act like Cain really had any authority to say anything, but what woman didn't want a knight in shining armor on occasion? I guess I wouldn't be getting that from either of the Michaels brothers.

"Rosie!"

Maybe I spoke too soon.

Cain's voice cut through my inner battle with myself as I tossed my suitcase into the trunk of my blacked-out Honda Accord.

"What do you want, Cain?"

"Come back inside. Please."

"For what? So Brent can give me more details about how he's going to screw someone else and have me listen? Or so you can sit silently while he talks shit? As much as I love being the source of your entertainment, I think I'll pass." I slammed the trunk harder than necessary and rounded the car, pulling open the driver's side door—but I didn't get in. Like a true glutton for punishment, I watched him from over the roof of the car, waiting for him to say something.

Cain rubbed his tattooed hand across the back of his neck, looking down at the ground. After several tense seconds, he brought his attention back to me. "Where are you going?" he asked, taking a few more steps toward my car.

"I don't know," I admitted, my eyes narrowing as I tried thinking about where my first stop would be. Probably the motel on the outskirts of Ridgewood. It'd be the most inexpensive. My heart hammered in my chest as I made a snap decision to pull down one more layer of vulnerability I couldn't really afford to gamble with. "Come with me."

Cain's eyes darkened with my request, and instantly I could see the turmoil behind his light brown eyes. "It's not that easy. Brent's my brother..."

"He'll get over it," I argued, doing my best to keep the desperation out of my voice. I knew I was walking a fine line between being vulnerable and being desperate. I *wasn't* desperate, but Cain held a piece of my heart in his hand and I'd be lying if I denied that I wanted him to run away with me.

"We both know he wouldn't, he'd—"

"Cain? The fuck are you doing?" The screen flew open and hit against the side of the house as Brent's voice boomed from across the front yard. Cain's spine went ramrod straight.

Brent's eyes bounced between me and his brother, narrowing as he assessed us, drawing his own conclusions. Being unapologetically myself, I tossed him a snarky smile, knowing he was about to either explode on both of us, or turn around and slam the door in our faces.

Cain turned to face his brother, shrugging nonchalantly. "She ran from the house like a bat outta hell. I came to find out why."

"Not so sure it looks that way from where I'm standing, *brother*."

Resting my hands on my hips, I watched the two men face off, one looking skeptical while the other looked like he was trying to come up with an iron-clad excuse to save his own ass.

"Not sure what you think it looks like, but I was just making sure your bitch knew to respect our property next time she walked out of the house. She slammed the door so hard it rattled the front windows," Cain spouted, the lies tumbling from his mouth effortlessly as he turned back to me and his features hardened.

"She isn't my bitch anymore," Brent scoffed, stomping down the two steps of the weathered front porch. "Kind of seems like you want her to be your bitch, though."

A satisfied smile curled at my lips—my earlier suggestion of crawling into Cain's bed had clearly resonated with Brent. It got him thinking. Doubting himself and his brother's loyalty.

My intention was never to cause a rift between them, but rather remind Brent that being in his presence was *my* choice. Despite my current lack of income, I knew my damn worth, and with the snap of my fingers, I could have another man lined up if I wanted.

My smile was short-lived though, because nothing could have prepared me for Cain's response, and the wound it would ultimately leave on my heart.

Cain tossed his head back and laughed. What was normally a rare, yet beautiful sound with the power to inflate my heart, came out villainous and cruel. "Why the fuck would I want your sloppy seconds, Brent?" His eyes connected with mine as he delivered the final blow that would ricochet through my darkest moments for years to come. "She's nothing but damaged goods. Trailer trash. You couldn't pay me to give her my cock."

I knew words could hurt, but I hadn't realized just how badly until then.

Without hesitating, I flung myself into the driver's seat and cranked the ignition, not bothering to let it warm up before I tossed the car into drive and sped away, my tires squealing against the asphalt. I blew through the stop sign at the corner of their street, needing to get as far away from the Michaels brothers as quickly as I could. It took everything I had not to glance in the rearview mirror as I hightailed it out of their neighborhood and in the direction of the most expensive hotel in Ridgewood.

Forget staying at a cheap motel. I had some money tucked away, stashed because my subconscious *knew* something like this could happen, and I couldn't think of a more perfect reason to pull a little cash out.

A high thread count and some room service would be exactly what I needed while I licked my wounds for the night.

Why would I sit around in a crappy room and dwell on the words of two certified jerks? Tomorrow was a new day with back-to-back job interviews and a whole lot of promise for my future.

Glass half full, right?

Fuck Brent, and fuck his brother even more.

I was Rosie Adler, and if there was one thing I'd learned over the years, it was that the only person on this planet I needed was myself.

Certainly not a six foot four, tattooed, sexy as sin man

who looked like he could murder your enemies with his bare hands, but around you was a complete marshmallow.

Definitely *not* Cain Michaels.

CHAPTER TWO

Rosie

Present Day

"**F**uck, mia preferita, you feel amazing," Sly grunted as he slammed into me, his beautiful Italian accent even thicker during sex. He reached his large hand up and kneaded my boob. "God, I'm so close. I don't think I can hold it much longer. You...feel like paradiso."

My legs wrapped tighter around his body and joined at the ankles as I attempted to shift the pressure to stimulate my clit. Not that I hadn't already orgasmed. But twice never hurt.

Sly's grunts and groans filled the air as he drilled into me, a thin layer of sweat coating his back like he'd been running a marathon. We'd only been at it for less than five minutes, but his chest heaved with exertion.

I did my part in letting out small moans at the right times, digging my nails into his back. I was good at pretending to be super into it—I'd had enough practice at faking it over the years. Thankfully, Sly couldn't see me rolling my eyes and glancing at the diamond Rolex I hadn't bothered taking off when we got naked.

It wasn't his fault I was bored. My head wasn't in it—I was tired and stressed, more in the mood to be alone than to be naked and sweaty, but I'd hoped a good romp in the sheets would take my mind off the world around me.

Two more grunts and a slam later, Sly's rutting was over. His body fell to a heap on top of mine and I allowed him around sixty seconds of caressing before I gave him the boot. "Alright, Sly, off."

His gaze slid to mine as I stared up at him. He smirked, dipping down to kiss the side of my mouth, his dick twitching inside of me before he slid out. He rolled off my body and dropped onto the bed.

"Sorprendente," he muttered, his voice soft. Bastard had already tossed an arm over his eyes as if he was going to fall asleep immediately.

I reached over to pull a cigarette off the nightstand and lit it up. The cherry glowed red as it caught, and I tossed the lighter aside. Filling my lungs, I let my eyes close as I willed myself to relax.

Anxiety crept into my chest, sitting heavily. No sooner had I inhaled a second puff, Sly pulled it from between my lips and stuck it between his.

This was our ritual. We fucked, played pass the cig, and we passed out.

Well, correction, he passed out. Some nights I laid there

for hours until I fell asleep. Other nights, I left and went home.

It wasn't that I didn't enjoy being with Sly, because I truly did. He was great. There was nothing I could pinpoint that made me dislike him, which was why I couldn't figure out why my feelings for him weren't stronger.

Being with him was easy and secure. At all times, I knew where I stood with him and after so many failed relationships, a man like Sly was exactly what I needed. A great lover with a wicked tongue, easy on the eyes, and extremely compliant. Whatever I wanted, I got—the man had never so much as thought the word no when it came to me.

It didn't hurt that he also looked hot as hell in his black jeans and leather vest. Just seeing him on his motorcycle, his bronzed skin covered in tattoos, his dark hair always combed to perfection, and the way he could wear a pair of dark aviators, was enough to get me wet.

I never would have guessed I'd be into the whole motorcycle club thing, but here we were. The best part—Sly never tried to lock me down. He took me at face value and never forced me to commit to a label I wasn't interested in. I wasn't his girlfriend; he wasn't my boyfriend. The simplicity of our arrangement was what kept me from going stir-crazy.

Finishing the cigarette, I watched Sly peel the condom from his limp dick, knot it, and toss it onto the nightstand next to its wrapper. My face contorted as I outwardly cringed, grossed out that he just tossed it haphazardly onto the same surface he puts things like his phone on.

And *he* made fun of *me* for taking a disinfectant wipe to

everything the second I stepped foot into his room. I wasn't a germaphobe, but bikers—*men*—could be absolutely fucking disgusting.

I kept my mouth shut and made a mental note to wipe it down at some point while settling into the softness of the cotton sheets. As my eyes shut, I felt his hand circle my middle, and he pulled me closer. There would be no falling asleep for me. His body heat was stifling.

His arm draped across my naked tits, while he gripped my waist and tucked me into his body. *Little spoon.* All I could think about was rolling out from under his grasp.

I *hated* cuddling.

After what felt like hours, the steady rhythm of his breathing told me he was finally asleep. Peeling his fingers from my areola, I scooted my body away and silently placed my feet on the cool hardwood below. I sat for a minute, listening to the low snores as they fell from his lips.

I really did like the man, but there was just something lacking that I couldn't put my finger on. Sly was all golden retriever vibes. And there was nothing wrong with that. Wasn't that what most women wanted? A loyal, loving man who spoiled them? I should want that too.

Maybe the problem was me.

Retrieving my thong, bra, and the men's button down I had worn as a dress today, I quickly got dressed, leaving the shirt unbuttoned. Grabbing another cigarette and my purse, I headed for the door. As I slipped through the crack just wide enough for my body, I lit up another smoke. The cherry was the only illumination in the dark hallway, and as the door clicked closed behind me, I leaned against it with my eyes shut, enjoying a drag.

"That shit will kill you, Rose."

His voice made me jump, not realizing someone else was in the hallway with me. I turned my head to the right where his voice had come from, and watched him push off the wall and stalk toward my direction.

Stopping in front of me, he plucked the cigarette from between my fingers and carelessly tossed it to the floor, snuffing it out with the sole of his boot. "You need to fuckin' quit."

"And you need to quit stalking me, Cain," I retorted, crossing my arms in front of my chest. His eyes trailed down my body, appreciating the swell of my tits, the curves of my wide hips, and the lack of thigh gap. All so different from the body of the girl he once knew.

The Rosie I had been...the Rosie I was...she wasn't me. She was the shiny exterior I showed the world, but I was tired of being her.

While some old habits die hard (and are super challenging to let go of), I was able to control my body.

Life had been crazy over the last two years and I'd decided I needed a change.

Oh, who was I kidding? My life has always been crazy, and I was constantly making changes to myself. But it was within the last couple of years, while watching two of my best friends find their happiness, I realized *I* wasn't happy.

Growing up, my biggest hardship was low self-esteem and an unhealthy relationship with binge eating. Eventually, I fell into the other extreme and became good friends with a little plague called the starvation diet. I trained my body to survive on water-based foods and extremely lean proteins (every once in a while) while I also obsessively killed myself in the gym.

For years I was a slender little minx, but it cost me my happiness.

I conformed to what I thought I needed to look like for society—what I needed to look like to fit into my "bad girl reputation" I had so eloquently placed upon myself. Slender. Dark hair. Big tits. Tattoos.

For what?

That was the million dollar question, and let me just tell you, it wasn't worth a goddamn penny.

Once I had my come to Jesus moment and realized I didn't need to be anyone other than myself, I said goodbye to the salads I forced down my throat and reacquainted myself with carbs. And if people didn't like it, they could promptly fuck off.

Then, I spent a small fortune at the salon to turn my jet-black hair back to my natural—*or as close as I could get to it*—brunette. I even treated myself to a few extra tattoos, because why the hell not?

Instead of a size four, I was now more of a comfortable eight/ten, and I loved myself more than ever.

So when Cain's gaze finally reconnected with mine, I jutted my chin out with confidence and gave him my award-winning attitude. "Why the hell are you out here? Enjoying the audio-version of the porn you'll never get to watch?"

His smirk made my stomach turn. The jury was still out on whether it was a good "butterflies" type or bad "want to upchuck all over him" type of turn.

Probably a little of both.

Cain, unfortunately, caused the butterflies in my stomach to flutter whenever I caught sight of him, which seemed to be more frequent lately. He'd aged like a fine wine. Thirty-five years old and a fine specimen of a man. He was covered head to toe in black and gray tattoos—at least I was sure he was. I hadn't ever seen him completely naked, but had seen him without his shirt many, many times. He had that rugged appearance that made my toes curl. His coffee brown hair was always messily pulled back into a bun at the crown of his head, and his facial hair was always scruffy, but in a way that worked for him. He had the zero effort thing down and in his favor. Add that to his blue jeans, t-shirt, and leather vest decked out with club insignia —*damn*, he was fine.

An ass, but pretty to look at.

"Hearing you *fake it* was the highlight of my night, Rose," he told me, his voice thick with sarcasm.

I flipped him the bird before pushing off the door I still leaned against. Giving him my back, I walked down the pitch-black hallway. Not many people were up in the bedrooms yet, it was hardly midnight, but Sly and I had snuck off earlier in the night. The vibration from the bass of the speakers rattled the walls from the music playing in the bar on the floor below us. "Stop calling me Rose," I called over my shoulder.

Cain's footsteps were heavy behind me as he followed. "Where are you hurrying off to?"

I took the opportunity of being cloaked in darkness to button my shirt. My feet were bare and I moved quietly, but he was hardly three steps behind me. When I made it to the back staircase, I stopped and turned to him, turning on the fake charm. "What do you want, Cainy-boo?"

I ran my finger down the soft leather of his vest and along the waistband of his jeans. My sarcasm didn't go unnoticed, and he boxed me in, caging me as my back pressed against the cool wooden banister.

"You know, *Rose*, your attitude isn't as off-putting as you think." He traced his nose against my cheek, tipping his lips toward my ear. "I *see* you," he whispered softly.

My body betrayed me, and a shiver ran over my skin. The cocky bastard knew it too, because he added, "I know this isn't one-sided. You're just fucking around with Sly and buying time until I finally claim you."

"You can't claim a woman who wants nothing to do with you, Cain."

"Your body seems to disagree with that statement."

"It's cold in here, asshole. My goosebumps are for lack of warmth, not lack of dick. We both know I'm not lacking in the latter, so just go ahead and fuck off back to where you came from."

He tipped his head back and released a husky laugh. "Hell hath no fury like a woman scorned, right, Rose?"

"To have fury toward you, Cain, would imply I care. Which I don't. Truly."

"Your words pain me, baby."

"Actions speak louder than words, Cain. Although you seem to have a knack for making your words pretty damn loud."

His features turned dark and his mood sobered. No longer smirking and laughing, I could see the fire behind Cain's eyes as he searched my face, looking for a glimmer of sarcasm or playfulness to indicate I wasn't being serious. But I was.

I forced myself to hold my own, to mask the feeling of inadequacy threatening to show on my face. As memories pushed their way to the forefront of my mind, I could feel the hurt surfacing.

No.

I looked away, but something must have trickled across my face, causing Cain to take a step back. "Rose, you know I didn't mean what I fucking said. I had to say it to save face in front of Brent."

Whipping my head back toward him, I snarled, "You knew how I felt about you, Cain. And you knew how he treated me. Yet you still sat there and called me—*to my face*—what was it again? Damaged goods, trailer trash? Wait... No... That wasn't all you said."

"You know I had to. If he knew I was after his girl, he would have murdered me. He would have murdered *us*."

"Bullshit, Cain. Brent and I were so on-again off-again, he wouldn't have cared either way. When I walked away from him for good last year, he didn't come running. Plus, *we* never did anything. You and I were nothing but unexplored feelings and lustful looks across the room. It's never been about your actions. In this case, Cain, it was about *your* words. How *you* treated me. I expected better from you. You were always the nice one."

"He's my fucking brother, Rose. What was I supposed to do?"

"It doesn't matter what you should have done, because

you did nothing. And now, I want *nothing* to do with you. I've let it go, Cain. Moved on. You should too."

Without waiting for his reply, I ducked beneath the arm keeping me caged against the banister, and took the stairs down two at a time, not sparing him a backward glance as I pushed open the door to the main floor of *my* bar, Andromeda.

CHAPTER THREE

Rosie

"Hey boss, you're here early today."

It was just past two in the afternoon the next day when I walked into Andromeda with an armful of supplies for the restrooms. Owning a bar wasn't as glamorous as it sounded and somehow, as a business owner, you ended up being your own bitch just to save a few bucks. I hoisted the bulk bundle of toilet paper onto the bar and peeled off my oversized cat-eye sunglasses.

"Hey, Indy," I greeted my lead bartender with a smile before shoving the sunglasses into my black leather crossbody purse.

Indy had been working at Andromeda longer than I had, and was my right-hand woman for literally everything. She had bright pink hair and snakebite piercings, and wore her eyeliner dark and thick. She was a 2000s punk wet-dream, and I was here for it. Loved her for her enthusiasm and A plus work ethic, too.

"I'll be in my office if you need me. Hold my calls and cancel my appointments. I have books to balance," I told her with a cheeky smile.

"Hold your calls from the phone we don't have and cancel your appointments with the ghosts I set up earlier this week? You got it, boss. Anything else?"

"Yeah," I told her as I pulled the bundle of TP off the bar and slung it over my shoulder like I was a hotter, edgier, beardless Santa Claus. "Keep being you, punk princess."

Her laugh brought a smile to my face as I rounded the corner. The hallway was secluded, but my office was even more so, hidden speakeasy style behind a row of mirrors. Which I had to mention was truly hysterical considering no one came down this hallway to begin with, but the previous owner was a paranoid idiot who'd made some poor life choices and was convinced every mob, gang, etc, was after him. With his paranoia in full effect, he installed several hidden doorways around the bar and a full wall of floor-to-ceiling bulletproof one-way glass, which allowed him to watch everything around him without anyone knowing he was lurking in the shadows.

Eventually, he went into a full mental breakdown and thought everyone—*everywhere*—was out to get him. His wife insisted they move out of Ridgewood and start over, so that's exactly what they did. Fast, too. Andromeda had only been open for a few months before it went up for sale, but as soon as I caught wind of it needing a new owner, I jumped.

Could I afford to buy a bar? Not really. But I'd sure as shit bust my ass every day to make it work.

With a few bats of my eyes at a dusty loan officer at the

bank, I was approved for the exact amount to buy the bar I'd fallen in love with the second I stepped foot in it on opening night.

Now I was riding down a path I had never expected for myself: a business owner in charge of giant adult headaches such as bookkeeping and business taxes. Did you know the government expects you to pay quarterly taxes? How the hell are you supposed to do that when business has so many ebbs and flows?

Yeah, I learned that term too. Ebbs and flows. And my high school economics teacher said I'd never amount to anything. *Joke's on you, Mr. Kromer.*

Most days I questioned why I bought this place. Then night fell, the ceiling twinkled like the night sky while the patrons happily drank and grinded, and I remembered why.

Pushing the frame of the mirror, the hidden door gave way, allowing me access to the darkened office hidden behind it. My fingers effortlessly found the light switch, and I flicked it on. Light swept over the room, a low warmth glowing over the furniture I decorated the area with once it became mine. Everything faced toward the mirrors—my desk, the couch. The idea of not being able to see my full surroundings made my skin crawl. I wasn't as paranoid as the previous owner, but I had plenty of experience with how people were, and I knew better than to give an enemy my back.

Or a friend, for that matter.

You never know who you can trust, and I was as distrusting as they came.

I could count on one hand the number of people who had my full, unyielding trust. I only needed three fingers.

I spent many hours concealed behind the one-way mirror, enjoying a full view of my bar. It didn't matter if it was day or night. I could stay in here for hours, cloaked in privacy, enjoying the scenery.

From the bar side, the floor-to-ceiling mirrors elongated the area, giving the space the illusion of being larger than it was. In my opinion, it also gave the space sex appeal, and from the number of women I witnessed watching themselves as they grinded against another sweaty body, I'd say I was right.

The one-way glass also gave me the opportunity to keep an eye on a certain motorcycle club—particularly their president—as they inhabited my bar night after night, from open to last call.

In an effort to secure himself more protection, the previous owner leased the upstairs of the building to Ridgewood's very own motorcycle club, Sinners Warlord, in hopes they'd have his back if and when he needed it. Though they may give off a 'cross to the other side of the street when you see them' vibe, they were really a group of leather-clad vigilantes who went around acting as though they were Ridgewood's personal scum exterminators. The beauty of it was, the Sinners worked alongside Ridgewood P.D. to help keep the streets safe, although if you asked either party to confirm their collaboration, they'd both deny it.

Thanks to the deal made with the previous owner, I was now stuck with the Sinners indefinitely. I really screwed myself by not asking more questions about the actual club when I signed my escrow paperwork to take over the building. I hadn't realized until later I completely overlooked the clause that said the upstairs tenants were locked into a five-year leasing agreement that couldn't be nullified by the purchaser.

In reality, the Sinners wouldn't have been a problem at all, had it not been for their club president.

What were the odds that Cain Michaels was the president of the fucking motorcycle club living above my bar?

Just my luck, honestly.

Once the paperwork had been signed and I closed on my bar, I dug deeper and found out as much as I could about the club and those involved. Two members in particular had caught my eye: Cain and Sly.

Cain because he was a giant pain in my ass—a part of my past that I thought was just that, in the past. Sly because he was hotter than the desert sun and looked like someone I could take on a ride.

For the last three months, I had been successful at keeping Cain at bay while having some good, filthy fun with Sly. Cain and I usually passed like two ships in the night, me avoiding him until we had business to conduct. And even though he left me alone for the most part, my body was acutely aware of his presence. I could feel his eyes on me always, and instinctively knew exactly when he entered a room.

The fact I was so in tune with him put a pit in my stomach. It'd been years and the bastard still had an effect on me.

Despite me never asking him to, Cain made himself Andromeda's personal security detail, watching the bar nightly from inside and reporting anything he deemed as suspicious to my *actual* security team. Whether he did this for the well-being of his club, or so he had a reason to show up to my bar every night, was something I had never bothered to ask him. Asking would require actually speaking to him, and when I spoke to Cain, stupid shit came out of my mouth.

I'd rather put my mouth to other uses. Like throwing back shots or sucking Sly's dick.

As though summoned by the devil himself, a knock bellowed through the door and pulled me from my thoughts. The knob turned and the door pushed inward slightly before Sly's painfully handsome face peered around the corner.

"Ciao, mia preferita. How is it going in here?"

Giving Sly a small smile, I picked up a pile of paperwork in both hands and waved them slightly, sighing deeply as I then released them from my grasp. The papers fell back down to my desk, landing messily in front of me.

"Ah, that well, then?" He crossed the room, letting the door close behind him. I heard the lock engage, shutting us into my office.

Sly always looked so perfectly put together, wearing his signature black jeans and t-shirt, and black steel-toed boots. He styled his hair with a small amount of product—just enough to keep it looking clean and tidy—and kept his facial hair short and impeccably groomed. Sly was literally the epitome of a wet dream. It's no wonder I had a hard time staying fully clothed around him.

"Brilliantly," I huffed as he came around my desk. I turned to face him, a mischievous smile circling at my lips. "It'd be a lot better if you swept everything off my desk and fucked me on it. At least then I'd be able to check one thing off my to-do list for the day."

Pushing my hair behind my shoulder, Sly brought his hand to the side of my neck, curling his fingers around it gently before he leaned down and kissed the place below his thumb. "I'd love nothing more than to do just that, but I have to go into the bar in ten minutes to speak with Cain."

"All the more reason to stick your dick in me now."

His vibrant hazel eyes met mine, and he quickly narrowed them, seemingly unamused by my suggestion. He thought purposely for a moment before telling me, "He loves you, you know. You may be mia preferita, but to Cain, you're the reason the sun rises each morning."

"The reason why the sun rises each morning has nothing to do with me, Sly."

He chuckled before pressing his lips to mine in a soft kiss. "You're wrong."

"I'm never wrong." I smiled weakly, knowing right now I most certainly was wrong. Or at least trying to live in denial. "Does it bother you? That Cain makes his feelings known to the entire club, yet the entire club knows you and I are sleeping together?"

"Sex is sex." He kissed the curve between my shoulder and neck. "You're not in a relationship, nor am I." Three soft kisses trailed up my neck, the last just below my jawline. "If you choose to spend your evenings in my bed, the only people who have the right to object are me and you. I'm certainly not complaining about our arrangement. Are you?"

Sly's fingertips brushed against the sliver of skin on my waist as he circled his fingers around my hip and pulled me flush against his body. Even now, I could feel the bulge in his pants, showing me he definitely wasn't complaining.

"Nope. No complaints from me," I breathed, allowing myself a moment to get lost in the simplicity of Sly's touch. He was *really* great at foreplay. A master at the art of seduction.

His lips caught mine, his tongue sweeping into my mouth, dancing with mine as he kissed me deeply.

All too quickly, he pulled away, leaving me wanting more. "Good," he said, smiling and tucking a lock of hair behind my ear. "So until something changes, we continue to enjoy the company of one another. Now, as much fun as pressing your naked body up against the glass and fucking you sounds, I really must go speak with Cain. You'd think he could see through the glass by the way he's been staring at it since I walked in."

Moving my gaze to the window, Cain was sitting at his normal high-top table near the back wall, chair turned so the back leaned against it. He faced the glass wall directly across from him, not taking his eyes off it. He took a cherry from a small bowl in front of him and popped it into his mouth, pulling the stem from between his lips.

My breathing hitched, and I turned my focus back to Sly. His eyes were on me as he watched my reaction, studying the way my demeanor changed despite me trying to remain aloof. Quickly, I snapped out of it—*somewhat*—and leaned forward to kiss him. "Tell him to get the hell out of my bar, would ya?" I laughed, but even to my own ears, my laugh sounded fake.

As he had when he first came into my office, Sly narrowed his eyes slightly, as though he could read right through me.

"Fino a stasera, mia preferita," he told me as he titled his head to kiss my cheek.

With one more beautiful smile, Sly slipped through my office door, heading in the direction of my worst nightmare and most vivid dream.

CHAPTER FOUR

Rosie

My finger felt numb as I laid sprawled out on the couch, skipping through the movie catalog on Netflix while I tried to find something to watch. It was nearly three in the morning and I should have been in bed, but after one of my bartenders called out tonight, I had no choice but to get my ass behind the bar and start serving. My feet felt like they were on fire after pouring drinks all night in heels, but what I was really irritated about was how my brain wouldn't go into shutdown mode. My eyelids were heavy, exhaustion plaguing me to the point where every cell in my body begged for sleep, but I just couldn't.

Closing down the bar meant I was far too tired to drive my ass across town to my condo, so I found my way to Sly's room instead. He was asleep when I let myself in, and rather than disturb him, I stripped out of my clothes and tossed on one of his t-shirts before padding down the dark hallway to the large space the club used as a living room. I needed to let my brain unwind and watch a little T.V. before I'd be able to fall asleep.

They kept their space simple and had only decorated their living room area with a couple of worn-down black leather couches and a seventy-five inch flat screen mounted to the wall. There wasn't even a coffee table anymore, since someone —*Damon*—ended up too drunk a few months ago and fell on top of it, smashing it to smithereens from his body weight, just like in the movies. I wasn't there that night, but I saw the aftermath, and the poor coffee table didn't stand a chance against the big, bad biker.

The room was cold, and I regretted not grabbing a blanket from Sly's room to bring with me as chills pebbled my skin. A momentary lapse in judgment had me reaching for the blanket draped across the back of the couch.

"I wouldn't do that if I were you." Cain's deep voice drifted through the doorway. Propping myself up on my elbows, I peered over the top of the couch to look at him. He leaned against it, arms resting above the doorframe. His shirt was off, tattoos and muscles on full display for me to drool over. He knew what he was doing. "I walked in on Nix earlier and he had the blanket wrapped around the waist of the woman riding his dick."

Fucking Nixon.

Another one of the club's gorgeous playboys who took every girl he could for a ride on his cock like it was the newest attraction at the amusement park. I loved to hate that guy and busted his chops whenever possible, but also appreciated the way I knew he'd have my back whenever needed. He was the club's teddy bear. Well, maybe just bear. Big and huggable, but absolutely vicious if you actually tried to hug him.

"What do you want, Cain?"

"You seem to ask me that a lot, Rose. I usually have the same answer. Do I need to keep repeating it?"

"Your answer is stupid. You will not get *me*. I'm not a possession to be had." Kicking my feet over the side of the couch, I sat up, turning my back to him as I clicked off the remote. If he was invading my space, I'd be leaving it.

"You're right. You're not a possession. But you're wrong if you think I won't have you, Rose. You've always been mine, even when I was too blind to see it."

His words were like a knife to my heart, slicing through the organ clean through. I squeezed my eyes shut, hoping just this once the phrase 'out of sight, out of mind' would have some truth to it.

Maybe if I ignored him, he'd go away.

Wishful thinking.

The wrinkled leather cushions dipped from Cain's weight as he sat down beside me. Our thighs touched, and though he kept his hands to himself, they balled into loose fists. "Can we please just have a conversation, Rose? This cat-and-mouse charade we've had going on for the last couple of months has been fun and all, but I'd really rather discuss the skeletons in our closets, so we can move past this."

"Stop calling me Rose, Cain."

"You told me once you hated the name Rosie because it was too delicate. Has that changed?"

I said that to him *one* time over seven years ago.

He was right, though. The name Rosie never felt like me.

Too sweet, too delicate. The name on my birth certificate was actually Rosalynne, but that didn't feel right either. My mom always called me Rosie growing up, so that's what stuck, and I only continued to introduce myself as Rosie because the only person who'd ever called me Rose was Cain. Even after he squeezed the life out of my heart and stomped on it, some sick part of me still wanted to keep the name reserved for him, and I never reinvented myself.

"No, that hasn't changed," I confirmed, not wanting to meet his gaze with my own. Sitting straighter in my seat, I went back and forth with whether I wanted to entertain him by finally allowing the conversation he'd been asking for. It was petty, I know. It'd been years. We were young and dumb, making our own rules as we went throughout our twenties, but there was a piece of me still unwilling to let go completely. It was a grudge I'd held for so long, and though I'd moved past it, I was admittedly too afraid to let him get close again.

Hypocritical since I not only forgave Brent over the years for his numerous fuck ups and constant disrespect, but with Brent I knew he was a relationship of convenience. I'd set the bar so low with him, it was lying on the floor. I mean, we literally broke up every other month, and I say broke up extremely loosely because we were never really in a full-fledged relationship.

But with Cain... Cain made me *feel*. I'd never been a woman who envisioned a white picket fence, a diamond on my finger, and a baby on each hip, but when my feelings for Cain developed all those years ago, it made me wonder if I was destined for a *different* type of forever.

Hearing him vocalize my every fear that night six years ago broke something within me, and it took a long time to heal from it. "You can call me Rose," I whispered, lost in my own thoughts as I realized that maybe the way to finally let go of the past was to let Cain share his side. It didn't mean I would give him my heart or trust him again, but maybe what I needed to get past my scarred emotions was to let him in, just a little.

"What I said that night...I felt cornered. You were Brent's girl. I was stuck between loyalty and love, Rose."

The word *love* startled me, and I whipped my head to him, seeing the look of someone just as haunted by the past as I was staring back. I shook my head slowly as a thousand and one thoughts flooded my mind. "You didn't love me, Cain. You barely knew me."

"How many nights did we stay up, just the two of us, talking until the sun rose? And all those times Brent was at work and we'd hop on my bike and just drive, only stopping to fill the tank or get a bite to eat? Those moments weren't just a means to pass the time, Rose. I'm not ashamed to admit that I fell for my brother's girl. Back then, I should have stood up to him. I should have fought for you."

An exasperated laugh burst from my chest at his admission, as all the hurt I had buried down over the years came roaring to the surface. "I'm not doing this, Cain. I can't do this with you. There's an expression, 'if he wanted to, he would'. Ever heard of that? You're the opposite of that saying. You didn't want to, so you didn't."

"I was a fucking idiot back then, Rose, but I've had time

to learn and grow. I know I fucked up, and I'm apologizing for it now."

"You're about six years too late, Cain. I've moved on from it, and so should you." My heart sank in my chest and I decided I was done with this conversation. I thought I could handle it, but the scars were too deeply rooted. Pushing to my feet, the cold wood planks sent a chill through me again, and my nipples hardened beneath the too-big t-shirt I was wearing.

As I took a step to walk away, Cain caught my wrist, his fingers encircling the smallest part of my arm as he held me in place. "It doesn't have to be too late for us." Cain's voice was low, practically a whisper, though I'm not sure he was capable of achieving that decibel.

Instinctually, I tugged against his grasp, but his hold was solid. I wanted to scream that it *was* too late, but even as the words formed in my vocal cords, and my mouth opened to speak them, no sound came out. Instead, I stared down at where he held my wrist.

"Rose, *please*." His voice sounded strained and plagued with emotion. Vulnerable. And that wasn't an emotion he showed often.

Not meeting his eyes, I reiterated the only words my brain could think to formulate. "I'm with Sly."

"We both know you're not *actually* with him. You may take up residence in his room some nights, but you're not his."

"You're wrong," I countered, shaking my head. My gaze slid up his body and met his heated stare. "Sly and I have an agreement that works for us. An agreement I have no interest in explaining to you, Cain."

Giving my wrist a firm tug, my body felt like a yo-yo as it whipped forward, and I collided with him. Falling onto his lap, he shifted his body, so he was partially laying on the couch with me sprawled on top of him. "*Ugh*, Cain, what the fuck?" I tried to scramble off, but his arms slid around my waist, locking me tight against him.

"Your body fits perfectly against mine, Rose," he rasped, his nose skimming up my neck. With his lips so damn close to my skin, I could feel the heat from his breath—a warm contrast from how cold the room was. Between the warmth of his breath and the slight brush of his facial hair against my skin, a shiver ran through me. Cain smirked triumphantly, letting his fingers trail up my arm as he did.

My stomach tightened as my body gave into the feeling of him beneath me. It took every morsel of restraint I had not to melt completely into him as heat rippled through me. I could literally feel my pussy get wet, and I clenched my jaw in protest.

Shifting my head toward him, I fixed him with a glare. It was the wrong move to make though, because as our breath mingled, I had to fight against the urge to close the distance between our mouths and give in to him completely. I was absolutely unaware of the restraint I could muster, despite the reaction I had to his touch.

The longer we held each other's stare, the less willpower I had to continue the charade of indifference. As much as I wanted to hate Cain Michaels, I just couldn't, and though I hated to admit it, being in his arms felt like *home*.

It wreaked havoc on my heart.

Softening in Cain's arms, I wrapped my fingers around his wrist and watched as the veins in his forearm flexed under my touch. His chest heaved beneath me and suddenly the air felt like it was thickening around us. I found it hard to breathe, but I also couldn't look away from him if I tried. Not when his eyes sparkled through the darkness, unspoken promises shining through, jolting me to my core. I knew I needed to move, but I was frozen against the only man who had ever truly stolen a piece of my heart.

"Do you remember that night when we still lived in Northwood? When you fell from the bed of my truck, and as I tried to catch you, we crashed to the ground? We landed in almost this exact position, Rose."

Cain's smile widened, and I got lost in the memory of that night.

The groves of the tailgate mixed with the effects of the tequila shots had me feeling slightly uneasy as I bounced from one side of the truck to the other, arms outstretched as though that would help my equilibrium and keep me upright.

My cheeks burned from the permanent smile on my face after Cain came to pick me up from Kodiak's, a popular bar housed inside of an old warehouse building. Danorah and I decided to call it a night, respectively, calling both of our boyfriends to pick us up. It was what we did—arrived together, then left with whatever guy we were seeing at the time to make sure we ended the night with a bang.

Literally.

To my surprise, Brent's phone rang repeatedly until clicking over to voicemail. It wasn't unlike him to not answer, but he knew my plan. He knew he was my ride home.

Within a few seconds, the darkened phone in my hand illuminated as Brent returned my call, only when I answered, it wasn't Brent's voice on the other end of the line. It was Cain's. Evidently, Brent had left with one of his buddies and left his phone at home. Luckily for me, Cain was more than willing to come get me.

Grabbing one last drink, Danorah and I headed for the dance floor for a few more songs until our rides showed up.

I hadn't finished dancing when he walked in and tossed me over his shoulder like a caveman, carrying me upside down through the parking lot until we made it to his truck, where he deposited me—right side up—in the passenger seat.

I swayed in my seat as he climbed into his cab and tossed an In-N-Out bag at me. "Animal style fries, to sober your ass up."

"Where's my Coke?" I asked with a slight slur.

The truck's engine roared to life, the vibrations tingling through the seat. Wordlessly, Cain held out a medium soda. I took it from him, bringing the straw to my lips and drew the sugary liquid into my mouth.

"Mmmmm," I moaned against the straw as I watched Cain from the corner of my eye while he reversed from the parking spot. "Kinda wish I had a chocolate milkshake, too."

He chuckled deeply and pulled a smaller cup from the cupholder between us, giving it a small shake to grab my attention. I squealed in delight and grabbed it with my empty hand.

Double fisting my Coke and my milkshake, I grinned at Cain, loving that he remembered my favorite things from the menu of my favorite fast-food joint.

"Thanks," I told him with sincerity and took a huge gulp of my slightly melted milkshake, sucking it down until I gave myself a brain freeze.

"Sober up, buttercup. I'm taking you somewhere."

"Oooh, where are we going?"

"One of my favorite places to go after a night of drinking."

Squinting my eyes and pursing my lips, I questioned, "But you haven't been drinking, have you?"

He smiled widely again, glancing at me before refocusing on the road. "No, but you have."

The drive was short, but toward the end, the road became windy and rocky, which was not great for my stomach full of alcohol, fries, and sugary beverages. By the time we parked, I felt a little queasy and needed air.

Throwing open the passenger door, I hopped out of the truck and did a three-sixty, looking at our surroundings.

"What is this place?" I asked, venturing away from the truck as I took in the dark meadow nestled between the ridges of the small mountain we'd driven up. Nearing the edge, my eyes immediately caught on the gorgeous, twinkling cityscape that was laid out before me.

Cain came up behind me, standing so close our bodies practically touched, though he kept the smallest of gaps between us. I was acutely aware of it, and for a moment, had a hard time focusing on anything else.

"Straight ahead," he told me, his arm reaching forward and pointing to where he spoke of. It brushed against mine, sending a current of electricity through me. "That's Northwood. And that," he moved his arm off to the right, "that's Bridge Point."

Feeling bold, I took a slight step backward, closing that tiny space between us. Turning my head to the left, I peered out at the darkness that stretched far and at the faint twinkling of the city that was far *off into the distance. "What's over there?" I asked, my voice breathy as the desire I tried to push away filtered through.*

His lips brushed against my ear, causing my lips to part from how absolutely erotic having him so close felt. I shouldn't have felt that way, not when his brother was technically my boyfriend. And as the thought of Brent trickled into my mind, everything suddenly felt so forbidden.

I took a step forward, allowing for more space than had originally been between us, and covered my chest with my arms.

My sudden change in demeanor must have pulled Cain from his clouded judgment too, because I heard him swallow thickly before he said, "Over there is Ridgewood."

Once my question was answered, the crunch of weeds beneath his footsteps alerted me he was walking back to the truck.

Following, I danced through the tall grasses, feeling light on my feet. When I stopped at the back of the truck, Cain dropped the tailgate, and I spared no time before hopping into the bed. The truck's bed liner was cold and rough against my palms as I used them to push myself into a standing position and kicked off my heels. My toes flexed beneath me, happy to be free from the confines of the too-tight shoes.

Twisting around to look at Cain, he stood at the tailgate with his arms crossed, watching me with a blank expression, though he was unsuccessful in hiding the amusement from his eyes as they floated up my body.

"Aw, c'mon Cainy-boo, don't look so drab," I mused, lifting onto my toes as I danced around the bed of his truck. The snack earlier had sobered me up a little, but I could still feel my body sway as I stumbled on the small ridges on the bed liner.

Reaching up to fist his disheveled hair that was growing far too long, Cain turned his body, giving me his back as he looked into the dark mountainside. An exasperated huff left him, and even through the dark, I could see the way his shoulders quaked as he expelled the air.

With his back to me, I twirled to the tailgate and balanced on the wide grooves, my feet teetering. Sober me would have had no problem walking across the small space, but with tequila pooling through my bloodstream, my head felt fuzzy and my stability swayed. A small squeak left me as my ankle twisted slightly, and I shot my arms out on either side to keep myself upright.

Cain turned back toward me and scrubbed his hand down his face. "Rosie, please be careful."

"Ugh, Rosie. Such a sweet name. I'm not a delicate little flower, Cain. I can handle standing on my own two feet." And I meant that in more ways than one.

But even as the words left my mouth, gravity did me dirty as I swayed and overcorrected, falling—almost in slow motion—off the tailgate.

Somehow Cain managed to catch me, his strong arms circling my middle, but my momentum was too much to stop and we both toppled onto the ground. Cain broke my fall, landing on his back with me on top of him.

With my body flattened against him, my eyes widened as I looked down at him with only a mere inch separating our lips. "Well, shit. That was my bad. Are you okay?" I asked, trying not to burst into a fit of laughter.

Cain reached up and tucked a piece of hair that'd fallen into my face behind my ear. "Never better, Rose."

My gaze caught on Cain's lips and I suddenly wanted nothing more than to slam mine against his and give into the desperation I'd felt for him for what seemed like so long.

But I couldn't. I wasn't with Cain. I was with Brent. His brother.

"Rose?" I questioned, swallowing thickly. My eyes bounced between his eyes and his lips, and it was an absolute struggle to fight against the deep-rooted urge to kiss him.

"Yeah," he murmured. "It suits you better."

God, I wanted this man. There was no doubt in my mind I was with the wrong brother. Brent was a fabulous lay and a fun guy to be around. We worked. It was easy, despite him being a complete jackass at times. Brent had low expectations for what we wanted from each other, and I was the same.

But Cain.

The things I felt when I was around Cain were on another level, and I was so incredibly conflicted about how I felt versus how I was supposed to feel around the brother of the man I was dating. There were so many things I wanted to say to him. So many things to admit —to confess. They were all at the tip of my tongue.

"Cain... I..."

His abrupt movements interrupted me as he pushed to stand and lifted me so I'd stand too. Confusion laced my brows together at how quickly he'd pulled us upright, and icy-cold rejection pulsed through my veins as Cain raked his hand through his hair again, cast his eyes downward and muttered, "Let's go. I should get you home to Brent."

I was jostled from the memory when Cain reached up to brush the hair out of my face, much like he did all those years ago. His touch made me flinch, the past rejection simmering through my blood as my thoughts swam with the swirl of emotions from that one, fleeting memory.

Cain had always been the only man who could make me *feel* deeper than I ever thought possible. The one guy who softened the exterior shell I'd built around myself to protect that stupid, fragile organ behind my ribs.

And I still fucking hated him for it.

Using his chest for leverage, I pushed off his body and stood, pulling Sly's t-shirt down as I did.

Looking down at him, the petty side of me reared her head as I twisted his past words and threw them back at him. Words that I doubted he'd remember even saying, but I would likely never forget.

"I should go. Gotta get *home* to Sly." It came out as a sneer, and as I turned on my heel and walked out of the darkened living room, I could feel moisture sting the backs of my eyes. I wasn't a crier, not unless I was deeply enraged.

Obviously, Cain had succeeded, yet again.

Rolling my eyes toward the ceiling to choke the tears, I used my finger to dab at my lower lashes and walked through the open alcove, into the club's hallway.

I hated how he made me feel like this—so vulnerable and scarred from the tumultuous wave of emotions he'd caused. From the moment I met him, I knew he'd left a permanent etching on my heart—a mark that could never be erased.

He was different.

Distinct.

Strikingly noticeable when all I wanted to do was ignore his very presence.

He wasn't the man I should have fallen for all those years ago, but I'd been marked by Cain in a way that still didn't fully make sense. My heart singularly beat for only him, despite my constant objections and effort to expunge him from my life completely.

Cain was determined to not only make amends, but to tear down the walls I'd built and crash through them like the wrecking ball he was.

And I wasn't so sure I'd be able to resist him much longer.

CHAPTER FIVE

Cain

She'd followed me for the last six years.

Her hazel eyes, her scent. Her take-no-prisoners attitude. Everywhere I turned, her memory lingered, reminding me of everything I'd lost but never truly had.

The things I said—I never meant them. And they imploded my entire world in less than ten seconds.

My entire life, I grew up enamored with my older brother. He had it all: our parents' adoration, nearly perfect grades, friends, popularity, and girls. Goddamn, did he have the girls. I learned everything I could from watching him. The way he'd speak to adults, his demeanor in front of friends, and the confidence he exuded in front of the opposite sex.

He was *everything*.

In the eyes of everyone in my life, I was an outcast. The complete opposite of my brother in every way possible. The guy who never did anything quite right. I never got the girl, only had one person I could qualify as a friend, and I was constantly straddling the line of fucking up. Despite that, I was fine with the way my life was going: I had the love and attention of Brent, and my brother was the only person I truly needed.

Until he wasn't.

I couldn't pinpoint exactly what changed with him, but something did. I'd watched it happen slowly, the transformation from the brother I knew to the brother I had trouble recognizing. Somewhere between starting high school and graduating, he stopped becoming everything I idolized, and I saw him for what he really was.

What's that saying? Rose-colored glasses, or whatever? Well, I'd finally taken them off. Whether it was Brent who had changed or me, I still wasn't entirely sure, but somewhere along the line the other shoe dropped.

To put it bluntly, Brent was a fucking dick.

And so was I, but I knew how to be respectful. *When* to be respectful. I could distinguish the line and know when not to cross it. That was an attribute Brent lacked, especially with women.

When he started bringing Rose around, I couldn't figure out their connection. She was fiery and stunning. Dark hair, bright eyes, pillowy perfect lips, and tattoos galore. I wanted to lick every single inch of ink on her body. Trail my tongue over each line until I reached her lips.

And her personality. God, her personality was the icing on the cake for me. She was *spicy*. Rose had a lot of attitude and put up a challenge at every turn. The push and pull from her was exactly what I craved in a woman.

She was an absolute fucking dream.

My dream.

But she was with my brother and I had no choice but to stand there and witness them together at every turn. Keeping my mouth shut like a goddamn monk while I watched their toxicity flourish.

Rose and Brent together were like oil and water. They didn't mix. She constantly gave him grief and attitude—fought him tooth and nail on everything. The complete opposite of what he typically went for. Brent liked his women to be compliant. Easy to manipulate and control.

That was *not* her.

I couldn't figure out why she put up with his shit, or why he put up with hers, and when I asked him about it, he told me to shut the fuck up and mind my business.

So I did. I watched from afar, observing and biding my time. I learned her mannerisms, figured out what made her tick. And when I finally saw her frustrations with my brother shine through, like a moth to a flame, I gravitated to her and became someone she could vent to.

Was it a little manipulative? Probably. But I wanted her to see what she was missing by being with him and not me. Along the way, though, she somehow became my best friend. Which eventually led me to catch stronger feelings, and those feelings turned into an avenue I *really* wanted to explore.

But again, like a good, loyal brother, I never laid a finger on her. Never did more than talk to her, even though it took exceptional restraint to not rip her clothes off and show her who the better man really was.

The night I called her damaged goods and ruined my connection with her was also the night I willingly severed ties with my brother. She didn't know it then—hell, she may still not know the full story—but when Rose left, speeding off in her car, I watched until it was out of sight completely. My chest felt like she had left behind a gaping hole from ripping my heart out and taking it with her.

But in reality, it was my own actions that ripped my heart out that day. I could have gone with her, but I chose my brother instead.

Loyalty.

What a joke that was. The second her car disappeared and I turned back to him, we snuffed out the lingering pieces of our relationship completely.

"You fucking my girl, Cain?"

"No, I'm not fucking your girl, Brent. You think I'd do that to you? To my own brother?"

"Sure looked like there was something between you two just now. You want to chase after her? Be her prince charming or some bull-shit? Go ahead. Go get the slut. We both know you'd happily accept my sloppy seconds—you always have. Bitch isn't even that good in bed."

I stepped toward him, bumping my chest against his. Though he was older, I was at least three inches taller and about thirty pounds heavier than him in muscle.

"Shut your mouth, Brent," I growled as my hands balled into fists at my sides. The ligaments in my joints strained from how tightly I curled my fingers. My nostrils flared as I tried to keep my cool. I was about four seconds away from punching my brother in his smug, unscarred, pretty boy face.

Feeding off my anger, Brent puffed out his chest and purposely bumped into mine as he attempted to assert his dominance. What he didn't realize was over the years, I'd become the alpha in our brother-hood. I'd just let him continue thinking he was.

"What are you going to do, Cain? You gonna hit me? You wouldn't dare to hit your big bro. What'd you say I was? Your idol?"

"I called you that when I was ten."

"Yeah, and you're still actin' like a little kid now, Cain. Nothing's changed. Now, back the fuck up. She's not worth it. Plus, she'll be back within a week, sucking my dick like she can't get enough. That's what whores do. They come crawling back out of their hole once they realize no other dude wants damaged goods. I liked that term too, bro. Good one. Damaged goods. Totally describes that b—"

A deafening crack permeated through the air. Blood gushed and covered my fist, rushing from Brent's broken nose as I hit him not once, but three times in the face.

I wasn't even a little sorry.

Brent clutched his nose. His brows furrowed together, wrinkling in the center. "The fuck, Cain? Seriously? Fuck you, man."

"No, Brent, fuck you. All these years I had nothing but respect for your ass, but I've sat idle too long while you treated Rosie like shit. It's not right, and I won't allow it anymore."

"Won't allow it?" He laughed sardonically. "Wow. You're more of a pussy than I thought you were."

My jaw locked—teeth grinding together as a low growl rumbled in the depths of my chest. "Unless you want a black eye to go with that busted nose, I suggest you shut your mouth."

Moving past him, I checked his shoulder and walked into the house, not stopping until I reached my room. The door rattled on its hinges from how hard I slammed it.

Pulling my old duffle bag down from the shelf in my closet, I *tossed it on my bed and rifled through the drawers of my bureau, tossing everything I owned into an unorganized pile.*

The way my stomach churned thinking about the likelihood of Brent being right—that Rose would take him back—was enough to make me realize there was no reason for me to stay in Ridgewood. I only moved here with him—with them—because Brent convinced me it was a good idea.

I refused to watch them repeat their toxic shit over and over, and even more so, I refused to sit back and not be the brother she ended up with.

My brother was a piece of shit, and it was high time I left him behind. Even if that meant leaving her behind, too.

For about a year, I went back to Northwood until I realized my hometown was not where I wanted to be. Realistically, I knew that before I went back, but I needed the stability of a roof over my head to figure out my next move. Moving back to my parents' house seemed like the simplest solution, and it was for a while, but being in your twenties and living with mommy and daddy fucking sucked. So as quickly as I could, I hightailed it out of there, tossing the same duffle full of shit into the bed of my truck, and headed toward Bridge Point.

Bridge Point wasn't bad, but it also wasn't great. If I wanted to work an industrial, warehouse type of job, I would have had everything I needed, but guess what? I didn't. Not one bit. So after four months I, yet again, tossed my duffle into my truck and tried a new town.

Shadow Hills.

It was small, but up-and-coming. The job options sucked, but nothing a quick commute into Ridgewood wouldn't rectify. So long as I stayed on the Shadow Hills side of Ridge-wood, I didn't have to watch Brent parade around with my girl on his arm.

Except she wasn't my girl.

Yet.

And right now, she pretended to be Sly's girl. It was a farce—I knew that. Her relationship with Sly was about as solid as the one she had with my brother, and I knew it was only a matter of time before she walked away from him, too.

The question remained, when she walked away from him, would she finally walk toward me?

BRINGING my elbows to rest on the long mahogany table, I clasped my hands together and cracked my knuckles, looking around at the men in front of me. Sinners Warlord—Ridge-wood's motorcycle club—wasn't your typical club. We were small, tight-knit, and formed to help the police department rid the city of the scum that inhabited the streets. Unlike the P.D., we weren't afraid to get our hands dirty. They had a code to abide by, one they couldn't bend for fear of losing their livelihoods, but for the Sinners, our main objective was to make Ridgewood a safe place, to *keep* it a safe place, by what-ever means necessary.

Pops, the club's former prez, was the epitome of every-one's favorite grandfather, but wasn't afraid of putting a bullet between the eyes of any rapist, pedophile, or abusive prick who crossed his path. His primary mission in life was to protect the women and children of Ridgewood. *All* women and children, not just the ones he knew. Pops had a moral compass and rules he required his crew to obey to keep us safe and make sure our loved ones were too. It wasn't uncommon for clubs to fuck around on their old ladies, but for the members of the Sinners, your loyalty had to lie with the one woman you gave yourself to. Family above *everything* else. Pops didn't take lightly to women being fucked around on. As far as club presidents went, he was an anomaly.

If you stepped out of line and strayed from the rules set in place, you were out. Done. Period. Pops didn't give second chances, and he also didn't believe in holding you to the club if your path led you in a different direction. If you were done with his rules or his club, he'd happily hold open the door and shove your ass through it.

Everyone knew the Sinners were doing more good than harm, even so, being an MC had a certain stereotype that the public couldn't separate from what the club was actually doing for the community. Which was fine by us. Things went bump in the night and we were the ones who added an extra *bang* to it before we swept the trash away.

Plus, it helped that back when Pops led the club he was golfing buddies with Chief Collier, and now that I'm prez, the current Chief of Police and I tossed back a whiskey together from time to time. Wes Duquette and I certainly weren't friends, but being that we were both in positions of power, we knew when the city needed us to discuss town politics and could do so harmoniously.

The gruff voice of my road captain, Silas, cut through my thoughts, pulling me back to our current predicament. "Word on the street's there's been two college girls roofied in the last week. One at Reggie's, and one at that new nightclub...er... what's it called?"

"Lawless." Preston smirked, tapping his fingers in front of his mouth. The club's newest prospect and resident party-boy was a frequent flyer at Lawless, Ridgewood's newest and hottest nightclub. True to the name, pretty much anything went at Lawless. I hadn't been yet, but I'd heard enough.

"But Reggies is in Shadow Hills, ain't it?" Damon asked. "Not quite our jurisdiction."

My lips pursed as I contemplated Damon's words, irritation zipping through my bloodstream at his lack of compassion. "Who fucking cares if it's Shadow Hills or Ridgewood?" I snapped, unable to help myself. "Either way, a barely legal girl was roofied and raped. The two could be connected, or they could be completely random, but I'd place bets on the former. Now the question is, what the fuck are we going to do about it?"

The men around the room grumbled and growled their agreement, while Damon's eyes met mine, a flash of anger momentarily turning his blue eyes navy. I raised a brow, silently daring him to open his mouth.

As I suspected, he stayed silent.

Damon, the club's enforcer, was the eyes and ears of the club. He made sure the members stayed in line and that our name was kept out of everyone's mouth less they were spitting compliments. Due to the nature of his job, Damon was a stickler for rules, laws, and guidelines. Apparently, he added city limits to that list as well.

"Either way, someone's targeting the college girls. Best we put a couple guys at each of the main bars and clubs for a while and keep our eyes peeled. If we find the fucker, we take him out," King, my Vice President, spoke up. "If someone sees him roofie another chick, we follow him out. We'll work in pairs. One makes sure the girl is safe, and the other takes out the trash swiftly."

Most of my men nodded in agreement, liking King's plan. My arms crossed in front of me as I sat back against the leather backing of the chair, my head snapping to my left with the sound of Nixon's voice. "There're more bars and clubs than there are us, King. How are we working the logistics?"

I turned back to my right where King sat and waited for his response. It wasn't unlike me to sit quietly and listen intently while the club worked through details on what needed to be done. I had overall say, and if I wasn't on board with a proposal, it didn't happen. It was important for me to listen to *everything* that was laid out—to scrutinize each and every detail to determine if ultimately my men would be safe.

After the Sinners agreed with Pops to appoint me as the new club prez, I gave them my word that I'd hold the club to the same standards he did. To keep my men safe and in line. I hadn't been the VP when the club voted me in. King had held that title for years, but had no interest in being fully in charge. Instead, they'd gone out on a limb and given me their trust. Traditionally speaking, I was all wrong for the position. Hadn't been in the club long enough, was too young, too new. But still, they'd chosen to vote me in as their prez.

I wouldn't mess that up.

"We'll rotate. Hit as many as we can. Visit the more popular ones over the dive bars—go where the women go. See what we see. I have a hunch it won't take us too long to find this prick." King's eyes met mine, and I nodded once with approval. He turned back to the room, addressing the group. "Is this vote unanimous or someone want to challenge it?"

Not a single member challenged the vote.

Pushing up from the chair, I stood and placed my palms down on the smooth wood table, leaning forward. Slowly, I met the eyes of every member of the Sinners Warlord before I concluded. "Let's find this fucker and put him in the ground."

CHAPTER SIX

Rosie

Social media offered me no entertainment as I laid upside down on one of my best friends' beige microfiber couch. My legs curved up the back and draped over the top, while my torso laid on the seat cushions, and my head hung off the edge. My wavy brown hair puddled on the carpet, the blood rushing to my head as I bounced my feet without a care in the world.

Tossing my phone onto the floor, I groaned and dramatically flung my arm over my eyes. "Ugh. I'm so bored, Noah," I whined, and I heard him scoff from where he sat on the floor beside me.

"Should have gone to Elle's instead then," he quipped without looking up from the file he was poring over.

Noah was one of my best friends, and a lieutenant for the Ridgewood Police Department, who was currently balls deep in a case. Paperwork strewn all over his dark cherry wood coffee table, his focus ninety percent on his work, ten percent on me.

I loved Noah like a brother—which really was quite a shame because he sure was pretty to look at—but unless his girlfriend walked into the room I knew his sole priority today would be his job, and I'd be hanging in silent company while I was here. The only thing that could shift his attention was the girl who he'd worked so hard to get to commit to him.

"You knock Lily up yet?" I asked innocently, swinging my legs off the back of the couch to sit up like a normal human. The blood rush to my head was fun for a second, but I had no interest in dealing with a headache for the rest of the day.

My question garnered a glance from Noah, and he blew out a shaky breath. Tucking his hands behind his head, he let the weight of it balance in his crossed palms. "No. No luck yet."

"It'll happen," I told him lightly as I reached out and placed my hand on his shoulder, giving it a squeeze.

Noah turned his head and gave me a pointed look, hurt shining through his eyes. "It's been months, Rosie, and it hasn't happened yet. We made appointments with our primary doctors to get started with all the tests, and labs, and shit to figure out why we're not getting pregnant."

I was at a loss for words, feeling very awkward because I didn't have an answer for him. Any words I said would never be the right ones, but falling silent also wasn't the right approach. This wasn't a topic I was well versed in, and I honestly wasn't educated in the process of dealing with infertility, or how to navigate the topic appropriately with someone who was living with it.

So instead, I stayed true to myself and did what I knew would bring one of my favorite people a little comfort.

I threw my arms around him and smashed a big, wet kiss on the side of his face. My lips connected with the spot just above his beard and I held him there obnoxiously hard, making sure to hum a big smoochy sound effect as I did. When I finally released his face, I told him, "You got this."

It probably wasn't the right thing to say in hindsight, but he knew what I meant.

Noah glared at me and wiped the spot on his cheek I had kissed, suppressing his smile as he did.

"What are you working on?" I asked, wanting to get his mind off of our current topic. He rarely talked to me about his cases, but I figured it was worth a shot. The worst he could do was deflect.

As he pursed his lips in thought, I knew he was debating whether he should tell me or not. I was a nosey bitch, but when it came to his work, I respected there were things I couldn't pry out of him. I still didn't know what he did when he went undercover almost a year ago, and it drove me absolutely batty.

"I can't really say much," he told me hesitantly. "But it has to do with the Sinners. How much longer are you stuck with them above Andromeda? I really hate that you are in such close proximity to them all the time."

"Oh, give me a break. The Sinners are harmless. Buncha modern day Robin Hoods walking old ladies across the road and shit."

Noah scoffed, obviously not agreeing. Lifting two manila

folders from the stack to his left, he shook them in his hand. "Yeah, okay. These files say otherwise."

I waved my hand in his general direction, brushing it off. "Yeah, yeah. So maybe they're a little rougher, but they're harmless as far as I'm concerned. I'm upstairs like four nights a week in Sly's room. They know better than to fuck with me —not only because I'm with Sly all the time—but because they better be respectful if they want to stay living above my bar."

"They're not as innocent as you think they are, Rosie. Something's definitely going on behind the scenes with them. There are things I can't talk about, but you promised me you'd be careful when it came to them, remember?"

"I remember, but you also won't tell me anything about it, so until I get some hard evidence, mister Lieutenant, I'm going to keep letting Sly satisfy my kitty cat."

"I don't need to know who's satisfying you, Rosie. Why don't we change the subject and you tell me why you're really here? What are you avoiding today? Because I know it's something."

"I have to be avoiding something to come hang out with my bestie?"

"That's usually your M.O., yes."

Slamming both hands on my chest, I rested them over my heart and pushed my lower lip out. "Your words hurt me Noah-ba-boah."

"Jesus Christ," he said, rolling his eyes at me. "Always so dramatic."

"And *you're* always so grouchy, mister."

He quirked an eyebrow, giving me a look that said '*spill it*'.

Ugh. The bastard always knew when I was keeping something to myself. I guess that's what made him such a great cop. He could see right through you.

I huffed dramatically and pulled my hair into a messy bun as I told him. "Cain. What else?"

"Now what?"

"He's just...*there*. Existing. I don't want him to exist."

Noah laughed sarcastically, knowing I was full of shit. "I think you'd be pretty upset if he didn't exist, Rose."

"No, I wouldn't." *Yes, I would.* "I just don't understand what he wants. I mean, obviously I do. He wants me. But why? It's been almost seven years. Surely he's not still holding onto something that didn't even really happen seven years ago?"

"Like you're not holding on to something that didn't even really happen seven years ago?" Noah argued. He loved to make me think about things in a different way. His favorite pastime was making me realize I was being an asshole.

Narrowing my eyes, I tucked my feet beneath me, curling onto Noah's couch. "I'm holding onto what he said to me as a reminder of why he'll never win me back. Not how I felt back then."

"Aren't they one and the same? It's okay to admit that you still care, Rosie. It doesn't make you weak."

"What does it make me then? If I were to admit that being around Cain fucking Michaels feels like I've finally come back home and that being in the same vicinity as him has the hole in my stupid fucking heart I thought was healed, not feel as empty? Because I can't admit that, Noah. I won't.

He hurt me and I won't allow myself to ever get hurt by a man again."

"It makes you human, Rosie. It's okay to give someone a second chance if you feel like they've earned it."

"He hasn't earned it, though, Noah. He's barely just waltzed back into my life and apologized."

Grabbing my face between his large palms, Noah squeezed my cheeks, forcing me to look him dead in the eyes.

"Who are you?"

"Rosie," I said through squished lips.

His eyes narrowed, and he shook his head slowly. "Rosie, who?"

Letting out a low growl, I rolled my eyes. Through my fish lips, I said with a distorted voice, "Rosie Adler."

Noah shook his head slowly, giving me a stern look. My answer wasn't good enough, and I knew exactly what his angle was. "Rosie. *Who?*"

"Rosie *fucking* Adler."

"There she is. Now, make goddamn sure he has to work for it."

THE MOVEMENT of my office door opening caught my eye as I laid on the plush couch in my office, ignoring the over-whelmingly long to-do list that sat on my desk. Opting for a little me time instead, I had one wireless headphone in, listening to my favorite true-crime podcast while I completed a stupid sunset landscape puzzle on a brain-teaser app I downloaded a few weeks ago. Sometimes just zoning out to simple things was exactly what the doctor ordered, especially when my mind was on overdrive.

I kept my eyes trained on my phone, but from my peripheral, I could see Sly come in. Per usual, he shut the door gently behind him before crossing the room. As he approached the couch, I slid my feet to bend my legs and pulled them closer to my body, allowing room for Sly to sit.

"Mia preferita, why the long face?" he asked as he took a seat next to me.

Toggling out of my puzzle, I paused the podcast and reached up to remove my headphone. "I'm just really in my head tonight. Salty for no reason."

"Did something happen?" Sly's eyes darkened as he asked the question. A smile played on my lips as I watched his reaction, loving that even though we weren't serious, he'd throw hands for me if need be.

"No," I told him with a sigh. "My thoughts just got the best of me again."

Sly held my gaze and slowly trailed his fingertips from my ankle up to my inner thigh as he scooted closer. "Sounds like you need una distrazione, mia preferita."

When he spoke in his native tongue, it did wicked things to my body. Though I couldn't speak Italian, I'd spent enough time around Sly to pick up on certain words he threw into his sentences, or just straight up asked him what the hell he said when I didn't understand something. The nickname he had chosen for me, *my favorite*, was a personal favorite because I knew it held double meaning. Sly had become a close friend, and him acknowledging me as one of his favorite humans was something I held near to my heart. He had my full trust, and that wasn't something I freely gave. Not anymore.

"A distraction is exactly what I need," I told him, letting my legs fall open. Though I wore my denim cutoff shorts, I knew they left little to the imagination, and with my legs spread, the fabric of my thong could be seen.

Without hesitation, Sly stood and walked over to my desk, snatching the keys that sat on top of it and unlocked the bottom drawer. I didn't need to look to know what he was pulling out of it, and instead, I unclasped the bottom of my shorts and pulled them from my body, taking my underwear off with them before tossing both to the floor. I kept my legs spread, and moved my fingers down to massage my clit while I waited for Sly to return.

The cushions dipped below my body as he settled one knee between my legs, keeping his other foot on the floor as he tugged my shirt up to expose my breasts. I had gone braless today, not giving a shit if my nipples showed through my loose graphic tee, because, why would I? If someone didn't like it, they could get out of my bar. Sly's hand reached up and roughly palmed my left tit, licking his lips as he did.

"Squisita," he said earnestly, keeping his eyes on my body.

"Translation?" I asked breathlessly, already so wound up with anticipation and my own touch. I hadn't heard him say that word before, and although I had a feeling what it meant, I wasn't sure.

"Exquisite, mia preferita, simply exquisite. Now, what setting?" Sly began clicking the button on my Rose toy, switching through the different vibration settings.

"Dealer's choice."

Sly replaced my fingers with his own, dipping into the wetness between my legs and pulling it upward to smear on my clit. He rubbed it in tight circles before abandoning it all together.

Slamming three fingers inside me mercilessly, he then brought the Rose toy to my clit, pressing it against me with just the right amount of pressure.

Immediately, I groaned with pleasure from the vibration. The fullness of his fingers was the cherry on top, making me squirm in pleasure against his touch. "The...*perfect* distraction," I moaned, lifting my hips to press into him and the toy further.

My body hummed as I rode Sly's hand. He was ruthless with the thrusts of his fingers, knowing exactly what my body craved from him and delivered it in the most toe-curling way. Grabbing my own breasts, I kneaded them, rolling my nipples between my fingers and loving the stimulation it caused. Heavy moans floated past my lips as I let myself drift away with the pleasure, my eyes rolling back as my body climbed toward release.

Sly slowed the thrusts of his fingers and removed the toy from my clit. When I opened my eyes, he was staring down at me, his eyes blazing. "Tell me what's got you in your head," he demanded in a tone that was sharp, yet somehow gentle. His fingers played shallowly, not entering me but still bringing me soft pleasure.

I knew what he was doing.

He was doing what he always did. Getting me to open up. To talk. He wanted me to admit my feelings.

Sly, on the exterior, was a hardened badass—a motorcycle

club member who kept to himself unless provoked. He wasn't a man you wanted to piss off. Cold and ruthless were traits painted throughout his interior, and although he didn't admit it, I knew he had some sort of ties to the mob. He hid it well from the MC, but the way he carried himself screamed trained upbringing. That should have thrown up so many red flags, but my gut told me Sly was trustworthy and had the best interests of the MC at heart. *That's* the type of man Sly was. On the inside, he was caring. Empathetic. He was loyal. And for being such an intimidating dude on the outside, the man was seriously in touch with his feelings, and for some reason, made it his mission to make me be in touch with mine.

Thrusting my hips upward, I chased his touch, growing frustrated that he'd stopped all movement of his hand and the toy. "Sly. Come on," I scoffed as I glared at him.

He laughed and brought the Rose toy back to my clit, the vibrations instantly pulsing through me and creating immediate pleasure again. Sighing, my head lulled back to the arm of the couch. Thank *fuck* he did that, because I was *this close* to snatching it from his hand and finishing what he started.

"Talk," Sly prodded as he clicked the button on the toy to change the vibration.

He was pissing me off. I didn't like that he quite literally was holding my pleasure against me right now. I knew if I didn't start talking, he'd stop playing.

"What do you want me to say?" I snapped. "Do you really want me to sit here and tell you I'm pissed off because, once again, Cain has pushed his way into my thoughts and won't leave them?"

"Exactly. Tell me why that's bothering you, mia preferita."

The vibration changed again, and I couldn't help but moan as the toy started pulsating against my clit, mimicking a sucking sensation. "Why would you want to hear about that when you're between my thighs, playing with my pussy, Sly? Does me talking about another man—*saying* that man's name as you pleasure me—get you off?"

Tossing his head back, Sly roared a laugh, his head shaking as he pushed two fingers into me. He wasted no time curling them upward to stroke my G-spot. The sensation stole the air from my lungs. "No, but it gets *you* off, and that's the objective right now, isn't it?"

"Cain doesn't get me off. The toy and your fingers get me off."

"Rosie. Talk," he repeated, clearly growing tired of my deflections.

Admitting defeat, I sighed dramatically, then began. "He haunts me, Sly. Everywhere I turn, he's there, and his gaze is heavy. I let him go years ago—I moved on. Yet, here he is again, stalking me silently. The last few months I've been able to brush him aside and ignore his presence, but suddenly, it's impossible. The *need* to be close to him gnaws at me. Thinking of him brings me both pleasure and pain."

His fingers stopped moving as my sentence finished, and I internally freak out, wondering if I've said too much. He may have goaded me to talk, but Sly was still my lover. My lover with his fingers very much inside me. And I just word vomited how I felt about another man. At his request, but still.

The feeling of wrong-doing washed over me—I might have just fucked up.

My face must have reflected what I was feeling, because Sly's spine straightened slightly and again, he pulled the toy away from me. "Your words don't hurt me, bella. In another life, you'd be my perfect match. But we both know in this life, we are simply a comfort for each other. I want you to speak freely about your feelings, mia preferita. I will always listen. Our understanding is mutual."

Shaking my head, I pulled my legs together until my knees met. "It's not right, Sly. I feel like a bitch. Especially right now —using you to get off."

"Mia preferita, I *offered* to get you off. You did not demand it. If this is you using me, then I use you too. You know...you know my heart is back in New York. And I know your heart is here—you just do not allow the barrier protecting your heart to come down. But the love is in there, I am sure of it."

The overwhelming feeling of weight on my chest was back, and I could feel emotions I had no desire in feeling bubble to the surface. All I wanted was to push them down and banish them away again. The motherfucker wasn't even around, yet the effect he had on me was excruciating.

Squeezing my eyes shut, I blew out a shaky breath and willed my racing heart to settle. "Distract me, Sly," I begged, and I wasn't a woman who *begged* very often, but right now I'd make an exception. I wanted to think about something else— *anything* else. "*Please.*"

Right now, it wasn't about getting off. I didn't give a damn about the orgasm that I'd now lost twice. Right now, all I cared about was pushing away the tears forming behind my eyes, and to get Cain Michaels as far away from my thoughts as humanly possible.

"Come desideri, la mia preferita."

Pushing my legs apart, Sly tossed the Rose toy behind him on the couch and placed a hand on each of my thighs as he positioned himself laying on his stomach, his face in line with my pussy. He descended on it, sliding his tongue through my slit, tasting my juices. He felt like heaven.

Still stimulated from him using the toy, I audibly gasped and slammed my head back on the arm of the couch as my hips pushed into his face. "*Fuck*, Sly, fucking *fuckkkk*."

He chuckled against me as he brought his tongue up and flicked my clit with its tip. Sliding his hand over, he slipped two fingers inside me, pumping a few times before adding a third.

Shamelessly, I rode his fingers, humping his face while I grabbed my tits as though they single-handedly had the power to keep me from levitating off the couch.

Sly's face shifted slightly as though something had caught his eye, but I couldn't bring myself to care enough to follow his line of sight. His magical tongue was pushing me too close to the edge, and I was so ready to freefall.

"Keep going. Don't fucking stop, Sly," I moaned, feeling myself climb higher and higher.

"He's watching, mia preferita. Even though he can't see through the glass, it's as though he senses you at the height of pleasure."

My gaze shifted over to the one-way glass wall of my office, and sure enough, Cain was staring at it as though he could see me ride Sly's face. For a moment, my brain allowed me to think that he *could* see through the glass, and that watching me was bringing him some sort of satisfaction. Then, I remembered the glass I could so clearly see through, was still very much a mirror on the other side.

Sly removed one of his fingers and made scissoring motions with the other two. With his tongue on my clit, his fingers moving expertly inside me, and my eyes glued to the man I would have given *everything* to, I felt my orgasm crest.

As though connected by a magnet, Cain prowled toward the glass, only stopping when he was right in front of it—so close he was practically touching it. His features carried a look I couldn't read, and as he stood there staring at his own reflection, he crossed his arms over his chest.

My breathing hitched before it began to sputter—the air struggling to fill and deflate my lungs.

Cain couldn't see me, but it sure as hell felt like he could. Unbeknownst to him, we were staring at each other straight in the eyes. And I was so close to coming—the pressure within me built to the point of explosion.

Sly's deep voice vibrated against my clit as he whispered, "Come for me, mia preferita. Come for *us*. Scream his name."

The last thing I remembered before I nearly blacked out from my life-altering orgasm, was the unintelligible string of moans as I came harder than I ever had on the tongue of my lover, while looking directly at the one man I hated to admit I wanted more than life itself.

CHAPTER SEVEN

Rosie

Andromeda was silent today. Eerily silent. The air was still and stagnant, the stale scent of alcohol from the night before lingering. Sitting on a barstool, I tapped my favorite pen against the counter and looked down at the list in front of me. Indy breezed around behind the bar, taking a small inventory and telling me everything we'd need for the weekend as I wrote it down.

I'd almost filled the small half sheet in front of me, and the mental total I'd created brought me more anxiety with every passing item added. This would cost me a small fortune.

I tried to push away the self-doubt and the nerves, and push forward the logical thoughts instead. Andromeda was thriving. It was successful, constantly packed, and we just won second place in the Best Night Life category for Ridgewood's Best in Business awards. I knew this weekend would be packed beyond belief, so I tried to not let the running tab of our necessities crawl its way under my skin.

We'd be fine.

Indy caught my eye when she stopped moving behind the bar and came to stand in front of me, forearms pressed into the counter as she leaned forward with a cheeky smile. I knew that look. The wheels in that pretty little head of hers were turning.

"Spill it, punk princess," I told her as I brought the pen to my lips, taking the capped side between my teeth.

"This weekend is going to be insane. I can feel it. Best Night Life? Hell ya, we are! So, to celebrate and bring in some extra cash, of course, I think we should do a signature drink this weekend only. Create something bougie, up-charge for it, and slap a punny name on it in honor of the award."

Her idea was brilliant, honestly. In the past, when we'd done similar, it'd been a gold mine. I pursed my lips in thought, the pen cap now tapping against my mouth. "Let's make it a parody. Call it The Runner-Up and make it a classic drink with a twist. Which cocktail was our best seller last week?"

"Probably the classic mojito. My fingers smelled like mint for three days after we got through Saturday night."

"What can we add to that to make it unique?"

"I'm not so sure it needs to be unique, boss," she quipped. "It's a runner-up, right? So it doesn't need to be too different from the original. A mojito is lime and mint, so what if we just throw some limoncello in too, and make it a limoncello mojito? Lime juice, mint, white rum, soda water, and a splash of limoncello. I can spiral some lemons and garnish the drink with the peel and mint leaves."

I jotted down limoncello onto my list and drew a star next

to lemons to indicate I'd need a lot of them. "Perfect, Indy. Great idea. Brains *and* beauty, aren't ya?"

"It's why you pay me the big bucks." She laughed as she rearranged the clear boxes of garnish.

I slid off my barstool and scooped my purse from where it sat beside me, turning back to her as I said, "Oh great! You think I'm paying you the big bucks? I'll cross 'give Indy a raise' off my other list, then."

Playfully, she picked up a damp dish towel and flung it in my direction. It landed on the edge of the bar. My fingers wrapped around it to toss it back, when suddenly the bright sunlight streaming in through the open side door dimmed.

"We're closed!" Indy called out, not bothering to stop her organizing.

Me, however... I looked at the door to see who was casting a shadow.

Looking back at me was a six-foot four motorcycle god standing in the doorway of my bar.

Our eyes connected, and for a moment, I forgot how to breathe. Cain leaned against the frame, his right arm propped against it like he didn't have a care in the world. He wore his signature jeans and t-shirt with his leather vest, all of which looked freshly laundered and not like he'd just hopped off his bike. Which, maybe he hadn't, since I didn't hear the familiar rumble of the engine enter into the parking lot.

"What do you want, Cain?" I sassed when I remembered how to form a sentence. From behind me, Indy snorted, and I tossed her a look. "What?"

"You just said that so damn loud, boss."

I scoffed, trying to play it smoothly by shrugging one of

my shoulders. "Whatever," I mumbled at her before turning my attention back to Cain. A smirk played on his lips, which I ignored and moved toward the hall, heading to my office.

The sound of his boots against the concrete floor echoed throughout the bar as he followed. Once in front of the mirrors that hid my office, I pushed the small perforation on the wooden frame on the mirror aside to reveal a keyhole. Reaching into my back pocket, I produced a single key on a thin, light blue lanyard, and shoved it in.

After it unlocked, I pushed the hidden door open and walked inside. The door swung shut behind me quickly, but unsurprisingly, the sound of what I presumed to be Cain's hand catching it before it closed fully caused the hinges to whine as he pushed it back open.

I expelled a dramatic breath and sat the shopping list and pen I still held on my desk. Placing both hands on the smooth surface, I let my head drop as I battled with the angel and devil on my shoulders on how to handle this.

Ever since our run-in a few nights ago in the club's living room, he'd infiltrated every thought I had, every moment of every day. But I still wasn't ready to just forgive and forget, despite Sly's words incessantly repeating in my head.

He loves you.

Maybe he did back then, but you can't love someone you haven't seen in years.

Can't you though? Your best friends both reconnected with the people they thought slipped away years later...

Clearly, they were the exception and not the rule.

My head turned slightly as my eyes wandered to the couch, the exact spot where just a few days prior, Sly gifted me an earth-shattering orgasm while I stared through the glass at the very same man who I could feel moving closer to me now. His steps were quiet, calculated, as he wordlessly crossed the room, stopping only when he was so close, I could feel the heat from his body radiate off him.

"Seriously, Cain. What?" I flinched slightly when his hand connected with my skin, just above my elbow. His fingertips trailed upward, lightly tracing a path up my arm, leaving goosebumps in place of his touch. Despite my efforts to remain unaffected and aloof, my breathing hitched, and I straightened instead of leaning forward on the desk.

Big mistake.

The slight change in posture caused my body to press against his, and as though acting on instinct, his head dropped lower, aligning with mine. His very presence made me second-guess myself. Made me second-guess my sanity for even slightly entertaining the thought of giving him another chance.

"I missed you," he muttered as his fingertips brushed against my shoulder, pushing my hair back to expose my neck. "This thing between us...it's not over yet. It can't be."

Something about his words snapped me back to reality, my mind wising up quicker than my body which was still melting against him. "You're right, Cain, it's not," I choked before taking a moment to regain my credence. Once I found my voice again, I turned toward him. We were practically nose to nose when I told him with confidence, "Because something can't be over when it never even started. This—" I gestured between us, "—is just...nothing."

A flash of hurt flickered behind his eyes before he masked

the pain my words had clearly caused. "I've never stopped wanting you, Rosie. You've always been with me."

Why was it that the use of my actual name, instead of Rose, sent my heart plummeting into my stomach? I didn't like it, and the fact that I didn't like how he hadn't used the name he always called me, bothered me more than it should have.

Yanking down the neckline of his t-shirt, he pointed to the space between his collarbone and his shoulder. "I got this right after you left him. When you left *us*."

I sucked in a sharp breath—not because of the black and gray photo-realistic rose he had tattooed onto his skin, but because of what he said. *Us.* He'd lumped himself in with my breakup with his brother.

Again, my mind bounced back faster than my heart. "A rose? You tattooed a fucking rose on your chest and thought it'd have me crumbling?" A manic laugh bubbled, and I tossed my hands into the air before connecting them with his chest and pushing. The momentum caused him to stumble a step backward, and I used the opportunity to put more distance between us. "I don't even like roses, you arrogant asshole. If you knew anything about me, you'd *know* my favorite flowers are dahlias."

Cain rubbed his hand against his beard, his eyes blazing with a heat I could feel from where I now stood across the room. My hands crossed in front of me as I stared back at him, refusing to back down. Stalking toward me, he closed the distance I'd made and this time, his hand wrapped around my throat. His warm, calloused palm encircled the vulnerable part of my body, yet not a single feeling of fear flickered through me. Lust, yes, without a doubt, but I wasn't afraid of the way he held me.

He used his grasp to turn my body and back me to the couch, where he sat down first, then pulled me onto his lap, still keeping his grasp firmly around my neck.

My knees came to rest on either side of him, the soft leather cool, contrasting against my hot skin.

Moving his hand from my neck, he placed it on my hip and pulled my body down onto his further. Through my thin jeans, my core connected with his hard cock, and we groaned in unison at the contact of our bodies. A jolt of electricity instantly zinged through me and radiated in my clit, causing it to throb. I used every bit of restraint I had not to rub against him.

"The rose is a symbol of you, Rosie, not your favorite flower." Cain's words came out breathy, and his eyes drifted to the spot where our bodies connected, though shrouded with several layers of clothing. When he slid his gaze to mine again, he brought his hand up, pushing back more of my hair before pressing it against my cheek. "I couldn't give a shit less about your favorite flower. In no way does that define who *you* are. I got the tattoo because I knew it'd be the only way to keep a piece of you with me at all times, long after you'd left."

The entire room felt like it was closing in on me in that moment.

"Stop calling me Rosie," was the only thing I managed to whisper.

Cain's brow shot up in question. "You told me a few nights ago to stop calling you Rose, and now you don't want me to call you Rosie? I'm confused..."

"You confuse me!"

"The feeling is mutual."

I licked my lips, desperately needing the moisture against them. "It doesn't matter, Cain. None of it matters. We can't go back in time."

"Then why are you holding words from seven years ago against me?"

"I'm not," I snapped. "I just have no desire to move backward. You are a part of my past, not my future."

Even as the words left my lips, I knew they were a lie. And as I watched Cain's face contort from lust to agony to anger, I felt it deep in my gut that I had just said the wrong thing.

"Tell me what I have to do to make this right between us, Rose," he sneered, his hold on my hip tightening. "Tell me what I have to do to get you to leave him."

"Leave who?" I questioned.

Cain snickered and lifted his pelvis slightly, pushing his erection against me. "The fact that you just asked me *who* tells me everything I need to know."

Sly, my subconscious told me, putting the pieces together.

A snarky response was at the tip of my tongue, but before I could retort, three things happened, seemingly faster than the speed of light.

First, Cain's large, tattooed hand wrapped around my hair tightly as he formed it into a ponytail at the crown of my head. Next, he tilted my head downward so we were staring straight into each other's eyes—his light brown met my hazel, and it was as though time completely froze. Our eyes spoke everything we held deep within us and it felt as though the world tilted on its axis. Memories flooded my mind, a full movie of every moment we'd spent together on hyper speed. Then, finally, he used the hand in my hair to pull me toward him, smashing his lips against mine.

I put up no fight as my lips parted on instinct, letting him gain access to my mouth immediately. His tongue swept against mine, connecting, exploring, while the hand in my hair kept me firmly in place against his. He kissed me hard, and I kissed back with equal fervor, loving the feel of his lips against mine.

My body went into overdrive and a spark ignited within me like never before, pulsating through my veins. Rocking against him, I moaned into his mouth from the friction my jeans caused against my aching clit. An overwhelming need for this man radiated through me, and I was certain I'd never felt this alive. Every inch of me trembled as emotions I'd long since pushed away came barrelling to the surface.

Cain kissed me until we were forced to break apart to breathe. The second his lips left mine, I felt empty and wanted to close the distance between us again.

"Tell me what I have to do, Rose. I'll do it. I'd do anything for another shot with you," he panted against my lips. His forehead pressed against mine, and I didn't dare open my eyes. I was still processing the moment, my feelings conflicting in every way.

If it was even possible, the room grew more silent than it had been. Only the sounds of our breaths evening out could be heard in the room.

Cain released my hair and lightly massaged my scalp, whispering, "Please, Rose. Tell me what to do."

This man had pushed his way in, chipping away at the

frosty tundra barricading my heart. Again, though years later, he had me wanting to explore what could be.

I *liked* easy. I liked no-strings-attached, easy companionship that I knew I could count on, yet still didn't force me to be tied down. The life I led was perfect for me—everything I wanted, in fact. It wasn't complicated. It wasn't riddled with frustration or heartache. I never had to worry about if I was making someone else happy, or if I was making them miserable. Sly and I had a fantastic arrangement and delicious sex, and he didn't expect me to be something that I wasn't. He didn't ask for more, or want more.

Cain would want more.

Could I give him that? Give him the piece of me that, other than his brother, no man had ever been given?

Commitment.

I could hardly even call what Brent and I had *commitment*, but it had been more than I'd given Sly.

Was I ready to let go of the simplicity of my arrangement, of my *life*, just to *finally* explore this connection between me and Cain? Clearly, after all these years, it hadn't gone away. At least not completely. And that had to speak for something, right?

Still, there was so much that could go wrong. So much potential for the frustration and heartache I'd successfully avoided over the last several years.

And I knew...I *knew*. Anything with Cain would be monumentally different than anyone who'd come before him.

I just wasn't sure I was ready for that.

He continued to search my eyes as I battled my thoughts,

so conflicted and ill-prepared to answer the question he'd asked me three times now.

Tell him what to do.

My heart seized, feeling as though he'd reached inside and was squeezing it tightly as he awaited my response.

I wasn't ready to give up what I had with Sly just yet. The ease, the comfort. I couldn't let it go for someone I knew could shatter my heart. So I responded with the only thing I could think would satiate him for the moment, the only thing I thought might buy me some time.

"Share me," I whispered. "Share me with Sly. I'll give you the chance to make things right, but on my terms. What I have with Sly is something you'll never understand, Cain. He's one of my best friends—a comfort. I'm not letting that go."

"I'm not sharing you with another man, Rose," he growled, his eyes narrowing with annoyance.

"You either share me, or you don't get me at all, Cain. The choice is yours." Pushing off him, I stood and practically ran over to my desk, grabbing the shopping list and my purse, before I bolted out of my office, leaving Cain sitting on my couch with a full view of me moving through the bar and out the doors, putting the much-needed distance between us so he could think about my offer.

CHAPTER EIGHT

Rosie

"Wait a second—back up, Rosie. You told him to *what*?" my best friend Elle whisper-shouted, her voice sounding a little strained with her question. A rustling of papers produced a deafening sound through the speaker, and I couldn't help but wince slightly because of it.

Readjusting my cell to cradle between my shoulder and ear, I pressed up on my tiptoes and reached for the bottles of limoncello to place in my shopping cart. "I told him I wanted him to share me?" It wasn't a question, but the uptalk in my voice made it sound like one. Hell, I was questioning my own sanity at this point.

"In terms of, what exactly?"

"You know," I told her, reaching for a third and fourth bottle. Once I laid them next to the others on the metal grates, I grabbed the phone again, holding it in one hand while I pushed the cart with the other. "Share me with Sly. I want my cake and I want to eat it too, babe."

That comment earned me a side-eye from the hunched over elderly woman in the aisle next to me. Holding a bottle of ten-dollar wine like her life depended on it, she scoffed before walking away as fast as her legs would carry her.

"So you want to have a threesome, then? With Sly and Cain?" Elle's voice sounded distracted as she worked, her always manicured nails typing away at the keys in front of her. Elle was a journalist for *The Daily Reader*, a passion she'd followed and stuck with since she was a teenager, evidently. I didn't meet Elle until shortly after I'd moved to Ridgewood. Who knew I'd become besties with a chick I literally bumped into while I was buying condoms in preparation of a rebound?

Funny how life works.

"Shockingly, a threesome never even crossed my mind. I didn't mean it so literally. Hey, how's it feel having your mind in the gutter? It's fun down there, isn't it?"

"Funny."

"Seriously, what I want is for Cain to give me time to come around to the idea of attempting to trust him again. And I want to do it without giving Sly up."

The typing on the other end of the phone ceased, and without realizing it, I had stopped walking, too.

"Rosie—" Elle started, but I cut her off, knowing her well enough to know what was coming.

"I know, Elle. I don't love Sly, so I should cut him loose. But he's like my favorite fuzzy blanket—warm and familiar, and comforting. It's not even about the sex, though that doesn't hurt, obviously. I just don't want to say goodbye to him yet."

"But is that fair to him?"

"I've told you about our arrangement…"

"Yes, but if the tables were turned, wouldn't it hurt a little knowing you were his second choice? You're treating him like a placeholder, Rosie."

The accuracy of her words stung. She was right, like she usually was, and I desperately wanted to ignore it. So I did what I do when I don't get my way—I lashed out. "Like you did with Noah when you were so hung up on Ryder you couldn't think straight?"

That actually wasn't exactly how her story went, but close enough.

God, I was a bitch.

"I'm sorry," I apologized immediately, sighing loudly. "That was fucked. You know I didn't mean it."

"Yes, you did, but it's okay. You forget, I know your defense mechanisms, which means I've also learned to let them roll off my back. But don't be a B, my friend. You know I'm here for you, always."

"Always," I repeated, because that's the thing about best friends—you can show them your ugly and they'll show you theirs, then you move forward together.

Too bad all relationships weren't like best friendships.

"So what are you going to do about Cain now that you've all but told him you're willing to give him another chance?" she asked, the sound of her fingers dancing across her keyboard beginning again.

Rounding the aisle, the check stand came into view, and I made a beeline to it, suddenly feeling like the store was closing in around me. Shifting the phone back to my shoulder, I placed the contents of my shopping trip onto the conveyor belt and muttered into the speaker, "I have no idea."

<hr>

IT WAS STILL EARLY, and yet the bar exploded with activity. People were crammed anywhere they could fit, whether it be the bar, a high-top, or the dance floor. Everywhere I looked, gazing out from my office, I was picking up on so many different vibes; I thought my head would explode.

Curiosity.

Lust.

Drunken stupors.

Irritation.

Happiness.

You name it, someone's face had it written all over it.

Andromeda was wild tonight.

Thank goodness I had the sense to fully staff the place and schedule everyone to work this weekend. My employees drifted around, working discreetly to keep the bar looking pristine and keep the alcohol flowing. Behind the bar, Indy and her team mixed and poured without even breaking a sweat.

Still, the mood that was radiating through the crowd was one I couldn't ignore: shit was on the road to getting rowdy. Which around here meant one thing.

Someone, if not multiple someones, was going to get dicked tonight.

By me.

Standing from the couch, I walked over to my desk and

opened the top drawer, grabbing a handful of the holographic dick confetti I kept on hand for when self-proclaimed alpha males started to get a little too cocky in my place of business. There was only one surefire way to knock them back down a peg. Just take a handful of holographic dick confetti and toss it over their head. Worked every time.

I shoved the tiny pretty dicks into my pocket and joined the chaos, letting my eyes drag over the sea of faces. Several members of the Sinners were lingering, taking long pulls of their beers or flirting with pretty girls. At the bar, Nixon and Preston—who I'm pretty sure was actually Nixon's little cousin—sat facing outward on the barstools with a girl standing between each of their legs. Nixon had his signature 'I'm getting lucky tonight' smile plastered across his stupidly handsome face, his hand gripping the girl's hip possessively, while Preston looked like he was more interested in the condensation on the bottle he was holding. Preston's demeanor, and the way his gaze kept shifting to my pink-haired bartender, told me he *wouldn't* be getting lucky tonight. Not with the hopeful woman in front of him, anyway.

Sliding behind the bar, I placed my hand on Indy's shoulder and asked, "How's it going?"

Even with the music playing at a decibel that had bodies gyrating, I never let the volume get to where you couldn't hear the person next to you speak. That simple reason was why I hated nightclubs. What was the point if you couldn't hear the people you came with? Yes, our music was still loud, but you weren't screaming over it to have a conversation. And judging by the crowds we pulled in weekend after weekend,

I'd say people either had no problems with it or felt the same as I did.

Shit, maybe I was just getting old.

"Fucking awesome," Indy told me as she smiled wide. "The Runner-Up is a hit, like I knew it'd be."

"Did I buy enough limoncello?"

"Nah." She shrugs. "But that's a good thing. Supply and demand, baby. They'll come back next weekend to see if we serve it again."

"Maybe we should," I countered. Looking at the stock, I noticed we were down to our last bottle. It was barely even ten—obviously I miscalculated how much we'd need.

"Probably not," she singsonged with a mischievous glint to her. She reached over and grabbed the tabletop specials board and produced a small piece of white chalk from her back pocket. Striking through the twelve ninety-five price, she wrote sixteen ninety-five instead, followed by the words ALMOST GONE with three lines aggressively written beneath it.

I laughed, watching her as she proudly slammed the sign back onto the bar and cupped her hands around the edges of her mouth. "LAST CALL ON THE RUNNER-UP! GET IT WHILE YA CAN!"

"You're ruthless," I told her as I still laughed. "What do you need me to help with?"

"Get ready to serve, boss. The ladies are about to flood us."

FOR A SOLID HOUR ME, Indy, and three other bartenders moved in sync with each other, pumping out drinks as quickly as we could. The limoncello ran out twenty minutes in, but that didn't stop people from asking us to create whatever other versions of The Runner-Up we could think of. Indy poured while I ran drinks up and down the bar, delivering the strange concoctions to eager mouths.

Around eleven, the roar of drink orders began to die down, and I finally was able to take a quick breather. Pouring myself a glass of water, I pounded it down, gulping the cold liquid until it was gone.

As I poured myself a refill, I noticed the gaze of a younger guy, probably in his early twenties, trailing my every move.

I hated when men did that.

"How's it going?" I asked him, then lifted the glass to my lips to drink again. This time, I didn't chug it, but sipped instead, not loving the way this guy hardly blinked as he stared at me. His gaze traveled from my eyes, down to my tits, before bouncing up to my lips. I didn't hesitate to roll my eyes at him and his boldness.

"Better now that you're talking to me." His tone of voice was full of cockiness, and the smug look on his face solidified everything I was thinking. He'd be the first one to get dicked by me tonight.

But first, no harm in messing with his head a little. "Smooth," I told him, packing on a sultry tone. Leaning my elbows against the bar, I brought one hand to rest beneath my chin, making sure my tits were pressed together.

Taking the bait, he leaned in forward too, a smirk pulling at his lips. His eye contact was too much, and the lack of glaze made me realize he wasn't even drunk. Not yet, anyway. So anything this fool said would be authentically him.

With a sly look, he reached up and rubbed his hand against his freshly shaven face, watching for my reaction as though that move of his was some sort of panty dropper. "I bet you can't wait to suck my dick later."

I couldn't help it. The bubble of laughter that erupted out of my chest was instantaneous, and my eyes widened with surprise. To my right, Indy's loud snort of laughter mixed with mine. I felt her eyes on me, waiting for my next move, knowing it'd be a good one.

I'd been hit on, propositioned, and spoken to in a lot of ways, but the words that had just flown out of this guy's mouth were a first, for sure.

Still, without missing a beat, I reached into my pocket and curled my fingers around the holographic dick confetti, securing a decent sized handful. I kept them in my closed fist and leaned back toward the guy. "Oh yeah," I began, laying on a seductive tone for just a second, before raising my voice so those around us could hear too. "I'm going to blow it, and twist it into a balloon animal, you fucking clown."

Then I flattened my fist, hollowed my cheeks, and blew the handful of dick confetti straight into the guy's face.

Around me, the bar erupted into laughter and cheers, watching as the guy blinked several times and batted at his face like the confetti hadn't fallen straight into his lap. Regulars of Andromeda started chanting "dicked, dicked, dicked, dicked," and the guy immediately slid from his barstool and practically ran out the front doors.

The laughter didn't stop until he was long gone, and I

stepped onto a stool behind the bar and gave a dramatic little bow. While laughing, I yelled to those watching me, "And that, ladies and gentlemen, is why you don't screw with the owner!"

Cheers and whoops sounded again, and deciding I was done with the shitshow for the night, I laughed my ass off the entire walk back to my office, ignoring the heavy gaze following me from across the room. I didn't need to look. I knew exactly who it was, and I knew at some point he'd be following me in here, too.

Until then, I replayed the look on the guy's face when the first holographic dick hit his cheek.

I fucking loved my bar.

CHAPTER NINE

Rosie

My back was to the door when I heard the gentle whoosh of it opening. I was sitting on the arm of the couch, my bare feet pressed into the soft cushion as I watched the bar start to wind down for the night. It was pushing two in the morning, and I knew Indy had already given everyone an opportunity for last call.

I'd been hiding in my office for hours now, watching Cain through the glass, as he sat and nursed the same beer. He glanced back at the mirror I was concealed behind several times, as though he could feel my heated gaze on him throughout the night.

At one point, Sly had paid me a visit, wanting to hear about what had Cain's panties in a twist the last few days. I'd word vomited, explaining everything I'd said to him, plus the conversation I'd had with Elle. Sly sat on the couch chuckling, unsuccessfully trying to hide his laugh behind the fist he held to his lips.

He agreed with Elle that Cain absolutely thought I meant I wanted to have a threesome, but promised to have a conversation with him if the opportunity arose to explain his side of our situation to him.

Not that I gave a shit, honestly. Cain could think whatever he wanted, but being that Cain held a higher rank in the club than Sly did—the *highest* rank—he wanted to show some sort of respect.

He'd also offered to step back from our arrangement so I could pursue whatever was unresolved between me and Cain, but I ended up begging him not to, in a very unbecoming, *un*-Rosie like way.

Whatever.

I knew the entire situation was a mess, but as the days passed, I felt myself sinking deeper and deeper into the hole I'd crawled myself into.

When Sly left for the night with my promise to join him in his room after the bar shut down, I sat in the exact spot I was in now and let my thoughts drift away from me.

Thoughts of Cain, and what could have been if I had left Brent all those years ago.

How different my life may have been if I hadn't kept letting Brent in, wasting years on a man I didn't really care about, all because having *someone* was better than having no one.

Now, as Cain strode into my office, my heart rate quickened with anticipation. "Have you thought about my offer?" I asked him, craning my neck to look at him. My tone was nonchalant, but on the inside I felt anything but.

"I told you I won't share you, Rose." He rounded the couch and lifted my legs, taking a seat on the cushion my feet had been resting on, then placed them back down into his lap. "I've always been the guy on the sidelines, the one wishing he had you when someone else did. It won't happen again, Rose. If you still want Sly, then you can't have me."

"Who said I want you, Cain?"

His hand skimmed up my bare leg, and he drew lazy circles with his thumb against my calf. "Because when two people are meant to be, those feelings don't just disappear."

A shiver ran through me, his words resonating somewhere deep in my soul. He was right, and I absolutely hated that he was right. I may have shoved my feelings deep down in the darkest caverns within me, but they were still there, begging to claw their way back through the dust, ashes, and rubble until they reached the very place they belonged.

My heart.

"You don't even know me anymore. For all you know, the Rosie you remember is dead and gone."

"I'm confident that the same woman I watched drive away is the same woman in front of me now. I've watched you these last few months, Rose. You've grown, but you haven't changed. You're stronger now, more independent. I'm really proud of how far you've come."

Emotion clogged in my throat, and I had to look away before I said something stupid, or worse...teared up. Cain always had a way with his words and knew exactly how to say everything I wanted to hear.

Unlike most men, though, Cain actually meant his words.

You could tell by the way he held your gaze as he spoke, and the sincerity in his tone.

"What happened to you?" I asked him, eyes cast downward as I watched the movement of his thumb brush against me. "When I took Brent back, you never came around. You never called. It was like you were a ghost. You two used to be inseparable."

His movements stopped, and he slid his hand back down to my ankle, wrapping his hand around it. "He never told you?"

I shake my head.

Cain's eyes narrowed, his face contorting into a look of sadness for a split second. "The short answer is I refused to stand by and watch you go back to him. I was done feeling like my heart was being set on fire every time he touched you or belittled you. That's all it ever was between the two of you, fucking or fighting."

"That's not al—"

"Yes, Rose, it was all you two ever did. And I was done. The longer answer is, after you took off that day, after I said what I said, I had words with my brother. He suspected how I felt, and said some shit. So I hit him, then went inside and packed my stuff. I lost both of you that day, but only mourned the loss of one."

It was too much. The honesty, the recollections. The room felt like it was closing in on me—the air suddenly feeling thick and humid.

The look in my eyes must have told him I was about to slide off the arm of the couch just to get some distance between us, because he reached his arms up and pulled me into his lap, securing his muscular, tattoo-covered arms around my waist.

"You can't run again, Rose. This time I won't let you. I'm here, and I'm all in. I want you. I want this."

"What about what I want?" I whispered, my voice strained and breathy. The room still felt stifling, as though a spotlight was turned on and shining directly above me, the heat radiating from the bulb. But there wasn't, and all the heat I was feeling was generating from my body. I could feel the warmth blazing from my flesh, and whenever I was hot, the shade of my skin took on a rosy red hue.

Cain's eyes dipped from mine, dragging down my body before settling his gaze in my lap. He moved his hands to my wrist and pulled off the black elastic I had wrapped around it. Taking the band, he stretched it around one set of his fingers and lifted both hands to my hair, scooping the wavy brunette tendrils up and securing them in a very messy bun on top of my head.

A small section of my outgrown bangs fell free, and he pushed it behind my ear. "If you don't want this, Rose, if you don't want *me*, then I'll respect that and back off. But I think you're just afraid."

"I'm not afraid, Cain. I just don't want to make the same mistake twice. You might think I'm holding a grudge, or I'm afraid, or whatever it is you're thinking, but what I'm thinking is that the only person I wholly trusted and thought would always be there for me, hurt me. And yes, they're just words, but that 'words can never hurt me' shit? They were wrong, Cain. Your words hurt me, and I've healed from it and have forgiven you, but like I've already told you, I can't just forget so easily."

"Why are you so against me trying to make it up to you?" he asked, looking at me with a glint of sadness in his eyes.

A pang in my chest hit me suddenly. It hurt me to see him hurt.

For several tense seconds, we sat in silence, me staring down at my hands as they sat in my lap, and Cain staring, well, at me.

"We're going in circles, Cain."

"I told you, I wo—"

"I *know*, you won't share me with another man—with Sly. And I get it. I don't think I'd be much up for sharing either, but for now, that's the only way you'll get me. So the ball's back in your court. You either get cool with the fact that I will continue to see Sly until I decide if this *thing* between us is *some*thing, or you don't get me at all."

Cain growled, an exasperated vibration pushing through his chest and out into a huff of breath. "And that's the only way?"

I nodded. "For now."

"And if I *share* you with him, you'll let me prove I'm the better man for you? The *only* fucking man for you?"

Slowly, I looked up, and our eyes met. "Yes," I told him simply, then waited for his response as a mix of fear, curiosity, and an emotion I hadn't felt toward Cain in a long time—*hope*—swirled in my chest.

His nostrils flared as he let out a breath through his nose, clearly dealing with conflicting emotions himself. He searched my face, his lips curling inward for a moment while he thought. I practically stopped breathing when he finally, albeit a little curtly, said, "I'll do it."

And I couldn't help the little smile that curled my lips upward, those words sounding like music to my ears.

My cake never tasted so sweet.

CHAPTER TEN

Cain

Roars of engines penetrated through the crisp night sky as I killed my ignition and used my foot to engage the kickstand. Pulling my helmet off, I ran my fingers through my matted hair, placing the helmet on the seat before pulling the elastic from my wrist and tying my hair back.

Within seconds, my brothers rolled up and joined me at The Bend—a large patch of dirt alongside the highway meant for truckers to pull off on, now used as a meeting point by the Sinners when we were on the road.

As the engines cut and the noise ceased, one by one they hopped off their bikes and came to stand near me. A few lit up cigs, while most just waited patiently for a briefing.

When they were all in front of me, I spoke. "I heard from Duquette about an hour ago. Another college girl was roofied last night, this time at Indigo Renegade. He left her in the alleyway, half naked and beaten."

"He's getting more violent," King said, stating the fucking obvious.

"And he's obviously a serial rapist," Nixon chimed in.

The men began to grumble amongst themselves, speculation of where he might hit next as the forefront of their conversation.

Behind me, the sun was below the horizon—the daylight fading quickly. I needed to assign them their positions and get my men in place to be eyes and ears for the night, so we could find this guy. Clearing my throat to signal I was about to speak again, I quickly made a list of the bars he hadn't hit yet. Not having eyes at Indigo Renegade last night had been a mistake, and I wasn't willing to make another.

"Tonight, I want eyes all over the city. We made a grave mistake in skipping over Indigo Renegade last night and a young woman was raped because of it. Every single bar and club needs to have at least one Sinner, preferably two. *Including* the ones he's already hit. We will take him down, and I'd prefer we do it sooner than later. Figure out who's going where, and get there. *Now*," I barked, and the Sinners sprung into action, splitting off into pairs and spouting off the locations of where they'd be. From the sounds of it, every bar and club was covered.

There was no reason to assign myself a place, or a partner for that matter. The Sinners knew exactly where Sly and I would be.

The thought of Rose being there now, alone, with this fucker on the loose, had my skin practically crawling.

"Everyone figure their shit out?" I asked, taking the time to give each and every one of my men a moment of eye contact as a sign of respect. Nods and gruff "yes's" filled the air as I made it around the half circle before me.

"You find him, you take him out. Be safe. Be smart. Make it home."

Some Sinners repeated the sentiment, while others simply nodded and hopped onto their bikes, bringing them back to life.

Dirt from The Bend floated up, creating a dust storm as they took off in sets of twos toward the direction of their posts. Sly hung behind, waiting for me as I watched everyone leave before climbing back on my bike. I pressed my boot against the kickstand, standing the bike up as I straddled it and gripped the handles.

He may have been a good guy, but he was still fucking my girl, and that made me like him a whole hell of a lot less. "You take outside tonight. Watch the door, see who's coming and going. I'll watch the inside."

I didn't bother waiting for him to say anything—the only response he'd have given would be agreement, so what the fuck did it matter? Instead, I cranked the ignition and hit the road.

I TRAILED her movements while she glided around her bar. She stopped at high-tops and greeted her regulars, checking on them and taking their empty glasses. Even while Rose concentrated on running her business, every movement this woman made was intentional. From the way she spoke to people, down to the way she constantly scanned her surroundings, making sure the bar was safe.

Although she should know better than to worry about safety when I'm around, especially hers.

Bringing the lowball glass to my lips, I took a sip of my tequila, letting the taste burn my mouth for a few moments before swallowing it down.

I hated tequila, but Rose still hadn't fully forgiven me, and seemed to find pleasure in reminding me of it. Instead of my preferred whiskey or bourbon, or hell, even a beer, she brought me tequila on the rocks, knowing damn well that tequila is my least favorite of all.

So every time I caught her glancing in my direction, I made a point to take a sip.

It'd been almost two weeks since I told her I'd "share" her with Sly, even though I had no intention of sharing her sexually with him at all. Still, every day between us was an improvement, but knocking down her walls had been more of a challenge than I thought.

At this point, I was just grateful for the time she'd given me.

Almost every night after the bar closed, I followed her to her office after she locked up, craving the time it was just us, tucked away from the rest of the world. Some nights I sat in silence while she caught up on clerical work, while other nights we sat together and talked about everything.

Connecting on a conversational level was never an issue with us. She had a way of getting the words to flow from me, and I knew my crew would be damn surprised if anyone ever found this out, considering with them, I was a man of few words.

The urge to kiss her again had been eating me alive—the carnal *need* to feel her skin against mine, to own her mouth was getting to be too much—but I held back, wanting to prove to her just how much I wanted her. She needed to see how much this time away had made me miss *her*. I wasn't in this for sex, and I knew if I did what I wanted and constantly kept my lips fused to hers, she'd think I only wanted her physically. And that wasn't the message I wanted to send to her.

The topic of my brother had gone unspoken in these last two weeks, but I didn't need to hear it to know how much he fucked with her mind over the years. I'd personally watched her withdraw and desensitize within that short year I'd been around them...I can only imagine what he did when I was gone. Still, I knew Rose would go to her grave swearing everything between them had been casual, but when you're with someone for half a decade, it's not just casual.

It just wasn't.

She could deny it all she wanted, though, because it didn't matter. As far as my brother went, I had no brother. Not anymore. My only brothers were the Sinners. The ones *I* chose.

Blood doesn't make you family, loyalty does.

I took another sip of my tequila and watched from my peripheral as Sly slipped into the chair beside me and shrugged off his black leather jacket.

Tossing the jacket onto the empty chair adjacent to him, he gave me a curt nod. "Prez," he greeted, his accent thick but his voice smooth as butter. "Any updates?"

"Not since earlier."

Rose's exuberant laughter echoed across the room, despite the bar being at capacity, as she leaned against the table of men. She gestured with one hand as she spoke, a wide smile pressed against her beautiful face. I recognized one of the men as that cop friend of hers, and judging by the way the other three men carried themselves, I'd guess they were also on the force.

The way they all watched her with stars in their eyes made me want to scoop them out of their heads with a rusty spoon and shove them down their throats.

"Green is not a good color on you, mio amico," Sly mused, leaning against his chair and crossing his arms over his chest. "Jealousy is a plague. It'll eat at you until it's destroyed everything you love."

My gaze snapped to him and I took in his laid-back appearance, casually watching Rose as she spoke with Ridgewood's finest. He seemingly had no care in the world about her interactions with other men, and it sat about as well as a bag of nails in my stomach that a man she was sleeping with had little regard for that. "Tell me, Sly. How does it not bother you that while Rose warms your bed at night, it's me in her head and in her heart?"

I wasn't a fool. I knew Rose had filled Sly in on everything—our past, our present, and hopefully our fucking future, too. Although I wasn't sure how much of our past he actually knew, the main point was, Sly was up to speed on this whole *sharing* agreement she and I had come to.

Sly sucked in his lips slightly as he narrowed his eyes at me. I took the time to set my glass down and cross my own arms over my chest, mirroring his calm demeanor as I leaned back against my chair.

"You want my truth?" he asked once I settled.

I nodded once, flicking my eyes to where Rose now stood behind the bar, engaged in conversation with her head bartender—the chick with pink hair. When I turned my attention back to Sly, he was staring straight at me, unwavering.

"I love her," he said without so much as a blink.

Beneath my crossed arms, my hands squeezed into fists, and my jaw clenched so tightly I thought I might crack my teeth. Around me the noise of the bar faded into a dull hum, and I began to lose focus of my surroundings as everything blurred from the rage I felt coursing through my body.

"I love her," he repeated, and I swear I was about to lose my mind when he lifted a hand, stopping me. "But I'm not *in* love with her, mio amico. She has told you about our arrangement, but I am confident she has yet to explain my side of it. My heart belongs to another, and our Rosie is aware of that. But I cannot have her, and because of that, I am here. The pain of not seeing her hurts less than the pain of seeing her with another."

"I think if anyone can understand that pain, it's me. I know Rose has told you our history."

"Sì, she has. It is why I know what's in your heart. I know your love because I, too, feel it, only for someone else. Rosie and I have an arrangement that benefits us both. It's not only physical, but deeply emotional. We are compatible on an incredible friendship level and can speak freely with each other."

I must have flinched at his words as they resonated with me, because he shook his head. I understood everything he was saying because it was the type of connection Rose and I had. Hearing that she had it with another man was internally gutting me. Scanning the bar again, I found her within seconds and let my sight linger as Sly continued.

"My words do not mean to harm you, mio amico, but to help you understand. Rosie and I are ninety percent friendship, and ten percent sex. The sex is an emotional comfort, not an emotional connection. Our bodies crave sex, and through each other, we are able to subside that craving. But since things have shifted with you, the sex has lessened. The last time she came by my doing was because she was looking at *you*."

Snapping my neck in his direction, I ran my hand over my beard as I narrowed my eyes in question. "What do you mean, she was looking at me?"

A wide smile crawled across his face, his pearly whites making me narrow my eyes at him even more. "Oh, mio amico, you have no idea, do you? She knows you stare at her through the glass of her office, watching, though you can't actually see, and she likes it. So much so, when I pleasured her a few weeks back, she came with your name on her lips."

Rather than respond, I reached for the remaining tequila and brought it to my mouth, quickly tossing it back. The soundtrack of how Rose may sound roared through my thoughts, causing my cock to stir in the confines of my jeans. Slamming the glass back down on the high-top harder than intended, I felt my nostrils flare as I scoured the bar, looking for the one person who could instantly ground me.

Like magnets, our eyes connected, and I slid from my chair, never breaking our connection from across the room.

"Let's go," I growled at Sly, not bothering to see if he actually followed or not. I had more important things on my mind. His recollection of Rose coming with my name on her lips was something I just couldn't ignore.

It changed things.

Put things in a different perspective.

Even when she was with him physically, that beautiful mind of hers was thinking of me.

And that told me everything I needed to know about where her heart was at, too.

CHAPTER ELEVEN

Rosie

The heat of Cain's stare intensified with every stride he took, and the closer he came, the harder my heart pounded in my chest. Behind him, I could see Sly meandering, looking relaxed while keeping a respectable distance as he followed.

The bar was packed tonight, and it took Cain several seconds to close the distance between us, pushing past patrons, weaving through connected bodies until he practically crashed into me.

A tattooed hand immediately tangled into my hair, wrapping the brunette strands around his fist until he held it tight in his grasp at the crown of my head. His other hand gripped my hip bruisingly, and he yanked my head back, tilting my neck just enough to crash his lips to mine.

A low growl erupted from his chest as he sank his tongue into my mouth, kissing me in a way that sent an obvious message to everyone around us.

Cain was staking his claim, marking me for everyone in Andromeda to see.

My hands clawed up the front of his shirt, bunching the fabric in my fists as he continued to kiss me with a passion that burned through my soul.

Releasing my hair, his warm, calloused hands sank down my body as he reached for my thighs, hoisting me into his arms. Curling my arms and legs around him, I pulled myself closer to his body and kissed him back, not caring who saw.

Let them see.

Let them talk.

Whistles and hoots erupted around us as we passed tables of my regulars, but I was also so lost to the kiss, I barely noticed them.

The air grew quiet around us as we descended the abandoned hallway toward my office, when suddenly my back slammed against the wall. A sharp exhale of breath assaulted my lungs, the wind knocked from my body.

Cain peppered kisses down my jaw to my neck, nipping and sucking along the soft flesh as I caught my breath, his firm hands still coiled tightly under my thighs.

To my left, Sly pushed aside the hidden lock and opened the door to my office, pushing it wide and walking through. Though out of my line of sight, I knew he was holding the door open, and as Cain pulled me away from the wall and walked through the doorway, I heard the lock engage behind us. With the flip of a switch, the lowest set of lights burst to life and cast a warm glow across the room.

Placing me onto my feet, I swayed slightly, my head feeling cloudy from the lust Cain ignited. I jumped when I felt a light set of fingertips brush the hair away from my neck from behind, and a warm pair of lips skirted softly across my skin.

"She's a vision, is she not?" Sly murmured, still pressing his lips against my neck. I could feel his smile... I knew what he was doing, ruffling Cain's feathers, and it clearly was working.

Cain's low growl vibrated through his vocal chords again and his grip from where he held my hips, tightened possessively.

I wouldn't lie and say I didn't like it.

"Strip her," Cain commanded Sly with a strained voice. He reached for my desk chair and rolled it over, settling it a couple feet in front of me before taking a seat, crossing his left ankle over his right knee as he leaned back. He appeared calm, cool, and collected, but I knew his heart was hammering just as roughly as mine was.

Sly grabbed the hem of my ribbed black tank top and pulled it up and over my head, tossing it to the side. His fingers brushed my lower back, moving slowly up my back until reaching the clasp of my bra.

My chest rose and fell rapidly as I struggled to maintain the level of calm I usually possessed. But I was finding it impossible to pull together a thought other than Cain was in front of me, watching as another man undressed me.

And holy hell, it was a turn on.

Skilled fingers unclasped my bra, releasing the black satin and lace from my chest. He tossed it in the same direction as my shirt before reaching around my hips and unbuttoning my denim shorts. Sly didn't bother unzipping them before he hooked his thumbs in the waistband, pushing the fabric down my hips and taking my panties with it.

The air shifted slightly as he followed the fabric to the floor, kneeling behind me, lifting one foot at a time. Pushing my clothes aside, he helped me step out of them.

Kissing up my legs until he reached my ass, Sly bit down on one cheek hard before he sucked the flesh into his mouth, swirling his tongue around the area to soothe it. As he came back to stand, he snaked his hand around my throat, settling his palm against it and gripped my jawline with his pointer finger and thumb. "Doesn't she look delicious, mio amico? Good enough to *eat*, wouldn't you say?"

Cain's eyes flared as he took in my naked body, seeing me without a stitch of clothing for the first time. Beneath his heavy gaze, I felt more on display than I'd ever felt, and a flood of memories infiltrated my thoughts—visions of the two of us becoming close years ago.

My eyes closed. I needed a moment to let the emotions pass.

When I opened them again, they connected with Cain's and the effect it had on my body was instantaneous. Heat burned through my core, catching fire from the inside. My pussy flooded with arousal from the way he was looking at me.

"Tell him what you want, mia preferita," Sly whispered against my ear. He splayed his free hand against my lower stomach, his fingers drifting lower until Cain's rough voice filled the air.

"Don't. Touch," he growled, and Sly's movements ceased.

"What do you want?" he whispered again, low enough so only I could hear. "Tell him."

With a smirk on my lips, I stared straight into the eyes of the man who'd once broken me. The man I never thought I'd let back in. The same man I knew had the ability to destroy me if he broke my trust again. "Kneel," I ordered, lifting my chin slightly. Sly's grip loosened slightly, allowing me to lift it more as I took control.

"Kneel?" Cain repeated, shifting in his seat so he leaned forward with both elbows resting on the tops of his thighs.

"Get on your knees, Cain, and kneel. Bow to your fucking queen."

We held each other's stare, neither wanting to back down. Around us, the air crackled, and I felt Sly's thumb brush against my neck, just below my jaw. His touch was reassuring —he knew exactly what this was. A tipping point. A way to push past my hesitations with Cain and take back my confidence in him—rebuild the trust.

Cain shifted his gaze from mine to Sly's for a fleeting moment before he pushed from the chair and sank to his knees in front of me. My breath caught in my throat as I witnessed the big, bad motorcycle club president fall to the ground for me.

"Now what?" he urged, awaiting my next move.

I didn't wait for Sly to continue instructing me...I knew exactly what I wanted. I was a slave to the lust, my body controlling my mind as I lost all sensibility for the man I've always craved. "Now show me how a good boy behaves and lick me."

Behind me, the faintest of groans pushed past Sly's lips,

and he shuffled forward just slightly, pressing his erection into my back to show me how much this was affecting him, too.

Cain's hand wrapped around my ankle, pulling it until my leg draped over his shoulder and his face hovered just above my pussy, so close his warm breath floated against my skin. My clit throbbed from the faint feel of air against it. I was so wound up, one touch was liable to set me off.

"You want me to taste you, Rose? Bruise my knees while I worship your body?"

I groaned, wanting *exactly* what he'd said. Sly pressed his palm into my throat more, forcing me to lay my head back against his shoulder as Cain settled himself further between my thighs.

Time stood still as I waited, my heartbeat ringing in my ears. I couldn't concentrate on anything but the anticipation. I felt paralyzed, waiting for not only the pleasure, but for the moment where everything changed forever between me and Cain. There would be no going back after this. We'd finally be crossing the line we'd never dared to cross before.

Looking down through my lashes, I saw Cain look up from between my legs and briefly lock eyes with the man behind me, a silent conversation happening through their stares. I could hardly blink before the air was stolen from my lungs with a gasp that quickly transformed into a moan as Cain dragged the flat of his tongue against my pussy. He groaned, moving his hands to my hips before diving in fully.

He ate me like he knew exactly what my body craved, prodding at my entrance before moving his lips to my clit and suctioning them around it, using the tip of his tongue to massage and play with it.

Pleasure sparked through my body, my hips rolling and seeking more of his touch—of his tongue. I was lost in the sensation. My eyes connected with Cain's as he stared up at me from his knees, his face buried in the very spot I pictured him in almost every single one of my fantasies.

A husky moan tumbled past my lips, and Sly took that as his cue to reach around and roughly knead my breast. "He looks at you as though you are his heaven, and his hell, mia preferita. His reason for breathing and the cause of his torment. You've made him wait for this for so long."

My brain screamed at me to deny Sly's words, to protest his profession when I was sure they rang hollow, but as I held Cain's gaze, my intention to deny them caught in my throat.

As though to prove my point, Cain repositioned his lips to envelop my clit, and thrust two fingers inside me, pumping them slowly through the evidence of my lust for him.

My body began to tremble as it climbed higher and higher toward release, a cascade of moans and curses pouring out of me with every rhythmic pulse of Cain's fingers.

Abruptly, he pulled away, his mouth and beard soaked from my wetness. "Support her," he barked at Sly, who slid his hands to my upper arms, holding me in place as Cain lifted my foot that was still on the floor, and slid that leg over his shoulder. He used his hands to bring me closer, grabbing my ass so roughly his fingernails bit into the skin as he held me tightly while coming to stand. I felt Sly's hands slide down my body, leaving a trail of goosebumps in the wake of his fingertips.

Once Cain was stable on his feet, he pushed my body even closer to him, causing my hips to drive forward. Spinning our bodies, he moved until my back pressed against the cool wall and repositioned his hands, one at a time, holding me where my ass met my thigh.

Then he reacquainted his face with my pussy.

The pleasure was immediate, and my hands flew to the top of Cain's head. My fingers raked into his hair, and I leaned my head back against the wall, moaning wantonly as my orgasm kicked into overdrive.

A few feet away, Sly leaned against my desk, his feet crossed at the ankles as he watched. He palmed his dick through his jeans, and I couldn't help but wish he'd take it out and jack off.

As quickly as the thought arrived though, it was gone, forced from my thoughts as Cain sucked my clit into his mouth. His tongue assaulted it relentlessly, and I cried out. "I'm about to come, I'm so fucking close!"

But as the sentence left my mouth, it ripped through me faster than I anticipated, and I writhed within Cain's grasp, his name tumbling from between my lips over and over again. Slowly, he moved his mouth from my pussy to my thighs, alternating between kissing and lightly biting them.

My body was still riding high as I felt his hands move again, situating on my hips, and he pulled me away from the wall, carrying me high on his shoulders over to where Sly was.

In a quick motion, he lowered me, but I barely had a second to register my feet touching the floor before he spun me and pressed down between my shoulder blades until the top half of my body lay flat against my desk.

"See what you do to us, baby?" he asked, grinding his hips against my ass so I'd feel his erection. As he did, I turned my head and laid it on my desk, at which point I was practically eye level with the erection Sly was sporting. Cain kicked my legs apart, widening them as he smacked my ass. Hard. "You're so fucking sexy. Do you know how long I've waited to touch you like this?"

Cain's fingertips dragged through the wetness between my legs, parting my pussy lips. I jolted when his fingers touched against my clit, still sensitive from my orgasm. Pushing back into his hand, I moaned, wanting him to trade his fingers with his cock and sink into me. "Do more than touch me, Cain. Fuck me. *Please.*"

"No," he growled, and the air shifted behind me as he dropped back onto his knees. He spread my ass cheeks, exposing every part of me, and brought his mouth to my pussy again. The change in positions had me crying out immediately, my eyes rolling back into my head as he thrust his tongue into me. "Cain, *fuck*. I'm still fucking sensiti—*ah!*"

But he didn't stop or even relent in his motions, still prodding at my entrance with his tongue, and brought his hand between my legs and used two fingers to rub my clit. "There are two of us, Rose. It's only fair that we get to watch you come twice," he muttered against me, barely moving his mouth far enough away from my pussy to speak, before picking up right where he left off.

Opening my eyes, I met Sly's lustful stare. "He's right, mia preferita. You are so beautiful at the height of pleasure. Let me see it again." He placed both hands down on the desk, leaning closer to my face.

"Your pussy has officially ruined me, Rose. Nothing else will ever taste so sweet. I hope you're prepared to be my every meal," Cain announced before sinking his teeth into the flesh of my ass. At the same time, he plunged two fingers into me, curving them to connect with my G-spot, and I was a goner. With two fingers inside me and another on my clit, my second orgasm ripped through me violently. My body convulsed and I thrashed against my desk, all control over my own limbs lost.

Incoherent words filtered through the room, my eyes squeezed so tight I was positive I was dreaming. But I wasn't, was I?

Because the man behind me was slipping his fingers out of me and grabbing me by the arms, pulling me to stand. He lifted me, his hands securing beneath my ass, and I wrapped my legs around him, too limp and hazy to do anything else.

Cain carried me to my couch and sat down with me straddling his lap. He peppered kisses all over, pushing back my hair as he held my face between his palms and searched my eyes.

"Get her a blanket," he barked at Sly, whose footsteps instantly thundered, echoing off the four walls. Within seconds, he draped a plush blanket over my naked body and Cain tightened it around my shoulders.

Sly sank onto the couch beside us and propped his elbow against the back of it. "How are you feeling, mia preferita?"

"Mmmmm," I hummed with satisfaction. "Like I was just given back-to-back orgasms."

"Just say the word, Rose, and I'll keep them coming," Cain promised, already pushing the plush blanket from my thigh and resting his hand barely an inch from my sensitive core.

I shook my head lazily, a smile pulling at my lips. There

was only one thing I wanted after coming twice and working a full shift at the bar. My eyelids already felt incredibly heavy, and a yawn threatened when I said, "Sleep."

I had no doubts I'd have the best night's sleep of my life tonight.

"It's too late for you to be on the road. Let's go upstairs," Sly suggested, pushing himself to stand.

"She'll be sleeping in my room." Cain's tone left no room for negotiation, and unsurprisingly, Sly didn't even try to argue. He just nodded acceptingly and flashed me a knowing smile. My heart jolted with my chest.

Everything had shifted.

Cain came to a stand with me in his arms and I wrapped the blanket around my shoulders tighter, keeping it around my chest, but letting it flow far past my body as though I had a plush, blanket cape.

I didn't hate it. I was a fucking queen, after all.

And as Cain trudged out of my office letting Sly lock up behind us, my heart danced with palpitations as I let my mind envision being in Cain's bed for the night, our bodies tangled together inside of his sheets, sleeping peacefully in his arms like I'd always dreamed about.

CHAPTER TWELVE

Rosie

My entire body hummed when I woke the next morning and stretched lazily. The sun streamed in through the curtains, the warmth from the rays penetrating through the black bedding on Cain's bed.

Turning onto my side, I stared at the man beside me who could double as a Greek God. He slept in only his black briefs, which left me with the most mouthwatering view as he laid on his stomach, his deliciously muscular tattooed arms curved under his pillow. His lips were slightly parted as he snored lightly, and a piece of his hair had fallen over his eyes.

When he'd brought me back to his room last night, I had expected him to fuck me, but Cain surprised me by tucking us both into his bed. He scooped me into his hold and pulled me close.

I absolutely hated cuddling, but I couldn't bring myself to pull away from him. Being in his arms didn't feel awkward like it typically did.

It felt right.

It should have startled me how comfortable I was with him. I was still afraid of getting too close. And I knew I needed to continue keeping him at arm's length, but fighting this was absolutely exhausting.

I needed to speak with Sly. I needed him to reassure me that throwing caution to the wind with Cain was the right thing to do, even if it meant potential heartbreak in the future. He was the only person who could see both sides of this scenario and detach himself enough to deliver me complete unadulterated honesty.

My mind begged me to be careful, but the heart wants what it wants and evidently can't be persuaded otherwise.

Crossing that line with Cain made me feel alive.

I watched him sleep for a while longer, contently listening to the soft expels of his breath puffing through his lips. I could have easily fallen back to sleep, but I knew I needed to get my day started, starting with a quick stop down the hall.

Cain barely stirred as I slipped from his bed. The floor was cool against my bare feet, and I ran my hands along my arms to warm up as I sought out my clothes from the day before.

His room was sparse, and it was easy to see my clothes hadn't made it upstairs with us. I glanced at the clock, seeing that it was still early—only seven—and I decided to brave the hallway in my birthday suit.

Cracking the door, I poked my head out and looked side to side, finding the hall completely empty. Slinking through the crack and shutting the door as gingerly as possible, I power-walked down to Sly's room and snuck in.

His room was darker than Cain's, the curtains fully closed and blocking the sunlight. My eyes took a moment to adjust, and when they did, I found Sly awake and smiling at me, leaning against his pillows with his phone casting a dim glow against his face.

"Ciao, bella," he greeted, lowering his phone. He pushed himself up a little straighter and patted the empty space beside him.

As I moved toward his bed, I caught sight of my clothes sitting in a pile on top of his dresser, and I stopped to put them on.

"Thanks," I said as I tugged my shorts up my hips, forgoing yesterday's panties because, ew. "I was thinking I'd need to borrow someone's shirt just to make it to my office this morning. Should have known you would have thought ahead."

I shrugged my tank top down over my chest, then crawled onto Sly's bed, settling close to him with my legs crossed.

"Did you have a good night, mia preferita?"

"You were there, you know how much I enjoyed it," I quipped, changing positions to lie next to him with my head resting on the pillow I used when I stayed over.

"You know I meant when we parted."

I sighed dramatically. "I know what you meant. We just slept, and it was great. I woke up with a lightness in my chest —like it felt right to be there. But Sly, I still don't know."

He rested his hand on my knee and stroked the skin with his thumb. For several seconds, I stared down at the motions of his hands, my brows furrowing as I realized the touch wasn't doing anything for me. Typically, when he touched me, little sparks of lust would trickle through my system, and for some reason, that wasn't happening.

Looking up at him, I gave him a small smile, not sure of what to say about that, if anything needed to be said at all.

"It's okay, Rosie," he said lightly, giving my knee a squeeze.

"What's okay?"

"Feeling differently about my touch now that you've experienced Cain's." His eyes met mine, and behind his vibrant blues, I saw no traces of hurt or anger shine through, and it confused me more than I thought it would.

"You're not mad?" I questioned, trying to keep my tone even, but my voice shook just slightly.

"Why would I be? Rosie, you'll always be mia preferita, but your happiness is what will make *me* happy. I know I don't need to remind you of our arrangement. It's been beautiful and everything we've both needed, but it's okay if it's no longer."

He brushed a piece of hair from my face and tucked it behind my ear. "I will never leave you, and so long as you want me around as you did last night, I will stay, but I will not hold you back from what your heart truly desires. It's time to stop letting fear drive you, amore mio. Let Cain prove to you what type of man he is now—he's been trying to show you for months. I did not know him then, but I know him now and his heart is good, and his love for you is unwavering. If you need me, I'll forever be by your side, but you *must* bury your hesitations and let your heart guide you back to him."

Sly was the most sincere man I knew, and my heart ached as his words settled deep within me. How could someone be so undeniably selfless and understanding? It pained me to know that while he was pushing me toward something that could be life-altering, he was sitting idle, unable to be with the woman *he* truly loved. He never fully opened up about his situation, but in this moment there was nothing more important to me than returning all the support and love he'd poured into our friendship, especially these last few weeks.

"When do you get to let your heart guide you back to *her*, Sly?" I asked, hoping he'd realize I wasn't the only one in the room who deserved happiness.

He offered me a weak smile, glancing down at his hands that were now crossed in his lap. "One day, I hope. Though time may not be on our side."

I wanted to ask another question, but he picked up his phone and resumed his scrolling, setting the boundary that the conversation was now over.

Scooting up the bed, I lifted his comforter and pushed my legs under, cozying myself under the covers. Sly leaned over to his nightstand before jutting his hand out, offering me my cell phone. I took it happily, grinning at him when I noticed my battery was full.

"Have I told you that you're the best and I love you?" I asked him as I found my string of text messages with Elle, sending her a message to meet me for brunch and mimosas in an hour.

The text was returned immediately, confirming what I already know. She'd be there.

"Sì, Rosie. And I, you."

CHAPTER THIRTEEN

Rosie

Elle and I had spent years finding the perfect brunch spot, trying out nearly all of them in Ridgewood and Shadow Hills. Several restaurants had been serious contenders for our number one, but when we sat down one fateful morning at The Breakfast Table in Shadow Hills, it was a done deal.

We'd been coming here as often as we could—at least biweekly—ever since. The staff knew us well. Shadow Hills was barely a blip on the map, after all.

What we'd both loved about The Breakfast Table was that they offered a brunch happy hour, with half off flights of mimosas and Bloody Marys, silver dollar pancakes for five bucks, and a whole array of other delicious foods for discounted prices. Elle and I would mix and match, eating and drinking until the brunch hour turned to lunch, and sometimes, even then, we'd still stay and order a third or fourth round of drinks, adding in some lunch entrees if we ended up with the day drinking snack cravings.

Today, a waitress by the name of Rachel, according to her name tag, seated us at a table by the window and handed us brunch menus.

"Start us off with a flight of mimosas, and the Mini Beni's please, Rachel. Thank you," I told her, setting my menu down in front of me on the table. She was a beautiful woman with a heart-shaped face and blue eyes. She had a total girl-next-door type of look about her, and a warm vibe.

I couldn't help but wonder if she knew how to bartend.

"A woman who knows what she wants! I like it," she said, jotting down our order on her server book. "I'll be right back with some water and your mimosas."

As she walked away, Elle cleared her throat and brought my attention back to her, my beautiful best friend sitting across from me. Although, my beautiful bestie was looking a little out of sorts today.

Her hair was piled messily on top of her head, a large claw clip keeping it secured, and she wore an oversized sweatshirt paired with yoga pants. Her face was bare, save for a little concealer and mascara. I guess I hadn't given her much time to prepare for our meetup, but in all the years I'd known her, this was by far the most dressed down I'd seen her out in public.

"You okay?" I asked, my gut telling me something was a little off. "Is everything good between you and Ryder?"

Elle and her husband, Ryder, had been married for a year or so, after spending ten long years secretly pining for each other while in relationships with the wrong people. It was a beautiful story in and of itself, but one filled with a lot of strife leading up to the ending they both wanted.

"Well, no, not exactly..." Elle drawled. She picked up her menu, letting her eyes skim over it, making me wait for her to finish her sentence. "I wish you hadn't ordered the mimosas and the Mini Beni's."

My face scrunched into a confused, *what the fuck* type look. Mimosas and Mini Beni's were our favorite. We ordered them every time.

"I'm pretty sure the hollandaise has raw eggs in it," she stated simply.

"Oookay?" I was confused as fuck.

She shrugged, still skimming the menu. Then she looked up at me, her bright blue eyes shining as a smile pulled her lips wide. "Can't have alcohol or raw *anything* when you're pregnant."

"YOU'RE PREGNANT?" I shouted, standing from my seat so abruptly the chair screeched back in protest. I rounded the table, grabbing her arm and pulling her up. Wrapping my arms around her, I hugged her tight as tears pricked the back of my eyes. Who knew I'd be so sappy when one of my best friends got knocked up?

"Okay, tell me everything," I told her, releasing her from my hug so we could sit back down. "I'm so happy for you! How far along are you? Give me details, even the dirty ones. I want to hear about the conception, too." I winked at her, and she shook her head, laughing as she rolled her eyes at me.

"I'm about eight weeks." She reached into her purse that was hanging on the chair and pulled out a black and white sonogram photo, passing it to me over the table.

I looked down at the photo, emotion sitting heavy on my chest. This wasn't my dream—the whole white picket fence with a couple of kids and a husband thing—but it was hers, and there was something truly special about having a front-row seat when your best friend's dreams came true.

"There's auntie's little poppyseed," I murmured, touching the small blip in the middle of the photo that I knew was the baby.

"Ryder came to the first appointment with me and we got to hear the baby's heartbeat. I don't really have many details to give you, honestly. This was our first month actively trying since I got off birth control, and I guess I'm just one of the lucky ones. I feel so grateful to have had it happen so quickly, but I'm still terrified that something will go wrong. My doctor said it's very normal to feel that way, and that we're not out of the woods until the twelve week mark. But the baby's heart-beat is strong and he or she is measuring on track."

"She," I said immediately, my eyes meeting Elle's across the table. "That's my niece in there."

Elle's hand fluttered down to her stomach. "I think so too."

From my peripheral, I saw our waitress return, tray in hand, balancing a flight of mimosas and two waters. We were quiet as she placed our drinks down in front of us, then Elle ordered herself a Strawberry Shortcake Short Stack and a decaf caramel latte.

"So, what's up with you? How's your love triangle going?"

"It's not a love triangle!" I snapped, but quickly checked my tone. There was no reason to get snippy when I knew she'd meant it in a carefree way. "But...they did share me. Kind of."

My admission swiftly brought back memories of Cain holding me on his shoulders while he ate me out with Sly watching. That'd been fucking hot. Just the thought had blood rushing to my vagina, my clit tingling as though it was playtime, again.

"Um...spill it. Now. Spare no detail, beginning to end. I'm talking *everything*, sister. Clearly, I've missed a lot."

Where do I even begin?

With a heavy sigh, I picked up the classic mimosa and tossed it back, letting the bubbly tang slide down my throat. As I placed the empty glass down onto the table and picked up the strawberry flavored one next to it, I opened my mouth and caught my best friend up on *everything* that'd transpired since we last spoke.

CHAPTER FOURTEEN

Rosie

"Hey, turn that up!" I shouted across the empty bar to one of my employees, Dylan, a young guy who started working here about six months ago. A look of confusion washed over his features, and I tipped my chin toward the T.V., indicating *that's* what I wanted turned up.

Thankfully, he needed no further instruction and reached for the remote to crank the volume.

"This is Amber Henry reporting live from outside Indigo Renegade, where last night a young woman was discovered in the back of the nightclub, badly beaten and disoriented. The woman was taken to Ridgewood General Hospital, where she underwent surgery that was considered life-threatening. We have not received updates on her current condition. A source close to the victim confirms she is not a heavy drinker, but started acting extremely intoxicated toward the end of her first drink early in the night. Police are not releasing any information on whether this may be connected to the other young women who were recently drugged and assaulted outside other Ridgewood nightclubs, but they are currently undergoing investigation. We will report back with any breaking updates. This is Amber Henry with RWC News, Channel 7."

"Fuck," I groaned, instantly feeling sick to my stomach. I'd heard of what happened at Reggies and Lawless, and had written it off as a fluke. But having it happen a third time…

Pulling out my phone, I went to my recent calls and clicked on Noah's name. "Pick up, pick up, pick up, pick up," I chanted as it continuously rang.

"Whitlock," he barked into the receiver, followed by, "Shit, wrong phone. Hello?"

"Hey, it's me, asshole."

"Hey. Work is a fucking nightmare right now, Rosie. Can I call you back?" He sounded exhausted—completely mentally drained.

"I'm actually calling regarding work, but I'll make it fast. Do you have more info on these girls who are obviously getting roofied? And should I be concerned about this dickwad showing up on my doorstep next? Or has my favorite band of misfits nailed the guy and the news just hasn't reported it yet?"

In the background I could hear dispatch speaking through the radio, the answers to my questions temporarily on hold so Noah could listen.

When it went silent, he groaned with frustration. "No, I have no information I can discuss at this time, yes, you should be concerned about him showing his face at Andromeda and no, we haven't nailed the guy yet because we don't know *what* his face looks like." He rattled off the answers, which did nothing to help subside the rolling in my stomach.

"We have no idea who this guy is, if he's working alone, where he's going to hit next—we know next to nothing. All our guys are working on this case, and chatter around the office says the Sinners are on it too. He's hit Reggies, Lawless, and now Indigo Renegade. Talk to Cain and tell him to be on high alert at Andromeda and to stick a few extra guys around. Until we figure out who this guy is, any bar or club could be hit next. So just keep an extra eye out, stay vigilant. Watch people's drinks—*yours* included—and if something seems off, call *me* immediately. The Sinners may be trying to help us, Rosie, but they're not the police."

My eyes met Indy's from across the bar. I'd sat on a barstool as Noah went into full lecture mode, and now my right-hand woman was readying herself for the details. "You got it, Captain," I told him, purposely calling him the wrong job title to try to make him laugh.

It didn't work.

"Lieutenant," he corrected.

I didn't bother explaining that I was trying to make a joke, and instead, decided to wish him luck. "If you or Lily need anything, let me know. I know there's a lot on your plate right now. Take care of yourself, and go find this fucker, would ya? The women in Ridgewood deserve to enjoy a night out without worrying if they're next."

"I will, thanks, and I'll let Lils know to call you if she

needs anything when I'm stuck at the station. Oh, and Rosie?"

"Yeah, Chief?"

Still not even a hint of laughter on the other end of the phone. Tough crowd.

"Let the police do their job. Seriously. Stay safe, and if you see anything, *call me*. Don't try to handle it yourself."

I waved my hand dismissively in front of me, even though he couldn't see it. "Yeah, yeah. Will do, Noah ba-boah."

The line went dead, and Indy descended quickly, placing a clear shot down on the bar in front of me.

I tossed the top-shelf vodka back, then pressed my elbows onto the bar and cradled my head in my hands. Suddenly, my temples were throbbing.

"We need to call an emergency staff meeting before we open tonight," I instructed solemnly, wondering how we'd all grow extra sets of eyes to keep an eye out for this prick.

"But, boss, it's already—"

"I know. We open in two hours, but we have to. The team needs to be aware and on their toes with this one. *All* eyes peeled at all times. We need to come up with a game plan."

"Alright, let's do it. I'll send out a text now and have everyone here within the hour."

"You're the best, and I appreciate you," I told her affectionately as she slid a second shot in my direction.

Instead of reaching for it, I stared at it for several long, worrisome minutes, wondering what the hell I was going to do to increase security and keep my customers feeling safe and comfortable. This could be detrimental to business. If people were scared, they'd stay home, and if they stayed home, I'd lose money, and if I lost money...

I needed to stop. My mind was spiraling quickly into the worst-case scenario, and we weren't at that point yet. The bridge we'd need to cross to get to that point was still very far in the distance, and there was no need for hysterics.

I was Rosie fuckin' Adler, and I knew what I had to do.

Unfortunately, I'd just need to swallow a bit of my pride to do it.

It hadn't even been seventy-two hours since I crawled out of Cain's bed and here I was, about to ask for his help.

Picking my phone up off the bar, I pulled up his contact and sent him a text, requesting his presence at my staff meeting. Because when you had to go against the devil himself, having a fallen angel on your side wasn't a terrible idea.

TENSIONS WERE HIGH TONIGHT.

The vibe in Andromeda was unlike anything I've experienced since I bought it; from both my staff and customers.

No one was dancing on the usually packed dance floor, and instead, everyone congregated around their tables, holding their drinks protectively in their hands as they hung out with the people they came with.

My staff had nervous energy, their eyes constantly scanning the bar, watching the door. They kept an extra close eye on people, especially those *without* drinks in their hands.

I absolutely hated it.

The usual happiness that radiated within these four walls

was gone and replaced with negative connotations. I was fairly certain if someone didn't bring the roofie-rapist down soon, it'd be my business going down instead.

From across the room, I made eye contact with Cain, who was watching me with a lowball of whiskey sitting in front of him that looked untouched. A handful of other Sinners were throughout the bar, keeping a watchful eye.

They were spread thin tonight, doubling their manpower here while other places in town only had one watchful Warlord. But Cain insisted on putting the extra bodies at Andromeda, a gut feeling telling him we're likely next, if not close to the top of this prick's list. And the last thing I wanted was for one of my customers, or one of my staff, to fall prey.

I blew out a shaky breath and weaved through the tables, sliding into an open chair at Cain's.

Wrapping his hand around the leg of my chair, he pulled it toward him until it bumped into his, and I was close enough for him to slide his arm around my waist. I let him hold me and leaned my head against his shoulder.

"I hate this," I complained. I was trying not to let the somber mood get to me and seemingly failing. Every inch of my body felt heavy with anxiety.

"I know." He pressed his lips against my temple in a reas-suring kiss. My stomach cartwheeled. "Where do you want to sleep tonight? I can take you home when you're ready if you want a break from this place."

A break sounded necessary, and the comfort of my own bed sounded heavenly. I wondered if he'd ask to stay with me. I'd let him, but I wasn't sure I'd have the lady balls to ask him myself. There was still some part of me holding back, afraid to fully give myself over and welcome the vulnerability for him to shatter me again. "Home sounds perfect."

And at that, I expelled a yawn, not realizing until just then how exhausted I truly was. Mentally, more than physically, but exhausted all the same.

Tugging my cell phone from my back pocket, I pressed the side button and illuminated the screen, seeing that it was only eleven. There were still three hours before the bar closed, and as badly as I wanted to duck out now, I felt obligated to stay.

As though sensing my inner battle, Cain raised his hand into the air to grab the attention of Indy, who came out from behind the bar and made her way to us.

She hopped into a chair, crossing her arms in front of her on the table. "Hey, guys," she said with a half-smile. "Weird vibe, right?"

"The weirdest," I confirmed at the same time Cain said, "Rose's exhausted. We're going to head out."

Glaring at him, I turned back to Indy and shook my head. "No, we're not. I'm not leaving you to deal with this on your own." I shook my hand dismissively at Cain. "Go ahead, and leave if you want."

He caught the hand that waved in front of his face and kissed my palm.

Indy beamed. She knew I'd been avoiding my attraction to Cain for months, but I'd never filled her in on the extent of it. "Honestly, boss, go home. I've got the bar and I have a feeling the occupancy will just keep minimizing from here. You've pulled hella late nights lately, so really, go home. We'll be fine."

"You're sure?"

"I'm positive," she replied. "Go get a good night's sleep. In the morning we can brainstorm ways to take some of the tension off tomorrow night."

"Okay," I said with a smile, then turned to Cain. "Take me home, big guy."

He raised his eyebrow with skepticism. "Big guy?"

Hopping off the chair, I plucked my phone from the table and shoved it into my back pocket. "Yeah, big guy. Have you looked in a mirror? You're a freakin' beast."

That comment earned me a cocky grin. "You have no idea."

Rolling my eyes, I walked directly across the empty dance floor and toward my office, not bothering to see if Cain was following. I knew he was. I could sense his presence all around me, as though he'd thrown a protective bubble around us.

It was oddly soothing.

After grabbing my purse, we slipped out the back door and through the alleyway. The small staff parking lot was where most of the Sinners parked their motorcycles, and I spotted Cain's immediately in front of the front spots. As we approached, he handed me his helmet. Taking it from him, I buckled it around my chin as he climbed onto the shiny black bike before I slipped on behind him.

As my hands wrapped around his middle, he pushed up the kickstand and cranked the ignition. The bike roared to life and he let it idle for a second before shooting off like a bullet, pulling onto the main road in the direction of my condo.

I didn't give him my address, nor had he asked for it, which in hindsight shouldn't have surprised me as much as it had.

Of course, Cain already knew where I lived.

CHAPTER FIFTEEN

Cain

Patience and persistence went hand in hand.

There weren't many occurrences where I didn't get exactly what I wanted. I worked hard for everything I had and was persistent in pursuing whatever I had my sights set on until the tables turned in my favor.

Pursuing Rose was no different. I knew I'd work tirelessly to win her favor again.

My patience came because it had to. Rose wouldn't let me in easily, and I'd made peace with that. It'd take effort on my part to *show* her my intentions and earn her trust back.

It was no secret she didn't trust me as far as she could throw me.

It's why I forced myself to give her time, even though it went against my nature to do so. I knew I needed to tread lightly and continue to prove myself to her for as long as it took.

Rose laid in my arms, her black shirt soft against my bare

chest. My fingers brushed her arm lazily, the room silent while we took our time waking up.

Last night when I brought her home, I gave her exactly what she needed, which was sleep. The peace that washed over her face when she crawled into her bed showed me how much she truly needed to rest.

The stress was eating her alive, and the heaviness of the week had been weighing on her. She fell asleep just moments after her head hit the pillow.

I hadn't bothered to ask if I could stay the night—I just did. While her eyes fluttered closed, I stripped down to my briefs, climbed in beside her, and fell asleep too.

Waking up next to Rose was quickly becoming my new favorite thing.

"So, I think we need to have a conversation." She broke the silence, shifting her head to look at me.

I wasn't sure what conversation she was referring to, but I was eager to find out. Nodding my head, I said, "I'm all ears."

"I'm not sure what your expectations are, but I want to lay it out there that I'm not into the typical relationship thing."

"I'm not asking you for anything, Rose. I'll take you anyway I can have you, so long as you're mine."

Her eyes burned with intensity. I could practically see the wheels in her head turning, the questions sitting at the tip of her tongue.

"I'm not ashamed to tell you I'm in love with you," I continued. "I've been in love with you since we first met—I was just too immature to admit it, let alone do anything about it."

"You can't possib—" she started, but I silenced her words,

smashing my lips to hers. A small whimper strained from her mouth into mine, and I deepened the kiss, only relenting when I was sure she'd let me finish.

"You think I can't possibly still love you after all this time, but you're wrong. I may have pushed it aside and hid it from view to get through the years that didn't have you in them, but it was never gone. Not completely. It's always been you, Rose." I pulled her hand to my chest, flattening her palm over my heart. "The only reason this thing has kept beating is because I hoped one day you'd come back to me and give me another shot. The chance I don't necessarily deserve, but will never stop trying to earn."

My words made my heart unsteady with racing palpitations. Most women would have become putty after a declaration like that, but Rose was no ordinary woman. Instead, she laid in my arms and assessed me with hesitation.

After several minutes, she argued. "And if I'm not ready to give you another shot?"

Her tone had a ring of airiness to it, like she was being playful without actually showing the playful side of her.

Wanting to draw it out more, I shrugged. "I could just kidnap you and hold you here against your will, if you prefer."

She laughed jubilantly, then pushed against my chest. "Oh, how very beastly of you, Cain! You could never kidnap me. I have friends who'd come looking for me."

"Who? That police officer friend of yours?" A smirk pulled at my lips, but I tried to keep a firm tone of voice, despite wanting to laugh with her.

"He's a lieutenant, and yes, Noah would come looking for me, absolutely."

"Ha!" I barked a laugh, my hand reaching around to her hip. Rolling her body, I positioned her so she was straddling me. She braced her hands on my shoulders, her long chocolate hair curtaining to one side. I schooled my features, and with as much seriousness as I could muster, told her darkly, "I could smite him and he'd be dead before he even found you."

"*Smite him?* You'd smite him?" She laughed so hard there were tears pooling in the corners of her eyes, and she dabbed at them with her fingers. Through the laughter she added, "What are you, a character out of some B-rated fairytale? A medieval henchman? Who the hell says smite?"

Tears freely streamed down her face as she moved her hands from my chest to her stomach, holding the flesh as she laughed. "Hurts...laughing too much..." she cackled.

I couldn't remember the last time I'd felt this elated in the presence of another person.

Seeing her like this, so carefree and wistful, had me thinking back when we first started getting to know each other. So many of the characteristics from the old *Rosie* were shining through, now mixing with the stunningly badass woman in front of me today.

I'd never get enough of her.

Reaching up, I pushed back some of the hair that fell in front of her face and tucked it behind her ear. With my touch, her laughter stopped. She swallowed thickly, leaning into my hand momentarily.

It felt like someone had reached into my chest and was squeezing the beating muscle I'd never let anyone into before Rose. Never let anyone in after Rose, either.

It was reserved only for her.

"Tell me you love me, Rose." The words tumbled from my mouth in a low groan before I could stop them.

She stiffened, her eyes falling to my lips, then to my chest.

"I'm not an idiot. I know you feel it too. I know you've *always* felt it, even back then. There isn't a world where you and I aren't meant to be together," I pressed, unintentionally holding my breath as I waited for her to say something.

She went to climb off me, but I wouldn't let her. Gripping her hips firmly, I kept her straddled over my torso.

"It doesn't matter if you love me, or if I love you, Cain. I will never be the woman you want or need me to be. At the end of the day, I will always choose myself over you. *My* goals, *my* dreams, *my* happiness. They'll always come first. No man has ever loved me the way I love myself, and I don't think that can ever change." She held her head high, but wasn't able to hide the quiver in her lower lip, and I felt a spark of anger ignite within my chest, knowing my brother was still at fault for how her brain had been rewired.

Once upon a time, Rose had given her love freely. She'd been easygoing and vivacious. Happy to love and receive love from everyone she met, because she genuinely loved people and having fun.

Now, she kept a wall up. A barrier. And not just from me —the way she interacted with people in general was more closed off than she used to be.

Brent had really done a fucking number on her, whether she recognized it or not.

"The only woman I ever want or need you to be is yourself. Where did you get the idea I would ever want to change you?"

Instead of answering, she sidestepped the question. "Being your old lady, marriage, a future with a family...I don't want any of those things, Cain, and I don't think I ever will."

I held her face between my palms, forcing her to look at me. Her skin was warm beneath my touch and I was tempted to pull her to me and kiss her again, but she needed to hear what I had to say. "Then it's off the table. I don't need labels and the progression normal society thinks we should have. We both know we're anything *but* normal. The only thing I want from you is *you*."

Without waiting for her response, I sat up, scooping my arms beneath her ass to hold her as I stood from the bed and carried her over to the oversized full-length mirror that leaned against her wall. Dropping her to her feet, I spun her body and held her back firmly against me as we both looked at our reflection.

"Tell me what you see," I coaxed, letting my hands roam her body softly.

Her eyes locked with mine in the mirror. "Why are you doing this? Your version of foreplay kind of sucks, you know that?"

"Just humor me, Rose. Look at yourself in the mirror and tell me what you see."

She rolled her eyes before disconnecting her gaze from mine and allowing them to travel the length of her body. "I see myself. Brown hair. Hazel eyes. Tattoos. Curves that haven't always been there, but that I'm proud of. I see me, Cain. What is the point of this?"

"Because you're not seeing what I see."

"We're looking at the same woman."

A low growl rumbled deep in my chest. "But you're not seeing her through *my* eyes. Do you want to know what I see when I look at you?"

She rolled her eyes at me.

Again with the fucking eye roll. One of these days, I was going to fuck the attitude out of her.

I didn't wait for her to answer me before I continued. "I see a fucking queen. I see strength and passion. An unmatched ferocity. A ruler with a level-headed tenacity that allows her to prevail through the chaos and ruckus around her. A kind and loving heart. I see a woman with compassion and empathy but who takes no shit from anybody. The *problem* with you, Rose, is that you think your *physical* attributes shape you. And they do, because you're the most irresistible woman I've ever laid eyes on, but that's only one component of what makes you, you."

She sighed with a shaky breath, letting my words absorb for a minute before verbally sparring with me again. "You speak as though you've known me for years, Cain. What makes you an expert?"

"I *have* known you for years," I argued. "Just because our time together hasn't been consistent, doesn't mean I haven't studied you closely in the months since you waltzed back into my life. And just because you were with my piece of shit brother back when we first met, doesn't mean I wasn't paying attention. I still know you better than I've ever cared to know anyone else in my entire life. Why are you making this into an argument?"

"Because," she stated matter-of-factly. She bit her lip, her eyes pressed into a glare as she watched my hand snake up her body and curl around her throat.

"You're impossible," I grumbled.

"Yep, I am. Now, are you going to fuck me? Otherwise, you're wasting my time."

Her words caught the attention of my cock, which hardened slightly. What I wouldn't give to fuck her, to claim her. But I was still resisting, and I'd continue to resist until I was the only man in her life.

Still, I slowly prowled to the front of her, more than happy to give her exactly what she's asking for, just in a different way. Sinking to my knees, I looked up at her heated stare, a cocky smirk lifting my lips as I peeled her sleep shorts and lace panties from her body. "Keep your eyes open, Rose. I want you to watch yourself in the mirror while I pleasure my queen's body. I want you to see yourself through my eyes, and watch how your body bends to my will."

Her breathing hitched, her hand automatically flying to rest on my head as I lifted her leg and draped it over my shoulder. Her pussy was glistening, already so wet and ready to be devoured.

A simple swipe of my tongue had her crying out and her nails digging into my hair.

"You're finished lying to yourself, Rose. Stop denying what you want. Go ahead and lie to me, but not to yourself."

My tongue swirled around her, the tip flicking against her clit as I alternated pressures against it, making her writhe against my face. I kept at it for a while before spearing her with my tongue and reaching my hand up to press my thumb against her clit.

A heady moan erupted through her throat, her voice strained as she delivered her first lie, "I don't want you."

I removed my fingers from her clit and dove two fingers inside of her, curling upward to stroke her G-spot, saying nothing in return.

"I don't love you, Cain," she hummed against my touch, her second lie almost as convincing as her first, though still strained from pleasure. Her hips rolled, matching the rhythm of my fingers.

I pressed my lips back to her clit, toying with it slowly, using my tongue. "Keep lying to me," I growled against her.

With a quiver, she blew out, "I can trust you."

I hadn't expected a simple lie to feel like a stab through the heart, and my movements faltered. "You *can* trust me," I growled against her core.

Her head shook, but instead of giving me another lie, she pulled me in by the back of my head, pressing me harder against her pussy. I took the cue and ate her with relentless ferocity. I could feel her body trembling, but I didn't ease up.

Her eyes closed, her head flew back, and I knew she was about to come.

"Open your eyes and watch yourself, Rose."

She was fucking soaked, her sweet desire coating my lips. Her eyes opened, and from my kneeling position I watched her watch herself, her face contorting into pleasure as she came. She moved her other hand to my hair, using both hands to hold herself steady as she rocked into me.

I fucked her with my tongue until she'd finished riding the high, before shooting to my feet. Gripping the back of her hair, I slammed her lips to mine and used my other hand to guide her upward, coaxing her to wrap her legs around my body. She did so effortlessly, and I turned us, pressing her body against the mirror.

"I will spend every waking moment of every fucking day proving to you that you can trust me. Nothing in this world is as powerful as what I feel for you, Rose, and I'll be damned if you go another day not knowing the lengths I would go through for you."

Roughly, she tugged my hair and brought my lips back to hers, possessing my mouth in a way I'd always dreamed of her doing. I rocked into her, my cock harder than stone, and desperately wanted to rip my underwear off and connect our bodies.

A whimper clogged in her throat, her legs gripping tighter around my hips.

Feeling myself start to lose control, I carried her over to her bed and tossed her down onto it. Staring down at her from the edge, I watched as she slowly unbuttoned her sleep shirt, peeling it off her body and tossed it to the side.

My willpower waned, but I still wasn't done proving to her that what I wanted from her was more than just anything physical. Until she realized that wholly, I wouldn't be fucking her.

As though she could hear my thoughts, her legs spread, falling to the side as she gave me a perfect view of her pussy. "Fuck me, Cain," she urged.

And I wanted to. *Fuck,* did I want to.

"Not until you trust me." My voice was strained. Resisting her was like resisting water after three days of walking through the desert. But Rose wasn't a mirage. She was here and in front of me, presenting her body to me on a silver platter. Resisting it was nearly impossible.

Leaning forward, I grabbed her by the ankles and pulled her toward me until her ass was on the edge of the bed.

Questions swirled behind her eyes, watching me as I sank to my knees again, and pressed her legs open wide.

"Cain, I—"

But I didn't want her words, I wanted her actions. Her trust.

I silenced her with my tongue and my touch, her words transforming into wanton moans as I pleasured her over and over throughout the morning, wanting nothing in return, but praying to a god I didn't believe in that she'd find a way to trust when I said I loved her and would never hurt her again.

CHAPTER SIXTEEN

Rosie

Two weeks had come and gone without another woman in Ridgewood being attacked, and it felt like the tension in the air had dissipated. But while my customers had bounced back, and Andromeda was bustling again, I was a little more weary.

Through the window of my office, I watched people dance, drink, and mingle. Their happiness did little to ease my stress.

"So, business as usual, then?" I asked Noah through speakerphone, holding my cell phone in my hand while I kicked my legs up on the desk.

He chuckled, the gruff laugh pouring out from the speaker into the space around me. "Yes, business as usual. We'll catch this guy soon, now that we know what he looks like."

The Ridgewood Police Department had combed through countless hours of security footage to find this guy, and finally did a few days ago. They knew what he looked like, how he spiked girls' drinks, and how he lured them outside without their friends noticing.

"When do I get to know what he looks like? *I'm* the one who should be on the lookout for him at all times."

"We can't release it to the public yet, Rosie, but rest assured, we'll have a heavy presence at Andromeda for a while. Not to mention the extra security detail you already have set in place."

I groaned and dropped the phone into my lap so I could rub my eyes with the heels of my hands. "For once, can't you break the rules?"

"No can do. I gotta go—stay vigilant, Rosie."

The line went dead before I could try to persuade him more, and I huffed out another angsty groan before picking my phone back up.

Texting Sly, I asked him to come to my office for a second, knowing he was already somewhere close. He didn't respond, but a few minutes later, there was a soft knock at my door before he let himself in.

"Ciao, bella. What's going on? Why do you look like you want to cry?"

"Because I want to," I whined as I rolled my neck from side to side, letting the joints pop to alleviate some of the tension. "I just got off the phone with Noah—Lieutenant Whitlock. They know who they're looking for now, but won't release the information to the public yet. How am I supposed to keep my bar safe when I don't even know what he looks like?"

Sly came around my desk and sat against it, stretching his legs outward as he crossed his arms over his chest. "Exactly how you have been keeping it safe. We keep an eye out. Watch the drinks. Watch the people. The Sinners have a set plan in motion—all our eyes have a job. You shouldn't worry about your safety, mia preferita. We're all protecting you."

"That's exactly what I'm worried about, Sly. You, and Cain, and the rest of your goonies, all protect me. But what about the rest of the people in my bar? Who's protecting them?"

"We are, as is your paid security team, and la polizia who circle the perimeter. We're all here, Rosie, protecting everyone. Though I can think of *someone* in particular putting a heavy emphasis on protecting *you*."

My head involuntarily shook. "I know, I'm sorry. This isn't like me. I feel like I'm losing my mind with stress."

Sly leaned over and pressed a tender kiss against the top of my head. "No, mia preferita, it's not, but I cannot blame you for the stress. Now, come with me. Let's get you out of this office and to where you flourish."

He stood, holding out his hand for me to take. I placed mine in his and allowed him to pull me to my feet, where he wrapped me in a warm hug before leading us out of my quiet fortress and into the bar.

"HEY BOSS, pass me that shaker, would ya?" Indy yelled over the music, tipping her chin toward the dirty cocktail shaker sitting to my left. I rinsed it before giving it to her.

The music was loud tonight, much louder than I like it, but in an effort to bring in some foot traffic, Indy had enlisted the help of her old college friend who abandoned his degree in social services in favor of becoming a disc jockey.

DJ Benny Beats (*truly*, that's the name he came up with), was giving me a splitting headache.

Placing three glasses on a tray in front of me—a martini glass, a shot glass, and a lowball—I made up the drinks for my server to take to a nearby table.

Across the room, Nixon and Sly each sipped on two fingers of whiskey, and I made a mental note to bring them a refill soon.

Though my feet were starting to ache from the five-inch heels I'd decided to torture myself with tonight, I was grateful for the distraction. It was easy to forget how much I genuinely loved owning Andromeda when I was often hidden behind a mountain of paperwork in the back.

Giving the serving tray to Dylan, I spun to grab another, adding a martini glass and a few shot glasses to it to prep another table.

From my peripheral, I saw a man slide onto a barstool directly across from where Indy and I stood on the other side. He was handsome enough, looked to be in his mid to late thirties, and wore a black button down and jeans. Tattoos peeked up from his collar, but didn't continue onto his neck. He struck me as a biker, but I knew he wasn't a Sinner.

It was unusual for clubs from neighboring towns to venture into Ridgewood, and though it did happen from time to time, they typically arrived in a small group—not just one guy.

He sat quietly, taking his time to look around at the crowded tables and dance floor behind him. His eyes lingered a little too long on a few of the women, and I noted they also lingered a little too long on some of the more menacing looking men.

I glanced at Indy at the as same time she looked at me. Our eyes met, and an unspoken agreement passed between us.

We didn't like this guy.

Maybe he was just a passerby taking in his surroundings. A traveler making a short pit stop on his way to the next destination.

But I doubted it.

I couldn't explain what it was, but his presence had me on high alert. It was likely that I was being paranoid, but still, I trusted my gut and it hadn't led me wrong so far.

"What can I get ya?" I asked him with a fake smile as I continued to pour the drinks I was working on.

His attention bounced between me and Indy before he focused solely on me. "How about a date?"

Wow, alright, let's just get right to it then. "Someone's feeling ballsy tonight."

"I'm a man who appreciates a beautiful woman, and I'd love to take you out so I can appreciate you further."

"Has that line actually worked for you before?"

The man laughed and nodded playfully. "Depends. Is it working now?" He crossed his arms over the bar and leaned forward a little, as though some invisible magnet was drawing him toward me.

No fucking thank you.

"Sorry, my guy, not working. I'm tied down."

"I don't see a ring on that pretty finger of yours."

A wave of disgust washed through me at how forward he was being. It wasn't like I'd never been hit on by customers, but there was just something about him I couldn't pinpoint...

"Many people don't wear rings," I snarled, hoping my attitude would be enough to stop him in his tracks. "Now, can I get you a drink?"

"How about I buy you a drink?" he countered.

An irritated sigh burst from my lips, and I picked up my Coke from in front of me and shook it lightly. "I'm good, thanks."

"Oh, c'mon. One drink never hurt anybody. Even if you do have a man, I don't see him. How about a shot?"

One thing I learned very early on as a new business owner, particularly a bar owner, was when to stop engaging with difficult customers.

This was that point.

Picking up the tray of drinks, I offered him a tight smile and rounded the bar to deliver them to the waiting table myself.

Weaving through the high-tops, I stopped at the group of women eagerly waiting for their drinks, coming up from behind them, so I could keep a full view of the bar. From my vantage point, I watched as guy-who-couldn't-take-a-hint retracted his hand, sliding it from over the bar, and placed it into his lap. His head subtly tilted left to right, looking to see if anyone had seen.

Fortunately for me, it didn't appear anyone had, as mass chaos hadn't erupted. Unfortunately for *him*, I saw enough to know exactly what he'd done. I knew what was sitting directly beneath where his hand had just slid from.

My soda.

Every nerve ending stood on edge, knowing he'd slipped something into my drink.

It seemed as though the roofie-rapist had found his way into my bar.

Adrenaline filtered its way through my body, sending trembles throughout as I reached into the back pocket of my jeans and pulled my phone out. I quickly opened my contacts and clicked on Noah's name, trying not to go into a full on fit of rage as I waited for him to answer the phone.

What I wanted to do was walk up to the man, grab him by the hair, and slam his face into the bar over and over...but I knew that was the anger talking. Though it sounded like the best course of action, since my law enforcement bestie wasn't answering his damn phone.

Ending the call, I slowly walked back toward the bar, never taking my eyes off the back of the guy's head. My heart thundered in my chest—a million things racing through my mind.

Should I send out a text and warn the staff? Call Cain and ask him to handle it? Do I handle it myself?

Every step felt like ten—like I was moving in slow motion.

Redialing Noah, I let a shaky breath move past my lips. I was halfway back to the bar, and Noah still wasn't answering.

"Hello?" his voice finally reverberated through the speaker.

But it didn't matter anymore, because Cain had made it to the bar first.

His hand slammed into the guy's neck before wrapping around the collar of his shirt. He ripped him out of his chair, dragging the man behind him as he raced toward the door. Struggling to keep up, the guy practically tripped over his feet as Cain yanked his body mercilessly through the small crowd. When he made it to the door, he tossed the guy out first before following.

Shit.

"He's here," I shouted through my cell at Noah. "Get here now!"

Disconnecting the call, I shoved my phone back in my pocket and elbowed my way through the congestion of patrons. Once I reached the door, I threw it open and pushed my way out into the crisp night air.

CHAPTER SEVENTEEN

Rosie

My head whipped side to side looking for Cain and the guy, but I came up short. I stilled, listening for the sound of...well, anything really. Voices, footsteps, the potential dragging of a body, but was met with the muffled thumping of the music from inside the bar, and the stillness of the night air.

Quickly, I scanned through the parking lot but saw no movement behind the cars. I decided to check the alleyway to the right of the entrance—if they weren't there, then I had no idea where Cain could have taken him. It wasn't like they vanished into thin air, so the alley was my best bet.

My heels clicked against the asphalt as I power walked. Pieces of loose gravel crunched beneath each step, completely diminishing my attempts at being quiet. Not that it mattered. Cain knew me well enough to know I'd be following.

When I rounded the corner, I was relieved to find them.

Okay, relieved was a weird emotion for the situation, but it's what I felt.

They were halfway down the alley, partially concealed by the bar's dumpster. Cain had his forearm pressed against the man's neck, his other hand pushing against his closed fist, applying pressure.

A lot of pressure, if roofie-guy's beet-red face was any indication.

Cain was eerily calm and his mouth was moving, like he was speaking in a low tone to the man he was choking the shit out of.

The sound of my footsteps drew both of their attention, their eyes both shifting in my direction as I made my way further into the alley. My gaze connected with Cain's, and I was a little startled by the darkness that reflected in them.

It was no secret the Sinners got their hands dirty from time to time, but seeing it in the flesh was different.

My eyes were glued to Cain's hands—the tightness of his fists, the pain I knew he was causing as he used his force to cause pain. The same hands that not so long ago were drawing pleasure from my body were now being used to distribute the exact opposite.

"Walk away, Rose. You don't want to witness what I'm about to do to this pathetic piece of shit." Cain's voice was sinister. Full of authoritative command. But he wasn't looking at me anymore. He was staring down at the man in his hold with a look just as menacing as his tone.

A slight hesitation prickled my body, but I wasn't about to listen to it or him. Instead, I waved my hand around airily, as though he'd just told me I wasn't needed for help in the kitchen or something.

The roofie-guy may have been a literal walking nightmare, but Cain was stealing my fun. It was *my* drink this jackass roofied, in *my* bar. And I wanted to be the one to teach him a lesson until the cops showed up.

Which, speaking of, weren't they supposed to be circling the perimeter? Where the hell were they?

"You can't just come into my bar and harass my customers," I argued with Cain, stirring the pot a little.

This time, he looked straight at me. "Harass your customers? Rose, he fucking slipped something into your drink! This is the jackass going around spiking drinks and raping women, and he set his sights on *you*. No one fucks with my woman and gets to live. So either walk away now, or watch me do something that you'll never be able to *un*see."

"You're insufferable," I half-laughed, half-goaded. He looked away, refocusing on roofie-guy. "I watched him spike my drink, and Ridgewood's finest are already on their way to deal with him. No need to further tarnish my already corroded image of you, Cainy-boo."

"Stop fucking looking at her, you sick fuck. You look at me," Cain growled at the guy, then adjusted his hold, causing me to jump in surprise when he swiftly jabbed the guy in the stomach with a weighted punch. He tried to double over from the pain, but the arm practically strangling him kept him upright.

"C'mon man," Roofie-rapist wheezed. "She...looks like she's...down for two dicks... I'm not...a...selfish man...you go first."

He'd barely finished the sentence when, in one blindingly fast motion, Cain slammed his body to the ground. His head hit the asphalt with a sickening crack, and Cain shuffled on top of him and issued blow after blow, landing against the guy's face every time.

My jaw slacked with mild surprise as I watched Cain unleash his rage. Not that I'd ever admit it to him, but it was sexy as hell to see him tear this guy apart—not just because he roofied my drink, but for all the other women he'd hurt.

Closing the distance, I moved toward them until the toe of my heel was close enough to push into the man's face, which I would have done if Cain hadn't been relentlessly beating this guy to a pulp.

"Alright, stop," I commanded, directing my attention at Cain. "You may have forgotten I'm a bad bitch, but I sure as hell haven't, so move, Cain. You don't get to have all the fun. I want to see his eyes bulge as I step on his trachea with my eight hundred dollar heel and watch him squirm until the cops get here."

Though my lips were moving and words were coming out, my demand was completely ignored as he continued to punch the man relentlessly. "Cain, seriously, take it easy."

Blood began pouring from the guy, his face transforming with every punch. Still, Cain ignored me and kept going.

Groaning, I placed my hands on my hips, doing the only thing I could do: watch.

Every hit made me cringe, the sight becoming more gruesome by the second. My stomach rolled, and I knew this would haunt me, but I couldn't look away.

"Rosie! What's going on?" Sly's voice carried as he jogged around the corner to where we were. "Is this him?"

His eyes flicked from the man to Cain's fist, as it landed forcefully against his nose. The cracking of bones filled the air and blood went flying. Even then, Cain didn't stop. The amount of blood pooling from this man's face created a metallic scent in the air and made me feel a little queasy.

The guy wasn't fighting him or even moving—far past the point of consciousness. For a moment, a fleeting concern of whether this was the right course of action drifted into my mind, but it was gone a second later. Tears pricked my eyes, conflicting emotions rolling through me as I continued to watch.

There was blood everywhere, the man's face so battered he was nearing the point of being unrecognizable. But it was sickly satisfying, and that alone made me feel like a terrible person.

"Brother," Sly called to Cain, and I knew he was thinking the same thing I was.

There's no way this guy was still alive.

Reaching up, I rubbed my temples. My heart was racing a little faster the more Cain rained punches down on the guy. "He's not listening, Sly. I already tried."

"Cain," Sly tried again, but the sound of fist connecting with bone just kept radiating through the space. He advanced toward Cain, catching his elbow before he could land another punch. "Brother, stop."

He shook Sly off his arm and continued his assault.

"Fermare," Sly yelled, and whether it be the foreign language or the tone in which Sly said it, it seemed to catch

Cain's attention. His fist stopped midair, and he turned to look at us, chest heaving.

Blood dripped from his closed fist and landed on the man's cheek. Cain looked wild, his eyes dark, face glistening with a layer of sweat. His stare penetrated through my soul, speaking through a simple look, rather than with words.

I wouldn't have let him hurt you.

I'd never let anyone hurt you.

He'll never hurt anyone again.

I love you.

Or at least that's what it seemed like was happening. My heart seized within my chest, the stupid thing sputtering and beating far faster than it should have been after just witnessing Cain go feral with rage.

Without a word, Sly came to a low squat and reached two fingers to the pulse point on the man's neck. "Dead," he stated simply, and stood.

Cain stood at the same time as Sly, and it was when my eyes followed him I noticed the red and blue flashing lights throughout the alleyway. Noticed the sound of doors slamming, and footsteps running toward us. Heard the shouts of, "Put your hands in the air!" and "Hands where I can see them!".

It made me feel numb.

The three of us complied, slowly raising our hands, but within seconds, Noah was there.

"You idiots, put your guns down," he grunted to the officers around him. His eyes never left me, pulling me in for a tight hug when he made it to where I was standing. "Are you okay?"

I nodded my head against his chest, letting myself close my eyes for just a second before I released him and stepped back. "Yeah, I'm fine. Took you long enough."

Noah looked around, taking in the scene in front of him. "I was all the way down at the station. Got here as quickly as I could. What happened?"

"Where were the guys that were supposed to be keeping an eye on the place?" Cain growled, finally saying something.

I watched him, looking his body over thoroughly for any indication that the blood he had all over him may have been his, but saw none.

"Who's the cop here?" Noah snarled back, glaring at Cain in a way I knew was meant to show who was in charge, but had me laughing on the inside.

I could feel the pissing match begin, and while Noah was a big guy—probably six foot one, and muscular—Cain was a beast in comparison.

"The piece of shit who's been spiking drinks made his way to Andromeda," I cut in, tired of their macho male bullshit. "He hit on me and I turned him down, and when I walked away to serve a table, he spiked the soda I had on the counter below the bar. I saw him do it, and apparently, so did Cain." I glanced in his direction, unsurprised to see he was already looking at me.

"I handled it," Cain added.

"Evidently," Noah retorted snidely. "Wish you could have left him alive. It would have been a helluva lot easier of a report to write up, so thanks for that."

Cain's hands balled into fists at his side, something that

Sly took note of. He slapped his hand against Cain's chest in warning.

Cain pushed his chest forward against Sly's hand, but didn't try to step past it. "You wouldn't need us if you did your jobs right."

"You're really pushing your connections, Michaels," Noah snarled back. He stood up straighter, his hands mirroring Cain's as they balled at his sides.

These two, I swear to God.

"I won't apologize for protecting Rose."

"You never have to apologize for protecting Ros*ie*," Noah said, his tone softer this time as he glanced at me. "Just try to think of my workload next time you decide to murder someone with your bare hands. Makes my job a lot harder when the P.D. has to cover your shit up. You guys may help us do the dirty work, but at any point we can easily put you away for *your crimes,* if we wanted to."

Cain grunted, but before he could respond, Sly cut in. "Thank you, officer. Can we go now? I'm sure Rosie would like to check on her employees and guests of the bar, and I'm sure you have to attend to this." He gestured to the dead body laying behind us.

Noah nodded curtly at Sly before pulling me in for another hug. He kissed the top of my head affectionately. "I'm glad you're okay."

"I'm always okay. Your misplaced faith hurts, buddy." I squeezed his midsection tight before adding, "But seriously, where were your guys tonight?"

He exhaled deeply with what I knew was a sigh of regret.

"I'm sorry. There was a rollover accident on the highway and they were the closest squad car. We had to send them."

"That sucks," I said, and he simply nodded.

Sly's warm arm slid around my shoulders as I stepped away from Noah.

"When she's done, take her to my room," Cain demanded, then turned to speak with Noah. Their bodies twisted toward the dead guy, their voices hushed.

Sly led me through the alley and back into the bar. I met Indy's concerned gaze the moment the door opened, and she practically sprinted to get to me, throwing her arms around my neck as her body collided with mine.

"Are you okay? I saw what the guy did, then what Cain did, and then you went after him, and I couldn't just leave the bar, but holy shit, Rosie, that guy slipped something into your drink." She couldn't take a breath fast enough, and her words slurred together as she held me tight.

"I'm okay. Are you okay?"

"Yeah, but don't kill me..." Her voice trailed off, and she released me, shuffling slightly on her feet.

I looked at her wide-eyed, my eyebrows shooting upward as I waited for *why* she thought I might kill her.

"I overreacted and panicked, and remade drinks for everyone who was sitting at the bar. I know he didn't spike anyone else's drink, but I went into panic mode and thought I'd feel better knowing there was absolutely no chance in hell anything was slipped into anyone else's."

Ugh, I freaking loved this girl. She had a heart of gold, even if she sometimes made rash decisions that hardly made any sense.

"It's fine," I told her, rubbing my hands up and down her arms. "I would never be mad over something as trivial as remaking drinks. You did what you felt needed to be done—you're my right-hand woman, Indy. I wouldn't call you that if I didn't trust your judgment."

She gave me a weak smile, and it suddenly occurred to me that I put a lot on this woman's shoulders. "Effective immediately, your new job title is bar manager, and I'm increasing your pay. We'll talk details tomorrow, but for now, I need you to do an early last call and close up shop. I'm exhausted, both mentally and physically, and it's time we all go home."

Indy beamed, pulling me in for another hug. "Thank you, so, so much. I won't let you down."

"You never do."

After I'd ensured that all of my employees were good and safe, I let Sly lead me up the stairs to the club's living space. I still couldn't wrap my head around why exactly they made the space above my bar their base, but as Sly and I walked down the dark hallway and passed all the closed doors, I felt grateful to have them there.

Sly opened the door to Cain's room and followed me in, flicking the light switch as we entered.

"Shower, mia preferita. You will feel better once you do."

I felt like a zombie as I kicked off my heels and made my way into Cain's ensuite. There were only a handful of rooms with bathrooms attached—the rooms were not initially meant to be bedrooms, the previous owner agreed to add only a couple of bathrooms up here—which forced most of the club's members to shower at their *actual* homes.

Yeah, there's a fun fact for you: not all Sinners live here

full time. But all of them had a room assigned to them for when they did stay, whether it be for club business or if they drank too much—they never had to worry about getting home.

When the scalding water hit my skin, my body hummed, and I let the tension melt away. I stood beneath the rain shower head until the water turned cold, then curled myself in the towel Cain had hung behind the door.

Emerging from the bathroom, I saw Sly sitting on the edge of Cain's bed with a folded t-shirt and my panties in his lap.

Shrugging, he handed them to me and said, "I thought he might appreciate you in his shirt, and not mine."

"You're probably right," I agreed, pulling the shirt over my head and down my body before tugging the underwear up my legs. Yawning, I crawled onto Cain's bed and under the covers, helping myself to his pillow.

Sly stood and walked to where I was curled up, and bent down to kiss my head. "He should be back any time. You will be okay?"

I shook my head no. "I will be okay, but don't leave. Not yet."

He chuckled, but took a seat on the bed next to me, keeping his boots off the edge. "He won't like this, but whatever mia preferita wants, mia preferita gets."

"Damn straight."

The last thing I remember before sleep, that seductive sandman, lulled me under, was Sly stroking my hair and softly singing something in Italian.

CHAPTER EIGHTEEN

Rosie

The slam of the door startled me awake, and I sat up fast, my eyes adjusting to my surroundings.

Warm light spilled from the lamp on the side table, illuminating the darkness just enough where I was able to get my bearings quickly.

Cain began tugging off his boot, holding onto his dresser to balance as he removed it completely and did the same with the other.

"Mio amico, how did it go with the lieutenant?" Sly asked curiously.

I crossed my legs beneath me, suddenly wide awake and anxious to know what happened after Sly and I left.

Cain said nothing, tugging his shirt overhead before working on his pants as he walked into his ensuite, the door slamming roughly behind him. Moments later, the shower turned on.

For several seconds, Sly and I simply stared at each other,

not sure what to make of Cain's abrupt departure to the bathroom. I'd never seen him like that before and though I knew Cain could hold his own, I couldn't help but worry a little.

I couldn't take the silence for long and asked Sly hesitantly. "Do you think he's okay?"

"Sì, mia preferita. Cain is fine. When he is forced to focus on the task at hand, he goes into another headspace. I imagine this time, however, his driving force was amplified by your danger, which is why we had such a difficult time rousing him from that headspace."

I nodded, not really having words to say in response to that. What could be said?

Sly and I sat in comfortable silence, listening to the sound of Cain's shower until the water cut off.

"I should go. He will want his time alone with you," Sly said, reaching over to press a kiss to my forehead.

"Please stay," I said, not ready for the man who'd unknowingly become my comfort blanket to leave yet. Part of me liked just having him there, and the other part wanted a buffer between me and Cain. Not a single part of me was afraid of him, but not knowing his mood, his *headspace*, as Sly had referred to it, made me want to tread lightly.

Cain emerged moments later with his dark gray towel slung low on his hips, beads of water dripping down his body from the wet hair that hung loosely around his face. I practically salivated at the sight, and my body responded instantly.

While I shamelessly admired his body, my eyes traveling down his muscular, tattooed frame, I realized I'd never seen him naked, and a red-hot urge to stand and rip his towel away from him slammed into me.

He smirked as though he knew my thoughts, and moved to his dresser, pulling out a pair of his boxer briefs.

"Out, Lucchetti," he barked at Sly as he tugged the briefs up his legs and beneath his towel, before tossing it aside.

The ridge of his cock bulged against the tight gray fabric, leaving little to the imagination. I squirmed a little on the bed, dying to press my thighs together, and suddenly unsure of what to do with my hands.

Still, I felt myself shake my head. "No," I told Cain. "I want Sly to stay."

"It's okay, bella," Sly said as he stood, but I reached up and caught him by the hand, pulling him back down. He lost his footing but caught himself as his backside landed on the bed.

"No," I repeated. "I want you to stay."

His brows came together in confusion, but I broke our eye contact and turned to Cain. "He stays."

"Fine," Cain growled, and took a seat in the plush wing-back chair sitting in the corner of his room. "What's going on in that pretty head of yours, Rose? I can practically see your wheels turning."

That was a loaded question if I've ever heard one.

What was going through my head?

So many things.

The night was on a constant loop—the only pause from it was when I fell asleep.

But what was in the forefront of my mind was my words from weeks ago, when I asked Cain to share me, and the memory of him and Sly in my office not that long ago.

And suddenly the room was stifling. I could feel the heat creep up my chest, settling on my cheeks. My eyes slammed shut as I felt a phantom tongue lapping at my cum between my thighs as it leaked from my body. Firm hands gripping my thighs. Hungry eyes staring into mine from across the room.

My body felt alight, slow tingles igniting every nerve ending. Beneath Cain's t-shirt I wore, my nipples hardened, and a gush of wetness dampened my underwear.

"I know that look." Cain's voice cut through my fantasy. "Do you know that look, Sly?"

"Sì," Sly answered. "The blush that's settled on her skin tells us all we need to know."

Opening my eyes, I saw Cain settled into his chair, his herculean legs spread wide as he relaxed into it. And if I thought his cock was big earlier, I was sadly mistaken. Fully hardened, his briefs could hardly contain it. The fabric strained, the head poking out from beneath the waistband like it was begging to come out to play.

Cain lifted his hands to rest casually behind his head. "What was it you asked me to do again? Share you?"

My stomach recoiled a bit with the mention of *sharing*, the roofie-rapists suggestion of him sharing me with Cain still fresh in my mind, but I pushed it away.

Cain *killed* that man for me.

So, I met his heated stare and rose to the occasion, even though my insides felt like Jell-O. "Yes."

Looking at Sly, he asked, "And is that what you want too, Lucchetti? You want to share her, right here, right now?"

Sly waited a beat before answering, and though it was gone within a split second, I could have sworn a look of hesitation washed over his features before he schooled them and answered. "Whatever mia preferita wants, mia preferita gets."

I raked my teeth against my bottom lip as he repeated his earlier sentiment.

"Take off your shirt, Rose," Cain demanded.

I removed the shirt without hesitation, tossing it across the room to him when it was off. The air was cool against my chest, and my nipples peaked again.

Picking up the shirt I'd tossed onto his lap, Cain brought the fabric to his nose and inhaled. "I fucking love that my shirt now smells like you, baby."

His eyes trailed down my body, stopping where my panties covered the rest of me. Without being told, I threaded my thumbs through my lace boy shorts and tugged them down, tossing them across Cain's lap next.

The air caught in my throat when he brought them to his nose and breathed them in, too. "This is my favorite scent. Fucking intoxicating."

From his words alone, a fire coursed through me and I felt my pussy get impossibly wet. My clit throbbed, my walls involuntarily clenching with anticipation. I fought the urge to reach down and relieve some of the pressure that had built.

I wanted Cain to do it for me.

Movement in my peripheral caught my eye, and the bed dipped as Sly sat. He rearranged himself, obviously as turned on as I was. He was still fully dressed, so I had to use my imagination as to how hard he was.

"Get naked, Sly," I said through a strained breath.

His eyes flickered over to Cain before he shrugged out of his leather vest, dropping it to the floor and he reached behind and pulled off his shirt. Digging into his pocket, he pulled out a condom and tossed it on the bed beside me, then stripped down completely. Sly clearly had no issue being naked in front of Cain, but even if he had, his eyes were glued to mine.

Neither of us moved, as though subconsciously waiting for Cain's next instructions.

"Push her down, Sly."

Sly reached out and pressed his hand against my chest, just below my collarbone, and lightly pushed me flat onto the bed. My feet stayed planted, my knees up, thighs pressed together. It did little to relieve the ache between my legs. So desperately, I needed more.

"Drop your knees, Rose. Show us how much you're enjoying this." Cain's voice was husky, but methodological. He had a plan. He was the maestro, the puppeteer. And goddamn if I wasn't fucking loving that right now.

My legs fell open, pussy on full display for Cain. He sat forward in his chair, pressing his elbows into his thighs, boldly staring at the place that was quite literally begging for his attention.

Sly moved around the bed, coming to the foot of it so he could enjoy the view as well.

"Tell us what you want, mia preferita." Sly's eyes sparkled as he palmed his cock, wrapping his fingers around the shaft.

"I want *everything*, but I'll settle for a face between my thighs right now," I taunted, hoping one of them would hurry up and oblige.

"You heard the queen," Cain barked at Sly. "Lay on the bed and let her ride your face. She takes her pleasure. Do *not* fucking touch her, Sly. You hear me?"

"I can handle that," Sly agreed, and crawled onto the bed.

He adjusted himself to lie down and I walked on my knees to him and climbed over his body until I was straddling his face, facing Cain.

Sly gave me a *sly* smile, then lifted his head to open mouth kiss my pussy. His hot, wet tongue swept through my center and collided with my clit.

The sensation jolted me and I lowered myself further onto his face, shamelessly riding his tongue as I grabbed at my breasts. We fell into a familiar rhythm, having done this time and time again. I tossed my head back in pleasure, unabashedly moaning loudly, not giving a shit about being quiet.

Sly knew my body. He knew what I liked, how to bring me to orgasm quickly, and how to withhold it. We'd become well acquainted under the sheets, losing ourselves physically in each other to satiate the craving for the people we couldn't have. But despite the pleasure he was drawing from it, this was different.

And as I opened my eyes and connected them to Cain's darkened irises, I couldn't help feeling like Sly was no longer in the room. My pleasure was Cain's, and the way his fists were balled tightly, resting on his thighs, and his jaw clenched, I knew he was struggling to keep his composure.

This sharing scenario was only happening because I had asked for it. Watching me with another man was killing him.

It was written all over his face.

Though my body was wound tight, my orgasm continuously building from the perfect strokes Sly's tongue was delivering, I felt myself pull away and move off of him.

Cain's brow furrowed in confusion before he slipped back

into the role of running the show. "Lay back down on the bed, Rose."

Sly rolled his body to give me space, before he ended up getting off the bed all together, standing at the foot of it again.

I did what Cain asked and laid back down against his black sheets. Like earlier, I kept my legs bent at the knees.

"Open your legs again, baby," Cain instructed. "Let us see how your pussy shines after being so close to release."

I dropped my legs, but this time as I did, I brought my fingers between my thighs and dipped two in, pulling some of the wetness to my clit, then began to rub it. My eyes drifted from Cain to Sly, then back to Cain, wondering who would make the next move.

Neither of the men said a word. Neither of them moved. They just watched as I finger fucked myself and rubbed my clit with just enough pressure to build my orgasm back up without teetering the edge of release.

I wanted to make this last.

I felt like a queen. *Their* queen. The queen to the king and a knight.

As much as that made my heart skip a beat, I knew this was also a one-time thing. They wouldn't share me again—I wouldn't ask them to. There were no longer any doubts in my mind of who I wanted to be with, or hesitations as to whether he'd hurt me.

I'd decided at that moment that Cain was worth the risk.

But that didn't mean I couldn't enjoy this moment while it lasted, either.

"Fuck me," I ordered to no one specific, more than curious to see who would make the first move.

Time seemed to move in slow motion while I waited spread eagle for someone to take the bait, and the more time that passed, the more self-conscious I grew.

After what felt like an eternity, but was likely only a few seconds because let's be honest, both of them looked like they were ready to devour me, Sly stepped forward. He yanked me by the legs until my ass hit the edge of the bed.

My hand patted the bed beside me in search of the condom he'd taken out earlier, and when I found it I tossed it at him.

He ripped the wrapper with his teeth and rolled the rubber down his shaft until it was firmly in place, then he aligned himself with my pussy, but he didn't slide in. Instead, his eyes connected with mine, a hint of mischievousness twinkling in them. An unspoken question passed between us, and I shifted my gaze to Cain.

Like earlier when I fucked Sly's face, Cain's jaw was clenched tight, and he looked like he was struggling to maintain his cool. He looked absolutely ready to explode, an unmasked fury overtaking over his features as he looked down at where Sly's cock practically nudged my pussy.

Sly rolled his hips slightly, and that's all it took for Cain to become unhinged.

His hand connected with Sly's neck and he ripped him away from me, and used the grip on him to forcefully steer him to the door. "Fuck this," he growled.

Cain threw open his bedroom door, shoving Sly through it as he snarled, "I'm not fucking sharing her. She's *mine*."

He slammed the door and locked it before turning back to me.

The laughter that bubbled up quickly died in my throat under Cain's intense stare, his eyes blazing as he stomped toward me. When his shins hit the bed, he stopped and tugged his briefs off, letting his cock spring free.

I literally gasped, my eyes widening as they connected with his not only gigantic fucking cock, but the row of piercings on the underside. Five steel bars formed a perfect Jacob's ladder, and to say I was surprised was an understatement.

Shocked, and now gushing with how wet I was, was more accurate.

Cain let his body fall forward, catching himself with one arm while his other hand enclosed around his cock. Bringing his lips to my ear, he whispered, "You're *mine*, Rose, and there's no way in hell I'd watch another man fuck you. Not when I can do it so much better."

He turned his face, and I wrapped my hands around the back of his neck and pulled him toward me, capturing his lips in a filthy, frenzied kiss.

As our tongues connected, he slammed his cock into me, burying himself until he was fully inside. I felt like I could feel him in my stomach as he began to move. The foreign sensation of his piercings against my inner walls was unlike anything I'd ever felt.

I cried out, the sounds muffled as Cain caught them through our kiss.

"That's right, baby. Let me hear you," he groaned against my lips.

Pulling my leg up, he held it to allow himself to get deeper, thrusting into me with a slow control.

"*Fuck*," I moaned. "Why'd we wait so long?"

His hips rolled into me and he pulled my other leg up, coaxing me to wrap my legs around his middle. "Because I knew once I had you fully, I'd never let you go, even if you fought me on it. Even if you tried to run." He reached down between my legs, finding my clit with his fingers. I moaned, my eyes rolling back into my head as my orgasm pushed forward at the speed of a freight train. "I've waited a long time for my chance to show you I'm the man for you, Rose. The *only* fucking man. I'll spend my life proving that to you. And I'll start by proving it repeatedly tonight."

Cain moved his free hand to my hip and guided it up, lifting it as he fucked me into another dimension while playing with my clit exactly how he'd learned I liked it.

"*Fuck*, fuck me harder, Cain. I'm going to come."

"Good. Coat my dick with your cum, Rose. Fucking drench it."

He added more pressure and fucked me with such force that the metal of the headboard slammed into the wall with every thrust.

A few seconds later, I cried out as my orgasm ripped through my veins. A current of pleasure shot through my entire body, down to the tips of my toes, every piece of me radiating with pleasure. Cain continued to slam into me, chasing his release, before he abruptly pulled out and gripped his cock tightly. He jerked himself twice before thick ropes of cum shot out onto my thighs and pussy. He grunted through his release, his hooded eyes on mine.

I ingrained that picture of him into my mind as one of the hottest things I'd ever seen.

Propping myself onto my elbows, I stared down at his cock in his hand, still fully erect. "How are you still hard?" I questioned. I'd been with guys who were half-mast after coming, but there was nothing *half* about what I was looking at.

"Do you know how long I've waited to get you in my bed, Rose? How many nights I laid awake, jerking off to the *thought* of you? Too many, baby. I've waited for this for too long."

I sighed contently, my stupid heart inflating at his confession of wanting me for so long. It hit so much different when you saw it, and not just heard the words.

It'd been a while since I was truly at a loss for words, but he'd rendered me speechless. There was so much I wanted to say, but now wasn't the time. Not when it was so obviously the time for us to connect in other ways.

This was more than just sex, and that absolutely fucking terrified me, but at the same time, it made me feel like my life had just begun.

For so long, I allowed myself to settle, but nothing about Cain felt like settling. It felt like living. Thriving. *Loving.*

My lips pursed in a smile. "So, round two then?"

With a wicked grin, he flipped me onto all fours, not bothering to clean up the mess he'd made. "Oh, baby, we've barely started," he cooed.

Nudging me to crawl up the bed until I reached the headboard, he gave my ass a hard smack, and groaned with satisfaction. "Hold on tight," he commanded, and I wrapped my hands around the metal slats at the same time he slammed his cock back into me, making me see stars.

Cain stayed true to his word and repeatedly proved how he was the man for me.

He proved it in every position on his bed.

In his wingback chair.

Against his bedroom door.

In the shower.

He proved it here, there, and fucking everywhere, until the stars I was seeing turned into rays of warm, inviting sunshine, and we both slipped into a deep sleep, satiated and spent, wrapped naked in each other's arms.

CHAPTER NINETEEN

Rosie

I couldn't help but feel like the world's biggest bitch.

Rationally, I knew I was overreacting, but irrationally, I felt like the guilt was eating me alive.

I'd barely batted an eye at Cain's abrupt and somewhat forceful removal of Sly from his bedroom on Saturday night. Distracted by the pleasure and the emotions of finally having come to terms with what I really wanted, I let him throw Sly out when I should have…I don't know?

Fought for him to stay?

The reality was, I hadn't wanted him there anymore. Didn't *need* him there anymore. I'd fully welcomed the potential of getting my heart broken again because the gain was worth the risk.

Cain was worth the risk.

It was a terrifying thought.

Leaning against the concrete wall of Andromeda, my body

slid to the floor, already exhausted for the day. Sitting on the asphalt, I kicked my legs out in front of me and lit up a cigarette.

Weeks had passed since I'd indulged, Cain's voice ringing in my head whenever I thought to have one, chastising me with the reminder that smoking kills. But after yesterday's all day fuck-fest, and this morning's pity party from feeling guilty, I felt like I deserved one to calm my nerves.

Inhaling, I let the smoke settle in my mouth for a moment before opening my lips just enough for it to billow out. My eyes closed, and for several minutes, I just relaxed with my head against the building and the cigarette dangling from my fingers.

The rumble of a motorcycle approaching in the distance cut through the otherwise stale air. I didn't bother opening my eyes as it pulled closer and came to a stop. The engine cut, and gravel crunched beneath heavy footsteps.

"Hiding?" Sly's smooth voice questioned. He swooped the cig out from between my fingers.

Opening my eyes, I found him crouching down next to me, taking a drag.

"Maybe." I took the cigarette as he passed it back, bringing it to my lips.

Sly settled on the ground next to me with one leg outstretched and the other bent. "I'm here to listen if you need to speak."

"How pissed are you?" I blurted. "That I didn't do anything to stop Cain from throwing you out of his room... *naked?*"

An echo of laughter erupted through Sly's lips, and he shook his head animatedly. "No, mia preferita, I am not mad at you. I am *proud* of you."

"Proud?"

"Sì." Sly reached over and grabbed the cigarette butt from my hand and tossed it to the floor. With his boot, he snuffed it out, then reached for my hand. He pulled it to his lips and kissed the back of it. "You finally stopped allowing fear to hold your heart in its grasp, and you are letting happiness in."

"Cain literally threw you out on your naked ass, Sly. You have to be a little mad about that."

"He did, but it was a move I anticipated him to make. Why do you think I hesitated to push myself into you, amore mio? I was *waiting* for him to allow his fear to stop holding him, and to fully claim what is his."

I glared at him, not loving the way he insinuated that I was property. He laughed in response and added, "So to speak, mia preferita. So to speak."

Nodding, I pulled my gaze from him and stared out into the street in front of Andromeda. It was a bright and sunny day, though the air was still a little crisp. The streets were quiet for a Monday afternoon, but the rumble of several motorcycles could be heard in the distance.

"Are the guys on their way?" I asked.

"Sì. Cain's called for a Church meeting. Damon needs to speak."

"About what?"

One by one, the Sinners arrived and filled the front row of my parking lot, my question left unanswered. They took their time, cutting their engines, pulling off their helmets. Cain was the first off his bike and he trudged his way to me with a smirk on his lips.

His hair was messy from his helmet, his eyes bright.

Reaching down, his fingers circled my wrist, and he pulled me to my feet so quickly my body slammed into his. Grabbing my chin between his fingers and thumb so he could tip my head, Cain's lips found mine, and he stole my breath with a kiss filled with passion and ferocity. It instantly set my blood on fire.

Whistles and whoops sounded around us, and instead of pulling away, Cain kissed me harder, his free hand finding my lower back, keeping me to him.

When we broke, we were both a little breathless.

"Hi," he said quietly, his forehead pressed to mine.

I smiled at the simpleness of his tone. "Hey."

As he turned back to face his men, his fingers laced with mine. He addressed them with a stern seriousness that wasn't there seconds ago. "Church is in ten. Whatever you need to do first, do it now."

Cain let them know the conversation was cut off by turning back to me, a hint of mischief behind the sparkle in his eyes. I'd acquainted myself with that look over and over again yesterday.

Running my hand up the front of his chest, my fingers grazed against the soft worn leather of his vest and danced across the patches of insignia. "So, ten minutes, huh? You didn't leave us much time."

He caught my wrist as it dipped to the waist of his jeans

and used it to tug me forward again. His lips grazed my ear as he leaned down. "Oh, baby, ten minutes is plenty of time for what I have planned for you. They're called a quickie for a reason."

With that, his hands were on my waist and he lifted me, tossing me over his shoulder as though my hundred and fifty-eight pounds were as light as a feather.

From my upside-down vantage point, I had a great view of his ass, which I hit with a closed fist—playfully, but with force. He could handle it. "Where are we going?"

"Hmmm," he mused as he nudged open the door of Andromeda with his foot. "You tell me. Office or my room?"

"How about neither?"

He stopped walking. "Neither?"

"Yeah, neither. Put me down."

Lowering me, I slid down his front. Once on my feet, I grabbed his hand and pulled him behind the bar.

"What are y—" he started, but his words were lost as I sank to my knees and quickly started to undo his belt, button, and zipper. Reaching into his pants, I pulled his cock out and pushed down the fabric that was in my way before closing my lips around him.

He grunted, his hands flying up into my hair as he pushed my head to take him further. I relaxed my throat and let him slide as far down as I could. My eyes burned immediately as I fought against my gag reflex.

Bobbing my head up and down his shaft, I swirled my tongue the best I could and reached up to massage his balls with one hand as I did. He groaned and shifted his hips forward, and as I looked up, his stare was already burning down into mine.

"You're so damn beautiful, baby," he praised. "Keep going like this and I'll finish way before our ten minutes are up."

My fingers wrapped around his shaft, stroking him with the same rhythm as I moved my mouth. Cain's breaths quickened, his body tense with his release that was right on the surface, when the door to Andromeda slammed open against the wall.

"Prez, we have a situation," Damon's voice boomed as he entered the bar.

Cain's grasp on my hair tightened, and I kept blowing him, ignoring the fact that Damon was looming just on the other side of the bar top.

"GOD DAMN IT, DAMON," Cain roared. "Fuck off, it can wait."

"No, it can't." Damon's voice was low and strained, but still harbored a ruthless edge. Was he rattled?

"FUCK." Cain loosened his grip and pulled his hips back, withdrawing from my mouth. His still-hard cock strained as he tucked himself in and refastened his pants. He looked down at me with a mixture of irritation and remorse. "I'm sorry, baby. If it were any other Sinner, I'd ignore them, but Damon—"

"It's fine," I assured him as I came to a stand, unapologetically wiping my mouth as I did. I offered Damon a smile, as though I wasn't annoyed.

Cain leaned down and gave me a dirty, rough kiss before turning to Damon. "If the fucking sky isn't falling, I will kill you."

Damon said nothing, but the two men seemed to communicate wordlessly.

"Church. Now," Cain barked, and Damon plowed his way through the bar and to the hall where the back stairs were. Directing his attention back to me, Cain grabbed my hand and kissed my open palm. "I'll see you tonight, but in case you're busy, I'll say this now. Meet me in my room after you close up, and I'll make this up to you."

"You're the one with the blue balls," I quipped, smiling as he leaned down and kissed me again.

It was like we'd done a complete three-sixty in a matter of forty-eight hours. All the walls, the hesitations, the back-and-forth...*gone*. Just like that.

And I couldn't stop myself from waiting for the other shoe to drop.

Yet, the man looking back at me had nothing but adoration shining through his eyes, despite his menacing exterior. Cain Michaels, president of Sinners Warlord, a man who I recently watched murder someone with his bare hands, was the same man looking at me like I hung the moon.

"I love you, baby," he told me, holding my hand until his footsteps carried him out of reach. I watched as he followed the path Damon had taken, making his way through the bar and out of sight as he headed toward the back staircase.

I stared at the empty space he disappeared through, my heart thundering. So quickly, everything had changed. My mind was reeling—that little voice in my head telling me to *be careful*.

But being careful already wasted so much time for us.

Through the past and present, Cain's shown me his faults,

his rage, his unparalleled determination, and now he was showing me his softer side. The tender side. The side he'd reserved for *me*.

So no, I wouldn't be careful—it was time to throw caution to the wind and follow Sly's advice to let my heart guide me and let the fear go.

Other shoe be damned.

CHAPTER TWENTY

Cain

When I walked into the room where we held Church, it fell silent. All eyes shifted to me, and their instant readiness for my words sat heavy.

Things felt off, and as I took my seat at the head of the table, my eyes met Damon's. He nodded slightly, and I relaxed into my chair, ready to start. "I called this meeting to talk to you all about what happened over the weekend, but Damon has a more pressing update he'll be starting with."

The Sinners looked to their enforcer, and he cracked his knuckles like he was ready to fight one of his own. "There's whispers on the road—the Sinners have become a target. Turns out that piece of shit Cain put in the ground was part of The Reaper's Wings and they're not too happy they've lost a member of their crew."

The words had barely finished leaving his mouth before I exploded. My fists connected with the table. I saw red as a newfound level of rage consumed me. Flying up from my seat, unable to contain my anger, I roared, "Those bastards should have thought about what type of scumbag they initiated!"

He wanted to hurt Rose. Tried to drug her so he could fucking rape her.

The Reaper's Wings was the club that operated out of Bridge Point. They were ruthless motherfuckers—part of the one percent. Word was they dabbled in the weapons trade, mixing business with the Italian fucks who ran the industrial part of their city.

Rifton, their club prez, was supposedly real close with some guy they called Caduto, both of whom were as shady as they came.

"Settle," King mumbled under his breath. The one word cut through the sea of red.

I lowered back into my chair, still seething, and forced myself to calm the fuck down so I could address my guys. "As most of you already heard, Saturday night I killed a man who spiked Rose's drink. The same piece of shit who's been drugging and raping women all over the city. The P.D. did what they always do for us and swept it under the rug. Played it off to the media that they were still looking for the guy who killed him, but suspect it was an unresolved gang-related hit, seeing as the guy had some questionable prison tats."

Taking a minute, I looked at each of the Sinners. They wore stoic expressions, many had clenched fists as they too struggled to keep their composure.

My little firecracker had become quite popular amongst the Sinners. A little sister figure—someone they held with high respect.

And now that I'd publicly marked her as *mine* less than an

hour ago, I imagined their perspectives shifted slightly. She went from just being someone they respected to someone they *protected*.

It was the way of the Sinners.

Once you'd committed to a woman, she became your old lady in every sense of the word, and therefore, became family to everyone in the club. I could practically see the wheels turning in everyone's heads, the pieces of information I'd given being processed.

"What's the plan, Prez?" one of our newest prospects asked, clearing his throat after, like it embarrassed him to speak up.

"The plan is...we wait it out. We listen, and keep our eyes peeled. We assess whether we're dealing with rumors or facts. If we've pissed off The Reaper's Wings, they'll let it be known. Until then, business as usual."

Immediately, the Sinners started speaking at once, some more quietly than others. A few were pissed, standing in their chairs and yelling from across the table. Some sat back and watched, their arms folded across their chests.

It was the first time I'd ever felt like I fucked up as their prez...like their trust and confidence in me was slipping through my fingers.

"If anyone has a *better* idea, I'm all ears," I bellowed, garnering their attention back. "Is it fuckin' ideal that we sit back and wait? No. It isn't. But unless we want to barrel into this situation headfirst and risk walking into a goddamn ambush, there's not much else to do. The Reaper's Wings are shady motherfuckers who don't give a damn. They have a reputation that precedes them—they don't care whose blood is on their hands or what repercussions there may be for it. *We* don't act like that. We have a code. And it's time you all remember it."

My chest heaved. There was more I wanted to say, but the more I did say, the more I risked exploding at them. Again.

Thankfully, King, my VP, took over.

"Now, I know a handful of you are newcomers, but most of you aren't. Pops was real clear on his intentions for this club. Protect each other, protect our women, protect our community. Just because Pops isn't the prez anymore, doesn't mean his legacy doesn't live on through Cain. If you all don't like the way he's running his club, you can see yourself the fuck out, or shut the fuck up. Like it or not, Cain's right. The best course of action at this point is to observe."

He turned his attention to Damon and tipped his chin toward him. "Our enforcer's out there listenin' and watchin'. If anything changes, we'll reconvene and go from there. Until then, we listen to our prez and remain idle, but vigilant."

A trickle of pride spiked within my chest, and I nodded in thanks to my second-in-command.

The Sinners were quiet after that. Their attentiveness shifted back to me.

"You are all my family," I began, my voice controlled despite the hesitancy I was feeling. I hated being vulnerable, but I knew what needed to be done to restore some of their faith in me. "Not so long ago, I had a brother, and he was the most important person in my life. My loyalty to him was unwavering—until it wasn't. He showed me his true colors and destroyed the respect I had for him. He went from being the one person I'd do anything for to the person I loathed the most. I cut him out of my life and now he may as well be dead for as little shit I give about him or his miserable existence.

"Point is, I didn't choose him as my family, and didn't hesitate to walk away from him, either. I *chose* the Sinners. You're all my brothers, and I'll protect this family at all costs. If you don't agree with how I run things, that's on you, but you will *respect* the choices I make. We've dealt with a lot of shit lately and haven't had time to decompress. So let's do that. Family dinner this Sunday in the side lot—show up any time after four. We'll go as late as Rose lets us."

Nods of understanding bobbed amongst the men, and that was enough for me.

Standing, I left the room, went to the club's living space, and sank onto the worn leather couch. I leaned forward with my elbows on my thighs, cradling my head in my hands. My head was throbbing, the tension radiating outward from my temples.

What a shitshow that had been.

I could hear the Sinners leaving, and my thoughts drifted back to when I had first joined the crew as a prospect, so hopeful to earn my way into their ranks.

It happened by chance—right place, right time.

My bike had broken down on the side of the road shortly after I moved to Shadow Hills. I commuted on the highway almost every day, to and from my shitty job in Ridgewood, when the damn thing just quit on me. I'd called for a tow, and the driver hauled my busted motorcycle back to a hole-in-the-wall garage called Dave's in Ridgewood. They weren't super busy that day, so the owner had time to look at it right then and there.

That's how I met Pops.

He lectured me about not having the know-how to fix my own ride and took me under his wing, showing me the basics. He gave me a job and told me to quit my other one. Introduced me to my *family* and taught me everything I needed to know about leadership, loyalty, and club business. I owed my adult life to Pops. Without his trust in me, I wasn't sure what I'd be up to right now.

A knock rapped on the edge of the doorframe to the living room, pushing me from my thoughts. Heavy footsteps followed as whoever was interrupting my silence came further into the room.

"Fuck off," I growled, even though I knew it wouldn't deter them.

"I know you're not talking to me like that, boy," King shot back. He took a seat on the couch next to me, relaxing into it with his feet crossed at the ankles. "Pops taught you better than to disrespect your elders."

"You're twelve years older than me, King, in your late forties. Hardly qualifies you as an elder."

"Still older than you by over a decade. What has you so pissed tonight?"

I dug the heels of my hands into my eyes, welcoming the pain that shot behind them from the pressure. "The better question is, what doesn't? Rose was drugged, the P.D. gave me attitude about his death, and now there's talk of The Reaper's Wings putting a target on us. Then, to top it off, the Sinners think I'm not doing my job right. That enough of a reason for you?"

"Alright, let's break this down one problem at a time, like Pops used to do when one of us would go off the deep end."

"Can't we just get Pops on the phone? The last thing I want is to talk about my problems with you. What next? Are we going to do each other's nails and braid our hair, too?"

"Your hair's just a little too short for me to braid, and Pops is in Turks and Caicos with his newly wed old lady. You're stuck with me, so like I said, let's address this one problem at a time, like Pops would."

Groaning, I sat back, mirroring King's relaxed position. "Rose was drugged."

"She was, but she didn't consume the roofied drink. She's fine. Next?"

I forced the irritation of his quick dismissal back down. "The P.D.'s questioned me twice now."

"Likely because you're close to this particular case, Cain. Had it been any other woman at any other bar, they wouldn't have batted an eye. But because it was Rosie and her bar, they're making sure all their i's are dotted and their t's crossed."

"The lieutenant is one of her best fucking friends!" My voice raised in argument, and again, I pushed the vexation down. "The lieutenant is one of her best friends. He, out of all people, shouldn't be giving me grief about killing the man who wanted to *rape* her."

"He is one of her best friends," King repeated. "Which is exactly why he's being extra careful with this case. There's a lot at stake, a lot of blurred lines and conflicts of interest. Step out of the situation as Cain and look at it from an outside perspective. It needs to be handled with concentration and care."

Looking away, I found a fist-sized hole in the wall across the room that one of the Sinners had punched through the drywall, and stared at it until my body forced my eyes to blink.

"The crew doesn't trust my judgment," I stated hollowly.

King leaned forward, resting his forearms on his legs. For the first time, I saw softness behind his hardened eyes. "The crew trusts you, Cain. It's why they appointed you as prez. You're doing right by them, they can just see how close this all is to you, and I'd imagine that puts them on edge. No one wants a target on their back, especially from The Reaper's Wings. They're a trigger-happy shitstorm and the last thing anyone wants is to deal with those fucks."

"Yeah."

He clapped his hand against the top of my leg. "You out of that head yet? How'd I do?"

"You're no Pops," I deadpanned.

"Yeah, well. Quit sulking and go do something that makes you feel alive." He stood and left the room without another word.

Kicking my feet up on our new coffee table, I ran my hand down my face and thought about King's theory on why the P.D. was breathing down my neck about this when usually they don't. About how The Reaper's Wings putting a target on us was the worst possible thing that could happen. Heading into Bridge Point to talk to Rifton was a terrible idea, but if Damon came back with any credibility that the threat was real, I just might have to.

No matter what, I needed to keep my family safe.
Even if it risked my own life to do it.

CHAPTER TWENTY-ONE

Rosie

"I think I want to go get a tattoo today," I said to Indy as I sat across the bar, watching her wipe down the counter.

The day was still young—it was only six and after last night I felt like I needed a little me time. A tattoo sounded like the perfect way to squeeze in a little self-care.

Cain had come down to the bar a while after the Sinners' meeting ended and spent the night kicking back whiskey until we were slow enough for me to take him upstairs. He had a good buzz going, and instead of picking up where we'd left off earlier, I tucked him into his bed and crawled in beside him.

Stress rolled off him in waves as we laid in bed and he filled me in on the meeting. He was hesitant at first to tell me everything, but eventually, thanks to the liquor, he fessed up. It bothered me that Cain was worried about this other MC, but the last thing he needed was for me to seem fearful. It'd just add another layer of pressure, and he didn't need to worry about me anymore than I knew he already was.

Once he'd gotten everything off his chest, his features turned from tumultuous to lust. As he smashed his lips to mine and rolled on top of me, our movements became frenzied. We both rushed to pull my underwear down enough for him to push inside.

He fucked me deeply, roughly, and frantically, his body telling me what his words wouldn't convey about the things he was keeping locked inside.

His hands roamed my body, but there was nothing tender about his touch. He was possessive and greedy—clinging to me like I was his lifeline—and though I never wanted to be responsible for another person like that, never wanted to feel like they needed me for anything, I didn't shy away from it. In fact, it spurred me on, and I wanted to give him everything he needed from me.

When we came, we came together, and even though we'd fucked hard and fast, I'd never felt closer to him.

It scared me. *He* scared me. But he also made me feel *so* alive.

"What would you get?" Indy asked, tossing the bar towel onto her shoulder. She leaned against the counter, giving me her full attention. "And where are you putting it?"

"Why do you have to ask hard questions?" I quipped, not having an answer for her. I thought for a couple of seconds, my lips pursing. Grinning, I told her, "Maybe I'll get your name tattooed on me."

"Or you could get mine." Warm lips pressed against my neck, kissing the soft flesh before skating up to my ear. "Put it right along your inner thigh. *Fuck*, that makes me hard just thinking about it."

Indy scrunched her nose.

Shaking my head, I pushed him off me. "Down, boy. I'm not getting your name tattooed on me. Not now, not ever. So get that idea out of that thick skull of yours."

Reaching into the back pocket of my jeans, I pulled my phone out and opened a new text message, wanting to see if my artist, Ramon, could even squeeze me in today.

I turned back to Indy after I sent the text. "I'm thinking I want the night sky across my back. A bunch of small stars to symbolize Andromeda. The moon. That sort of thing. I'm making it sound ugly, but Ramon will make it amazing." I shrugged.

"I think it sounds beautiful," Indy complimented. "I hope your guy can get you in! You deserve a night off."

"Oh, speaking of time off, the Sinners are having a family barbeque on Sunday if you want to come in earlier than your shift and hang out with us. Guy Fieri over here is going to be grilling all day, so there should—*in theory*—be tons of food. Then again, the Sinners are pigs, so you should probably show up early in the night to eat."

I tossed a glare at Cain, who shrugged.

"What can I say? We're growing boys." He laughed, bending slightly to trail kisses up and down my neck again.

"You're a bunch of grown ass men..."

"Exactly. We like to eat." He reached down and cupped my pussy through my jeans. "Speaking of, let's go to your office. I'm starving."

The pressure from the seam of my jeans and Cain's hand

sent a spike of arousal through my clit, and my hips rocked slightly into his hand, chasing more of his touch. By then Indy had walked away, and since her back was toward us, I let him keep rubbing me through my pants.

Warmth bloomed through my body and I had to bite down on my tongue to keep from moaning aloud. I let my head fall back against Cain's shoulder. His hand moved upward, his fingers pushing past the waistband as he shoved his hand inside. Arching my back, I ground my ass into his crotch, his cock hard behind his jeans.

This was so fucked up to do with Indy in the same room, but I found it really difficult to care once Cain's rough palm pressed against my clit and his finger dipped inside me.

I was about to suggest that we *do* go to my office when my phone rang. Picking it up off the bar, I saw my tattoo artist calling, and pulled Cain's hand out of my pants as I connected the call.

"Hey, Ramon," I answered. "How are you?"

Cain brought the finger that was just inside me to his mouth and licked it clean.

Damn, that was hot.

"I'm good, Rosie. Glad you texted me. I actually had someone cancel last minute and can take you tonight depending on what you're wanting."

"I was thinking a back piece of the night sky. Small stars, the moon, and whatever you want to add to it. We can start it today, and if needed, I'll schedule the rest of it later."

"Cool, cool. I have a couple hours, and can do that. Can you come now?"

My gaze moved to Cain, slightly disappointed we wouldn't have time to have a quickie in my office.

"Yeah, now is good. I'll be there soon."

Ramon ended the call, and I shoved my phone back into my pocket. "Hey, Indy, I'm headed out. I'll be back late tonight. Call with any issues, okay?"

She was stacking clean glasses, getting ready to open. "Sure thing, boss! Have fun!"

I started walking toward my office, and Cain followed.

"I'm coming with you," he informed me, as though I wasn't already aware. We'd practically been inseparable these last few days.

"I know," I quipped back. "How do you feel about driving?"

It'd been a while since I'd been on the back of his bike, and the thought of taking a ride with him was exhilarating. I missed it. The feeling of freedom that being on the back of his motorcycle had. The wind whipping through my hair. My tight grasp around his midsection as he sped us down the roads.

He pulled his motorcycle keys from his front pocket and spun them around his fingers with the keychain loop. With a wicked grin he said, "Thought you'd never ask."

———

AN HOUR AND A HALF LATER, I was laying face down on a flattened tattoo chair with the needle from a tattoo gun scraping my flesh.

I *lived* for this feeling—the addictive pain vibrating into my skin as my artist created something unique and beautiful.

Ramon had drawn up a stunning tattoo to fit across the width of my back, spanning across my shoulders. A dark black and gray rendition of the night sky glittered with shimmering stars and a crescent moon. He'd been practicing a glittering ink technique, and I was eager to see how he'd use it to make the stars come to life.

Cain sat on a leather stool next to me and watched Ramon create his magic. My hand sat in his lap, and I mindlessly drifted my fingers across his leg, listening to the loud music in the tattoo shop.

Only Ramon and one other guy were working tonight, and we practically had the shop to ourselves. Half walls separated the stations for privacy, and an antique wooden desk sat in the front. Art hung on the walls, all with small price tags under them, showing they were for sale.

I'd been coming to this shop, Inked Hypocrisy, for years now, and the only thing that's changed had been the art on the walls and a few of the other artists. What drew me in initially was the shop's name, but what kept me coming back was the attention to detail that only Ramon could achieve.

When I first sat down in his chair and asked him why the hell the tattoo shop's name was Inked Hypocrisy, he chuckled and simply said the owner wanted to call out everyone who put on a façade. They tattooed clients who, on paper and on the surface, were sophisticated, and clean-cut professionals, but if you were to strip them down, you'd find the most salacious of tattoos inked into their skin.

Honestly, it made sense.

"It looks fucking amazing," Cain mused, leaning closer to watch as Ramon shaded what I assumed was the moon.

He leaned closer, his lips dusting the shell of my ear. "I can't wait to stare at it when I fuck you from behind."

Ramon grunted, hearing him. "Should I add your name in there somewhere?" he teased.

"I will *kill* you," I threatened at the same time Cain laughed and told him, "I suggested earlier that she get my name, but she wasn't in love with the idea."

Ramon lifted the tattoo gun and wiped the spot he'd been working on with a paper towel. "I can't imagine why."

Another hour passed before Ramon finished. He stood and grabbed more paper towels, folding them, then spraying them with soapy solution, cleaning the excess ink and blood off my back.

"Alright, have a look." He handed me a mirror, and I walked over to the full-length one hanging on the wall inside his station. From the reflection, I could see my tattoo.

"Holy shit," I breathed, completely blown away by what he'd done.

"I'm not going to wrap it. I prefer to let them breathe. When you sleep tonight, try to sleep on your stomach. You know how to take care of your tats, so I'll spare you the lecture, Rosie."

"Thank you so much, Ramon. You killed it once again."

"Any time. Always happy to tattoo you."

The tattoo looked stunning—far better than anything I had dreamed up in my head while he worked on it. Layers upon layers of dot work in shades of grays mixed with whites, blacks, and blues created a dark, glistening backdrop. Strategically placed on my right shoulder was a thin-lined crescent moon with its own glittering craters, and he'd even added in some wisps of gray to create a foggy cloud effect.

Cain's eyes raked over my back, admiring the tattoo before they met mine in the mirror. "It looks amazing, Rose."

Dropping my gaze, I took a step backward to get a closer look at the detailing, lifting the hand mirror to reposition my view.

Cain reached into his pocket and pulled out his wallet, handing Ramon a small wad of hundreds. "Do me a favor and get the hell out of here for about ten minutes."

As Ramon left, Cain stalked the few steps toward me. He wrapped his arm around my lower back and pulled me to him, and let his tongue find mine.

"You didn't have to pay for my tattoo," I said through the kiss. "How do you know you even gave him the right amount?"

He pulled away, his eyes searching mine. "I gave him plenty, trust me. Now, let me get a closer look at it."

Cain turned my body and pressed down on my spine, forcing me to bend and support myself with my hands flat on the tattoo chair.

"So beautiful," he muttered. His lips dragged across the back of my neck, but he was mindful not to touch the raw part of my skin.

His hands weaved around my body and he unbuttoned my jeans, sliding the zipper down next.

"What are you doing?" I asked, like I didn't already know. As if I had any intention of making him stop.

"Picking up where we left off at the bar."

From across the shop, I could see the other tattoo artist in the corner working on his client—a muscular guy getting his spine tattooed. Both were facing away from us, the sound of the tattoo gun barely audible over the music that played through the shop's speakers.

Ramon was nowhere to be found.

"Cain," I hissed when he pulled down my pants and underwear, leaving them mid-thigh.

I knew no one could see, but still. This felt a little too open of a place to screw around in.

Looking over my shoulder, I watched Cain unbuckle his pants and pull out his cock. He gripped it and rubbed the underside against my ass, so I could feel how hard he was, and each of his five piercings.

He knew I couldn't resist that damn Jacob's ladder inside me. I swear he'd already ruined me for anyone else—the way the piercings felt was otherworldly.

Without warning, he brought his cock between my legs and slammed home. We both groaned at the same time.

Slowly, he pulled back before sinking into me again, letting my body adjust to his size and the angle. With my jeans still around my thighs, it was impossible to spread my legs, so it felt even tighter around him than normal. I waited for his hand to wrap around to stimulate my clit, but he surprised me by clicking on a bullet vibrator and pressing it against me instead.

My knees buckled with the unexpected intensity, but his other arm came around my stomach and held me up. "*Fuck*, Cain, where did that come from?"

I moaned, my body moving against the vibrator as he held

himself still inside me. Everything faded away, making me forget where I was. I could have been on live T.V. for all I cared, so long as he didn't fucking stop.

He kissed the side of my head and began to move. "Stole it from your room when I was at your house."

His movements increased, thrusting his hips into me while he held the vibrator to my clit. My body was tingling from head to toe, already desperately horny from earlier.

"There's no way I'm lasting," I moaned, my eyes clenching shut. I rode out the pleasure, my body climbing higher.

It felt like my soul was leaving me. I shut my eyes tight, and the vibrations from the toy melded with the sounds of the tattoo gun and the bass of the music. Two of my senses completely numbed heightened the one that mattered most: the sense of touch.

And every single place Cain's body touched mine felt like it was an inferno.

It was all I could do not to scream when my orgasm hit, slamming into me so powerfully I lifted onto my toes and fell forward more on the tattoo chair. Cain slammed into me harder as he chased his own release before coming inside me.

When he pulled out and tucked himself back into his shorts, he turned off the vibrator and shoved it back into his pocket before helping me get situated.

"You ready to go home, baby?" Cain asked, lacing his fingers through mine.

I was still coming down from my post-orgasmic high, so I simply nodded.

He led us through the tattoo shop and pushed through the door, bringing us out onto the dark street. Pulling my helmet off his motorcycle, he placed it on my head and secured the strap beneath my chin before doing the same to his. We'd only brought the small helmets since we weren't traveling too far, which I was grateful for because as it was, my ponytail was already sticking to my newly inked back and it made me wince. I couldn't imagine a full helmet and having to wear my hair down right now.

We climbed onto the bike and, once again, I wrapped my arms around his middle as he pushed up the kickstand and started the engine.

A few minutes later, we were on the road, and I found myself suddenly intrigued by exactly *whose* home he was taking us to.

CHAPTER TWENTY-TWO

Rosie

There were days like today where the Sinners forgot they didn't own this bar and did whatever they pleased. Two o'clock on a Tuesday and no less than fifteen bikers crowded my *closed* bar, played pool, and enjoyed some drinks. I, on the other hand, frantically fluttered around, trying to get everything restocked, cleaned, and ready before the weekend.

"Hey, baby, can we get another round over here?" Nixon called out from where he sat at a high-top, his dirty boots kicked up onto the chair across from him.

"Get it yourself, asshole! The bar's *closed*, in case you missed, oh, I don't know, the lack of staff and patrons!"

He chuckled. Next to him, Preston hopped up and made his way behind the bar.

Before he touched anything, he looked over at me. "I used to bartend. Do you mind?"

"Be my guest." I gestured to the bar. "But if you break

anything, you're replacing it, *or* working it off when we're *actually* open."

He grinned, his tone cheerful as he said, "You've got it."

I watched as he moved around my bar with a natural ease, popping caps off bottles and pouring hard liquor into their respective glasses. I was impressed. For a kid who looked a little rough around the edges, he seemed to have a talent for bartending. It was easy to see by the way he handled himself.

"You looking for a job?" I asked, knowing I could always use an extra set of hands.

He shook his head. "Nah, but thanks. As much as I enjoy mixing a drink here and there, I'm not a customer service type person. You wouldn't want a bartender who'd beat the shit out of your customers."

"You could always dick them instead," I retorted with a laugh.

His eyes widened, his head whipping toward me. "Do what, now?"

"Oh, you heard me," I teased. "You can dick them. I keep holographic dick confetti in my office to blow in the faces of jackasses who deserve it. Embarrass the shit out of them. It's much more effective than a fist, and you won't end up with a felony assault charge, either."

"She's not lying," Cain inserted, walking up and leaning against the bar. "She really does have dick confetti and throws it on people. Though I disagree about it being more effective. I still prefer to work things out with my fists."

He grabbed my chin and tipped my head back, kissing me roughly. I grinned into the kiss, immediately feeling myself get turned on.

Every day with Cain made me regret every day without him.

Breaking the kiss, Cain stepped behind me and wrapped his arms around my middle, careful not to press into my back. My tattoo was tender, but because of the thin line work it was far less painful than most of my others had been.

Cain began to speak with Preston, getting to know him better. I relaxed into him while I listened, tilting my head back onto his shoulder.

They talked about club life, and why Preston wanted in. What growing up with Nixon was like, and Preston's goals for the future. He was young, only twenty-three, and so excited to be given a chance with the Sinners.

When the door slammed open unexpectedly, the entire bar fell silent, turning to look at who was coming in. I went to pull away from Cain and deal with it, but he pushed me behind him. His hand never left my arm and I read that for what it was; to not move.

In the doorway stood two men, dominating the door-frame. They both wore scowls, along with their leather vests and dirty jeans. Tattoos covered every inch of visible skin, even their faces.

I always tried not to judge a book by its cover, but these dudes looked intimidating as hell.

All around the bar, Sinners stood and moved closer to the door. A few moved a hand behind their back, and I knew they were readying to grab their guns if needed.

"Where's your prez?" the man on the left barked, taking another step into the bar.

Sensing a threat, a few Sinners mirrored that step as they drew closer to him.

Without hesitation, Cain released my arm and stepped forward. "Right here. What can I do for you?"

I went to take a step forward to be closer to Cain, but from my peripheral, Sly caught my eye. As if he knew what I was about to do, he flattened his hand by his side to tell me to stay still, and gave me a look of warning.

The guy looked Cain up and down, then his eyes drifted behind him to me. I lifted my chin.

"You fucked with the wrong crew," he stated as he looked around at the Sinners. The other guy made no move to enter the bar further, but stayed watching closely from the doorway.

"I don't know what you're talking about," Cain told him, revealing nothing.

The guy's eyes snapped back to Cain, and he smirked, flicking a toothpick out of his mouth onto the floor. "Figured you might say that. I'm here to deliver a message. Watch your fuckin' backs, *Sinners*. You see, us Reapers live by a code—an eye for an eye. You owe us a fuckin' eye."

Cain's hands balled into fists, his whole body tensing under the guy's words. As he stepped forward, about to explode, I threw myself at him and grabbed his bicep to stop him from making a mistake.

These guys weren't the type you fucked with, and any reaction Cain revealed right now would be detrimental.

"Get the fuck out of our bar," he hissed, taking another step forward despite the hold I still had on him.

The guy put his hands up mockingly and walked backward

toward the door. His buddy opened it and they both left without another word, letting the door slam shut behind them.

"Fuck," Cain roared, turning around almost violently to face his men. "Church, *now*!"

Pulling me into a tight hug, he kissed the top of my head. "I'm so sorry, Rose. *Fuck*, I'm sorry."

"This isn't your fault, Cain. Take a deep breath and go talk it out with the Sinners. You guys will come up with a plan on how to handle this."

"Go lock the doors, and under no circumstances unlock them again until your staff shows up for work in a few hours. Better yet, go into your office and don't come out until I'm back."

"You're overreacting." I ran my hands down his chest in a way that was meant to be comforting. "I get why, but it'll be fine. It'll all work out. Go. Talk to them. Come up with a plan."

I lifted on my tiptoes and pressed my lips to his, wasting no time pushing my tongue into his mouth to find his.

He grabbed onto my hair and deepened the kiss, pressing his lower body against mine so I could feel the way his cock was hardening.

Even under pressure, the man still found ways to make me feel like I was the most important thing in his life, even though right now, his crew needed to be.

Pulling away from him, I gave him one more quick peck before I fulfilled his request and went to lock up the bar. He watched as I did before retreating upstairs to go figure out what the hell he was going to do about the threat of 'an eye for an eye'.

CHAPTER TWENTY-THREE

Rosie

My eyes strained as I stared at the computer screen, attempting to figure out how to make QuickBooks do what I needed it to do. It was time I hired someone to balance my books, but I was having a hard time relinquishing that portion of control. I was meticulous and liked things a certain way, even if that meant I was killing myself slowly by having to teach myself new programs and do everything without help.

Giving up, I sat back in my chair and tried to clear my head. My stomach growled, the not-so-subtle reminder that I hadn't eaten since I forced down a banana at breakfast. Now, it was nearing seven at night, and my empty stomach was rolling.

Two days had passed since The Reaper's Wings stopped by the bar, and though tensions were still high, the Sinners hid it well. Especially Cain.

It worried me how when he returned from his emergency

Church meeting, he was eerily calm and had seemingly turned off any and all emotion toward what happened. I wanted to ask what was said in their meeting, but I wasn't sure it was my place.

Cain and I hadn't defined our relationship.

Not having a label didn't bother me, but it did put up a giant question mark on what information I was privy to when it came to the Sinners. So I waited, hoping he'd open up on his own, but considering it was now Friday and he still hadn't, I assumed whatever was said was on a need-to-know basis.

The middle of the week at Andromeda had been slow. During the day, Cain surprised me by insisting on doing the mundane day-to-day things with me as I prepared for the weekend, and for the club's family barbeque on Sunday.

The first night, Indy and the staff shooed me out early, which I resisted at first, but after gearing up for an argument on why I should stay, Cain came up from behind me and tossed me over his shoulder. He seemed to do that a lot.

I had to admit, though, being able to leave and have the confidence to know that everything was under control was a godsend. Since then, I'd let Indy handle evenings at the bar.

Two days full of multiple stops at grocery stores, countless hours on the phone with my liquor distributors to reorder for the next few weeks, and even lunch with Elle, and Cain never complained once. Not when she spent the majority of the time grilling him with every question she could think of. Nor when he'd endured enough of his awkward interview, I asked him to go to the store across the street and buy me tampons because I felt like I was getting my period.

Elle had laughed as he obliged and I revealed I wasn't

actually getting my period and just wanted to see how he'd react. He hadn't asked what brand I needed, or what size, so I wasn't holding much hope, but when he returned with the *exact* tampons I used, I shut up real quick.

So did Elle.

It seemed no detail was too small for Cain to pick up on, and I couldn't say I hated that about him. I spent many years on and off with his brother, and the man didn't even know my favorite color by the time we broke up.

Blue, by the way.

Cain not only knew my favorite color, but had even sought out blue dahlias for me. I wasn't normally a 'buy me flowers' kind of woman, but something about him showing up yesterday with them hidden behind his back as he leaned against the doorframe of my office had me dropping to my knees instantly.

"Let's go grab some dinner," Cain said from where he laid on my couch. "Maybe take a ride after?"

Standing from my chair, I walked over to where he was, and he shifted his body so he was sitting. His hands found my hips, and he pulled me down to straddle him. I lowered myself until I was sitting on his lap, and he buried his hand in my hair.

I smiled, then closed the distance to kiss him softly.

His lips were tender against mine, and when our tongues met, a heavy sigh exhaled through him as he relaxed under my touch. The moment the air left his body, my heart broke because I could feel it... The turmoil. The stress and the anxiety. The guilt, and even the fear.

Breaking the kiss, I wrapped my arms around his neck and

held him to me tightly. He buried his head into my chest, needing this as much as I did.

We'd been through so much in a short time.

After a moment, my stomach rumbled again, ruining the surprisingly gentle moment between us.

"C'mon, let's go get you something to eat," he said, letting me slide off his lap as he stood up. He walked over to my desk chair and pulled my denim jacket off the back of it, holding it open so I could slide my arms inside. "What are you in the mood for?"

"Pizza," I blurted, because honestly, I'd been craving it since yesterday.

Cain laughed and said, "You've got it, baby."

Grabbing my hand, he led me through the back entrance and out toward the staff parking lot where his motorcycle was.

Moments later, we were on the road. The air was chilly—the fog began to roll in and added a saturation to the hues of bright oranges and reds from the sun setting over the horizon. Traffic was light, allowing Cain to weave past cars expertly until we were on the open highway.

For some reason I couldn't explain, being on the back of Cain's bike had me feeling giddy. Maybe this was my version of a heavy sigh, but if just for the moment, I felt light and carefree.

Tightening my thighs against him, I outstretched my arms and tipped my helmet-clad head backward. The tint on the helmet's visor made the sky appear dimmer, but still, I could see the stars beginning to come out against the darkening sky.

As I brought my head back up, I saw Cain steal a glance

over his shoulder. His left hand immediately flew to my leg as he pressed it against his body more, likely wanting me to hold on tighter. I hugged myself to his body as much as possible, and when I did, Cain accelerated.

The motorcycle flew forward and on instinct, my arms tightened around him, holding on as he raced down the highway. Adrenaline pumped through my veins, spiking when another motorcycle whizzed by us at an even higher speed and swerved directly in front of us.

Cain leaned on the bike and maneuvered us out of the way, just barely. He shook his head and glanced behind us, his shoulders tense. The other motorcycle strayed behind.

Seconds later, another motorcycle, or maybe it was the same one, caught up with us, hugging our right side. They were so close if I reached out I'd be able to touch the driver's shoulder. It was then that I realized on the back of his leather vest was a large emblem of a scythe with angel wings.

The Reaper's Wings.

A second bike pulled to our left, and Cain cranked the gas, jolting his motorcycle forward to get us away from them.

As we raced down the highway, they followed, boxing us in on each side. If we slowed, they slowed. If we raced ahead, they caught up. I tried to get a good look at them, but like us, they wore full face helmets and masked their identities. I had a sickening gut feeling, though, that these two were the men who walked into Andromeda earlier in the week.

For the next forty minutes, we were forced to play a game of close-quarters cat and mouse; them chasing us while Cain tried to put distance between them.

It dragged on and on, but there was nowhere for us to go other than straight on the highway.

They were relentless, not caring how far outside of Ridgewood they were traveling, or that with every mile outside of the city, they were even *further* away from their shitty town of Bridge Point.

I began to feel nauseous from the constant state of adrenaline; the stress started to make me feel like my stomach was eating itself from the inside. I wanted this nightmare to be over, and though it surprised me a little, I actually wanted to cry. Hot tears threatened to spill over my lashes, but I was doing a good job at keeping them from doing so.

Countless times, they almost ran us off the road, swerving into us and forcing Cain to manipulate the bike perfectly to keep us upright. I had no idea how fast we were traveling or where we were even going, but I found myself praying to a higher power to fucking *end this* sooner than later.

My heart hammered as I held onto Cain with my head pressed against his back. I faced the right, and every time the piece of shit on that side would get close, I tried to memorize another tattoo on his body in an effort to be able to identify him in the future.

And then as quickly as it had started, the chase ended.

The bikers from The Reaper's Wings jetted off onto the exit we were passing.

Looking over my shoulder, I watched as their motorcycles flew across the overpass and turned, getting back onto the highway going southbound.

Even above the roar of Cain's motorcycle, the sound of theirs faded into the distance.

Cain waited three more exits before he finally got off and pulled over into a dirt patch. Putting down the kickstand, he hopped off his bike, ripping off his helmet and tossing it down before doing the same to mine. His large hands grabbed my face roughly, and he slammed his lips to mine.

"Are you okay?" he frantically asked as he pulled away, still holding my face. He kissed me again before I could answer.

"I'm okay." But I was in shock. I could feel it in the way my body trembled and my brain was at a loss for words.

Cain kissed me again, then pulled me close, hugging me so tightly I thought my boobs might explode from the pressure. I pushed him away to loosen his hold.

"I'm okay," I repeated, not sure why I felt like I needed to. "That was...scary, for lack of a better word. What the fuck?"

"They were sending a message," Cain told me, void of emotion. Taking a step back, he pulled his phone out of his front pocket.

"King," he barked when he pressed the phone to his ear. He glanced at me. "Those pieces of shit *Reaper Winged* scumbags sent two men to tail me and Rose. They followed us almost entirely to Northwood before circling back on the highway."

He listened to King on the other end of the line, his eyes narrowing.

"No, I'm not fucking kid—yeah. Yeah. I lost track of how many times they tried to run us off the road and tried to cause us to crash."

Cain's eyes were downcast to where he scraped his foot against the dirt.

"I'm not sure. I won't risk Rose's life to get home tonight.

I'm thinking we'll get a room somewhere." His eyes connected with mine, silently asking if that was okay.

I nodded in response, wishing I could hear King on the other end.

"No, King, they crossed a fucking line. I don't just want to get back at them and send them a message, I want to destroy them. Take them down completely."

A low growl emulated from his chest, and he stared blankly out into the darkness.

"Call another emergency Church meeting right now—tell the guys. This just got a whole helluva lot worse for us and we're not just going to just lie down and take it."

My heart jolted. "Indy!"

Fuck. My staff needed to be on high alert, too.

"Keep one or two Sinners downstairs at the bar during Church and catch them up after. I want extra eyes around the bar and on the staff. When appropriate, warn Indy of what's happening so she's in the loop. We'll be home tomorrow."

Cain reached out and softly ran his fingers down the side of my cheek before he tucked my hair behind my ear.

"You guys stay safe, too. Update me if anything goes down."

He ended the call and pushed his phone back into his pocket, then bent to pick up our helmets. Handing mine to me, I took it, but made no move to put it back on.

"C'mon beautiful, let's go get some food and find a place to relax for a while. We'll do some quick research on decent hotels in Northwood while we eat."

"What will King say to Indy?" I asked, needing more reassurance that my staff will be protected.

If The Reaper's Wings sent guys to follow Cain, who's to say they didn't have people at the bar right this second?

"He'll tell her everything. King's not one to withhold information once we've decided someone is entitled to it."

His choice of wording instantly sent a spark of irritation through my chest. "So you've decided I'm not entitled to information, then?"

"What?" Cain asked, confused.

"You never bothered to fill me in on what happened during the last Church meeting after those assholes came to the bar. Am I not entitled to information?"

"Baby, of course you are." He stood in front of me, holding his helmet against his side. "I didn't think you *wanted* to know since you never asked. The last thing I wanted to do was add more stress to your plate by bringing it up when you hadn't asked for it, and I figured since you hadn't, you just wanted to push it away. Out of sight, out of mind—that type of thing. I dunno. Fuck, I'm sorry. I didn't realize."

"Alright," I said simply, annoyed that his apology could so quickly thaw my anger. "Let's just go, I need to eat. As you can see, the hangry is happening." I tugged on my helmet and kicked my leg back over the side of the bike.

Climbing back on, he popped the kickstand up and as he pulled his helmet over his head he said, "I love you even when you're hangry."

I WASN'T EXPECTING a trip down memory lane tonight, but as I sat on a small boulder overlooking Northwood while forcing myself to eat my meal from In-N-Out, I couldn't help but feel a sense of déjà vu wash over me.

In a lot of ways, history really does repeat itself.

Except in some capacity, the past seemed a lot more simple than the present.

My mind wandered while I admired the twinkling lights from the cities in the distance as they danced across the dark night sky. This place never failed to take my breath away.

"You know," I said, popping a small French fry into my mouth. Even though my appetite was gone and I was forcing myself to eat, it was still an unspoken rule that you had to eat In-N-Out French fries before everything else, because cold fries sucked. "If you had just once asked me to leave him back then, I would have without hesitation."

It wasn't really fair of me to bring up the past when there were bigger issues at play, but being in this spot—the spot where I fell in love with him—was dredging up old feelings.

Cain looked down at his burger and pulled the wrapper lower. He took a bite and chewed it slowly before he responded.

"The biggest regret I have in life was not fighting for you back then. If I could go back in time, I would do everything different. I should have shown you how much you meant to me and proven myself to be a man worthy of your love. There's nothing that pisses me off more than thinking about how I was always just his brother to you."

I finished my burger and crumpled up the wrapper into a tight ball.

He was never just Brent's brother to me. He was *always* so much more.

But what was he now?

Yet again, we'd fallen into uncharted territory and even though things felt more stable between us, there was still so much unknown.

After dropping my trash into the bag that sat on the ground between us, I reached up and pulled my jacket tighter around me. "And now? What are you now?"

At the same time, our heads tilted toward each other, and our eyes met.

"I'll be whatever you want me to be, Rose. Whatever you'll *let* me be. Your friend, your boyfriend. Lover, husband, protector. I want to be *everything* to you, but I'll settle for being whatever you need me to be."

Tears pricked the back of my eyes. I looked away and back out at the city lights. "You really do love me, don't you?"

"Love doesn't even begin to cover the depths of my feelings for you. I'd lay down my life if it meant you got to live yours happily."

I choked back a sob, flying to my feet and crashing onto his lap. The rush of emotions that ricocheted into me had me feeling completely out of sorts, as though I was experiencing everything from the outside looking in.

After years of a revolving door of short-term boyfriends and one-night stands, I wasn't even sure how a love like this was meant for me. But I *felt* it—this love—within every fiber of my being. Wiping away a few tears that had fallen, I swallowed thickly. "God dammit, Cain. I'm not a crier. But I love you, you big sap. Who knew such a tough exterior would house such a beautiful soul?"

He swiped at another tear with his thumb, banishing it from rolling any further. "I love you, baby. I always have."

Though my heart soared, my stomach sat in a knot. "What are we going to do about The Reaper's Wings? I'm worried, Cain. They're not just going to disappear."

"I know, and I don't want you to worry about it. I will take care of everything, okay? I'll probably have to take a ride to Bridge Point and go work it out, prez to prez."

"I hate that plan—there has to be another way."

Cain took my hand and laced my fingers through his. "It might be the only way since they've now escalated from just threatening to actually showing us they mean good on their word."

"Do you think they'd go after my staff? The bar?" I asked, feeling my stomach roll. If The Reaper's Wings knew where to find the Sinners that easily, it meant Andromeda had a target on it, too. If there was true danger at my bar, I needed to be there. I walked back toward the bike. "Take me back to Ridgewood."

He followed, hot on my trail as we pushed our bodies through the overgrown brush and back to the dirt road. "No baby, let's just get a hotel for the night and head back early. It's already getting late and—"

"I don't care, Cain! If these shitbags end up in the bar between now and us getting back tomorrow and they do something to my staff, I'll never forgive myself. Please. Just get us home."

I thought he'd put up a fight—argue with me about why we needed to stay, but he didn't. Instead, he searched my eyes, and whatever he saw behind them convinced him to take me home.

"Okay."

"Thank you," I breathed through the knot in my chest.

He handed me my helmet, and I tugged it on, waiting for him to get on the bike. Once he did, I curled myself around his back and settled in, trying not to think about the distance we had between us and Ridgewood, or the fact that I just might freeze my ass off on the way there.

CHAPTER TWENTY-FOUR

Rosie

By the time we made it back to Ridgewood, Andromeda was long since closed. When we pulled in front of my condo, we were cold, wind-blown, and exhausted from the night. Cain sent a message to King to let him know we'd made it back without issues, then slowly undressed me and nudged me into the bathroom for a shower.

The warm water washed over me, offering a slight reprieve from the tension that'd settled into my bones. I stood there for a while before the shower door opened and Cain stepped in. Despite the exhaustion that plagued his features, he reached for my shampoo and squeezed a generous amount into his palm, before lathering it and bringing it to my scalp. Massaging it with his fingers, he washed my hair, working the soap down to the very ends, before using the excess to wash his own.

When our hair was clean, I returned the favor by cleaning

our bodies with my body soap, scrubbing away the night we'd had.

Once all the suds had washed away, Cain tangled his fingers through my hair and kissed me gently, letting his actions speak the words he was holding inside. Our bodies reacted, yet neither of us attempted to turn the kiss into more, content with just basking in the closeness of each other.

We held each other and kissed until the water turned cold, then dried off and met under the covers of my king-sized bed.

Even though cuddling wasn't my thing, I found myself craving the comfort of his touch and scooted closer to him, nestling into his side. Within minutes, sleep swept him away, and his soft, rhythmic breaths acted like a sound machine as I fell asleep too.

HEADLIGHTS ILLUMINATED through the window as a car passed by, temporarily lighting up my bedroom. Cain and I spent the day in bed, only getting up for necessities. We drowned ourselves in sex, hardly stopping long enough for Cain to take King's and Damon's calls, fully aware we were using each other to hide from reality, but for just one day, we allowed ourselves to. The Sinners were under Cain's strict instruction to go to their *actual* homes for the night unless stationed as extra eyes around the bar.

King looped in Indy last night, and after I spoke with her this morning to let her know I wouldn't be coming in, I'd called the head of my security team and asked him to stay extra vigilant.

There was no point in cowering from The Reaper's Wings. We wouldn't allow their threats to have a chokehold on us, but we'd absolutely make sure we protected everyone as best as possible.

"Maybe we should call off the barbeque tomorrow," I suggested as I trailed my fingertips along Cain's chest.

He adjusted the arm that wasn't wrapped around me to rest behind his head. "I mentioned that to King and Damon while you were in the kitchen earlier. Neither of them thinks it's necessary. If we cancel family dinner, in some capacity, we're letting them win. It sends the message we're afraid of them."

I understood and couldn't fully disagree with him. Still, an anxious feeling sat deep in my gut. I'd learned a long time ago to always trust my intuition, and I knew as confidently as I knew the sky was blue, that this war between the two clubs was just beginning.

Sensing my nerves, Cain pulled me closer to him and let his lips graze my temple. He held me close, and the steady beating of his heart soothed me. "It'll be okay, baby."

"Alright," I said, with only a hint of uncertainty.

Cain gripped my chin, tipping my head back. He offered me a small smile before pressing his lips against mine. Our kiss started slow, but as he deepened it, the fire within me roared to life again. Rolling on top of him, I straddled his body, and I kissed him roughly as I took what was mine.

INDY, Cain, Sly, Nixon, and I hit the ground running to set up family dinner, and within thirty minutes, the employee parking lot looked fit for a motorcycle club barbeque. Several six-foot folding tables were set up with simple plastic table-cloths, and enough chairs for at least fifty people, not that we were expecting that many. A few coolers were packed with beers, water, and even some juice pouches, in case anyone brought their kids.

Cain lit up the two charcoal barbeques King had brought from home, prepping them to throw the meat on. Steaks and brats were on the menu for tonight, and a bunch of random side dishes the guys had brought.

Once most of the Sinners had shown up, I noticed the majority of them had come by themselves instead of bringing their families. I couldn't say I blamed them with how high tensions were.

But as soon as the guys came together, they loosened up and started to enjoy themselves.

Sounds of beer caps popping off the bottles, chip bags opening, and husky laughter brought a smile to my face. They were happy—a little less serious and more carefree. It looked good on them.

Cain looked pretty good too, doing something as domestic as flipping steaks on a grill.

Walking over to him, I lifted on my toes, leaning to press a kiss to his cheek. At the last second, he turned his head and crashed his lips into mine, prying my mouth open with his tongue. Tingles immediately overtook my body, and my arms had a mind of their own as they wrapped around his neck and pulled him closer.

Catcalls and whoops erupted from the guys, and one even yelled, "Get a room!" Smiling against his lips, I smacked my hand against Cain's chest as I pulled back.

With a wide grin, he turned and refocused his attention on the grill.

"Maybe I should have picked up an apron for you. Who knew you'd be such a master at the grill?" I half-teased, half-complimented.

I watched as he hung the tongs off the grill's handle and switched to the other one, grabbing a plate from a nearby table to stack bratwursts on, handing it to me when he was done.

"Baby, go eat if you're hungry because once you put those down, they'll be gone," he encouraged before yelling, "these guys are monsters when it comes to food!"

A couple of the guys raised their beers in response, but Nixon patted his stomach and shouted, "Damn straight, Prez!" His cousin Preston nodded enthusiastically from where he sat on top of the table.

"If that table collapses under your weight, don't say I didn't warn you," I play-scolded as I sat the plate down on the table across from him with the rest of the food.

Everything looked delicious—I couldn't wait to dig in.

As I stood there looking at everything, Sly came up beside me and pressed a kiss to my temple.

"Ciao, mia preferita. You'd better eat before the guys swarm."

I wrapped my arms around his middle, giving him a tight hug.

Reaching for an empty plate, I handed it to Sly before

grabbing another for myself. "So I've heard. If I'm eating, you're eating too."

He grinned and used his plate to gesture at the food. "Ladies first."

Before reaching for the tongs to pick up a brat, I snuck another glance at Cain, who was chatting with King while he flipped the steaks again. For the first time in the last forty-eight hours, I felt like I could breathe a little. Things felt good...happy. Settled, if only for the moment.

If the Sinners were enjoying themselves, I would relax and enjoy myself too. I exhaled a deep breath and refocused on the food spread out in front of me.

Working my way down the table, I loaded my plate with a little of everything to try. "Everything looks so damn good. Can you grab me a water?"

Sly was opening the cooler, grabbing himself another beer. "Of course."

He tucked the bottle under his arm and I followed him to another table with a few open seats. As we walked, the familiar rumble from a couple of motorcycles neared, and we both stopped in our tracks.

The employee parking lot was down a side street, around the corner from the main road the bar was located on. It was a dead-end road and not many people came down it.

Thinking I was being paranoid, I took another step toward the table before I stopped, frozen in place. The growl of the engines amplified, and three bikers came into view.

And the moment they did, they each withdrew a gun. With fingers on the triggers, they pointed them.

Everything seemed to move in slow motion until it didn't.

Then everything happened so fast.

The *pop, pop, pop* of the gunshots rang out, deafeningly loud. All around, the Sinners stood and pulled out their guns, springing into action.

My adrenaline instantly spiked from the noises that erupted, my body reacting through panic. But before I could move...run...duck... A searing pain tore through me and I screamed, my lungs burning from the intensity of my roar. At the same time, a body slammed into me—Sly, I think—and sent me flying backward.

Another round of *pop, pop, pop* rang out.

A sickening crack mixed with the sounds of uproar, and the last thing I remember was someone in the distance yelling my name.

Then everything went black.

CHAPTER TWENTY-FIVE

Cain

By the time The Reaper's Wings had come into view, shots were fired.

Immediately, I drew my gun to fire back, but as I screamed Rose's name and watched her head slam against the pavement, I faltered.

My body flew forward, and I took off running toward her, not caring that there was a firefight happening right in front of me. The only thing I could focus on was getting to Rose.

Rose, whose body was covered by Sly's.

Rose, whose blood was pooling and seeping out from beneath her as she laid unconscious on the asphalt.

From all around, gunshots rang out, and the Sinners continued to unload their mags. The Reaper's Wings engines revved as they circled at the dead end and hightailed away from us. One of them bled from his arm as he sped off, and I silently fumed that somehow a shot to the arm was the only one we'd landed.

But the damage was already done.

As I made it to Sly and Rose, I dropped to my knees and rolled him off her slowly. He groaned as his back hit the floor, and my eyes connected with the blood pouring from a shot to his chest.

"Fuck! Sly, hang on, brother." Shrugging out of my leather jacket, I bunched it up and pressed it against his wound.

"WE NEED SOME HELP OVER HERE!" I bellowed as my eyes raked over Rose's body, trying to assess her wounds while still maintaining pressure on Sly's.

Damon appeared, and I traded my hold on the jacket over to him. "Call 911," I ordered. Then my hands were on my woman.

Carefully, I positioned my arms under her neck and legs, and lifted her as slowly as possible while coming to a stand.

Indy appeared next to me, frantically yelling, "Oh my God, Rosie? ROSIE! Is she okay?"

"I need to get her to the hospital now. Give me your keys."

She patted her pockets wildly, tears streaming down her face. "I don't have them!"

"WHO HAS THEIR KEYS?" I roared, already moving toward the side of the lot where the vehicles were parked. Most of the Sinners had ridden their motorcycles, but thankfully a few had their trucks.

King appeared by my side, handing his keys to a distraught Indy who was trying to keep up with me. "Take my truck. I'll stay here, figure out who's hurt, and wait for the ambulances. I'll keep you updated."

All I could do was nod and glance one more time to where my men were, seeing who was injured.

Indy unlocked the truck and opened the cab door for me. Stepping on the running board and hoisting Rose onto the back seat, I climbed in with her and slammed the door.

"Indy, breathe," I demanded, exhaling a shaky breath as I watched her adjust the driver's seat so she could reach the pedals. The truck's engine roared to life at the touch of a button, and she immediately threw it into reverse and got us onto the road.

Rose laid unconscious the entire drive to the hospital, and the whole time I felt like I couldn't breathe.

When Indy pulled in front of the ER, she barely came to a full stop before I was out of the truck with Rose in my arms.

Storming through the automatic doors, I ran in, commanding the attention of any nurse or doctor who would listen. "I have a thirty-two-year-old woman who is unconscious and bleeding from the back of the head and the arm. Possible gunshot wound. She needs immediate help."

Time stood still as questioning eyes from around the room bore into me.

An overwhelming sense of hopelessness sat in my chest. "Please," I rasped.

Doctors and nurses rushed to us with a wheeled bed, taking over and pulling Rose carefully from my arms. They placed her on it, popping the rails into place before immediately taking her away from me.

"Wait!" I called, springing forward to go with them, but a nurse pressed her hand against my chest, holding me back.

"Sir, let the doctors do their job. Come with me, let me get some information from you about the patient. Are you okay? Do you need to be seen?"

I shook my head. "I'm fine."

The nurse led me to a set of chairs and sat, urging me to do the same. She gestured to another nurse, who was standing off to the side, and took the clipboard from her. "Let's start with her name and the basics."

"Her name is Rosie Adler," I told the nurse, staring at the doors the doctors just took her through.

"Date of birth?"

"April 1, 1990."

"Your relation to the patient?"

My heart sank. Rubbing my palms across my face, frustration pierced my chest, and part of me hated myself for the lie I was about to tell the woman who was helping me, but I knew it'd be the best way to get information later. "Her husband."

"And your name?" she asked without batting an eye.

"Cain Michaels."

"And your contact number, Mr. Michaels?"

"(555) 555-6150."

"Thank you. That's all I need from you right now. I'm going to have you wait here for a while until we find out what's going on with your wife. If you need anything, let us know."

As the nurse stood to leave, the automatic doors of the ER opened again and a team of paramedics rushed in with a man on a gurney. He had an oxygen mask covering his face, but I knew immediately by his clothing, and the mess of dark hair, that it was Sly.

Flying out of my chair, I ran over to him, but the same

nurse I'd just been talking to stepped in front of me to block me.

"Let the doctors do their job," she chastised, holding her hand out in a *stop* motion.

The doors opened again as King, Nixon, and Damon rushed in, along with a crying Indy trailing behind them.

"Where is he?" Nixon asked frantically. "WHERE IS HE?"

He rushed to me, his eyes bloodshot and lined with tears. "Did you see him yet?"

"Sly?" I asked, but at that very moment, the doors opened again and two paramedics walked in wheeling a gurney. They took an immediate right and pushed through a set of doors and away from the small area where we waited.

"Let me go find out what's going on," the nurse said with a concerned look, before hurrying away, following where the paramedics had just gone.

"Preston," Nixon choked. "He stopped breathing twice before the medics got him in the ambulance, but they were able to bring him back. He's just a kid, man."

I grabbed his shoulder. "He'll be okay. Do you know where he was shot?"

"I don't know, Cain. There was so much blood. It was everywhere."

And as I really stopped to look at him, I realized he was covered in it.

"My aunt needs to know. I need to call her."

"Hey." I tightened my grip on him and pulled him in for a hug. "We'll call her in a few, okay? Sit down for a minute."

Nixon had a blank look on his face as he took a seat in a nearby chair, and immediately buried his head in his hands.

Turning to King and Damon, I asked. "What about Sly?"

"Bullet to the chest," Damon responded. "We kept your jacket on the wound and he was conscious when the medics took him, but barely. His injuries didn't seem as serious as Preston's."

"How's Rosie?" Indy interjected, directing my attention to her.

I sank back into the chair I was standing in front of. "I don't know. They took her a few minutes ago, and it's too soon for an update. She was still unconscious when they took her."

"Was she hit?" Damon questioned.

Shaking my head, I shrugged. "I don't know. I don't think so. It looked like her arm was grazed pretty good, but I couldn't find any entry points on her. There was just so much blood…"

Indy choked on a sob and walked across the waiting area, sinking into an empty chair.

"But Sly was on top of her. The blood was probably his," King stated confidently, though I knew him well enough to know by the look on his face he was anything but.

"Yeah," I agreed.

The three of us fell silent, and the two men sat down to wait with me and Nix.

I turned back to King, a thousand questions running through my mind, but one in particular kept haunting me. "How did this escalate so quickly? We haven't even had time to—"

"I know," he cut me off. "The Reaper's Wings are ruthless, you know this. Two attacks in forty-eight hours...we couldn't have predicted this, Cain. We weren't prepared. The Sinners... we may look similar to them on the outside, but we're the good guys. The guys Pops taught us to be. And we've been cleaning up the Ridgewood scum for so long, it was only a matter of time before it caught up with us. It fucking sucks, but try not to beat yourself up. This isn't just on your shoulders."

Swallowing thickly, I leaned forward with my elbows resting on my knees and dropped my head into my hands. He was right, but that didn't mean it wasn't just on my shoulders. I was the president of the Sinners Warlord and responsible for my men.

And I'd failed them.

We waited an hour before a doctor finally came over to us. He was around my age and wore dark blue scrubs. He looked like he was dreading this conversation. "Is anyone here related to Preston Patberg?"

Nixon shot to his feet. "I'm his cousin."

The doctor walked over to him, shooting the rest of us a glance.

"It's okay," Nixon told him. "They may not be blood, but they're family. How is Preston?"

"My name is Doctor Richards. I'm sorry to have to tell you this, sir, but Mr. Patberg suffered extensive trauma from his gunshot wound. The paramedics did everything they could to keep him stable, but unfortunately his heartbeat was too weak to sustain his injuries, and he never made it to the operating table."

"He...he's dead?" Nixon asked, his face white as a ghost.

"I'm so sorry," the doctor repeated.

"But how...he...he's only twenty-three..." Nixon stumbled over his words, his breaths coming through each word. His chest heaved, and I could see that he was about to crumble.

He brought his hand to his mouth, his eyes glistening as a thick tear rolled down his cheek.

"Thank you, doctor," I said, dismissing him and turning to Nixon. He was unnaturally still as he stared at the dirty linoleum.

I grabbed his shoulder, but he immediately shrugged my hand off and completely exploded.

"FUCK!" he yelled, picking up the folding chair he'd sat on earlier and slamming it to the ground. As he reached for another, King stepped in and grabbed his face between his hands.

"Nixon," he growled. "Calm yourself, *now*."

Nix tried to pull out of his hold and shoved him back. Instead of fighting him, King released him, and he turned and stomped out of the ER.

"I'll call you with an update," King grumbled, and followed where Nix had just gone.

"What the fuck?" I muttered in disbelief under my breath, dropping back into my chair.

Preston was just a kid, so young with his whole life ahead of him. Twenty-three was too young to die. He had so much going for him, and he'd barely just become a prospect with the Sinners. A choice he never should have made, but did because he wanted to spend more time with his cousin. That's what he'd told me—that one of his biggest reasons for wanting to be a Sinner was because of Nix. He looked up to him.

Nixon would blame himself for this.

But there was no one to blame but the scumbags who'd shot him.

Rubbing my eyes, I glanced at my watch, growing more worried by the second. Why hadn't they given me an update on Rose yet? Or Sly?

I tried to catch the attention of a passing nurse, but her head was buried in a clipboard as she scurried through the double doors and into the section of the hospital I wasn't allowed in.

Two more hours went by before a nurse emerged through them, and our eyes locked. I stood as she approached.

"Mr. Michaels?"

"Yes," I blurted before she'd finished saying my last name.

"Ms. Adler is awake now and is asking for you. Follow me, please."

All the air rushed out of my lungs with relief, and I turned to Damon. He pulled me in for a quick hug, clapping my back affectionately.

Over Damon's shoulder, I could see Indy laying across two chairs, asleep after crying for too long. Momentarily, I wondered if I should wake her.

"I'll wait here in case there's an update on Sly," Damon said, pulling out of our embrace.

I nodded and realized there was something wet on my face. I wiped away the tear and choked, "Thank you."

Following the nurse, she led me through the white, sterile

hallway. The fluorescent lights were blinding, and with every step, my heart thundered.

We took an elevator up two floors, zigzagging down another two hallways before we finally stopped outside her room.

The nurse blocked the door and turned to me. "The doctor will be in shortly to go over the details of her condition with you. If you need anything, you can page the nurses' station from the phone in the room."

"Thank you," I told her, and she spun on her heel and walked back down the hallway we just came from.

Placing my hand on the doorknob, I swallowed the lump in my throat and blew out an unsteady breath before I pushed the door, not entirely sure what condition I'd find the love of my life in on the other side.

CHAPTER TWENTY-SIX

Rosie

When I woke up, I was lying in a hospital bed hooked up to a bunch of machines. They were beeping steadily, and I took that as a good sign, but the debilitating throbbing in the front of my head reminded me I was here for a reason.

My mouth was dry, and I couldn't swallow—it felt like sandpaper in my throat. I wanted to sit up, and wasn't sure if I should, but I tried anyway. I was tired and weak, but after several minutes, I found the button to adjust myself. Once the bed was upright, I scooted myself up a little more.

Touching the thin layer of gauze wrapped around my head, my fingertips followed it to where it held thick cotton in place at the base of my skull. Looking down, I saw another bandage wrapped around the bicep of my left arm.

Recollections of what happened started flooding my memory—the barbeque, gunshots, the chaos. Being slammed backward, Cain screaming my name.

Cain.

Where was Cain?

Patting the edge of the bed, I looked for the remote I knew held the button to page the nurses. I needed to see him. I needed to know if Cain was okay and to find out what happened.

What about the rest of the guys? Sly? Indy?

I tried not to panic completely, but my thoughts were spiraling.

I continued to press the call button for a nurse until one finally came in. She was an older woman wearing light blue scrubs and had her graying hair pulled up in a neat bun.

"Hi, Ms. Adler, it's great to see you awake. How are you feeling?"

Her voice was soft and maternal—soothing, but did little to put me at ease. She walked over to my machines and added some notes to the clipboard that hung by my bed.

"A little out of sorts and trying to piece together what happened. Is my...is Cain Michaels here?"

"He is, honey. Out in the waiting area of the ER still. Would you like me to bring him back?" She jotted down a few more things on the board.

Relief flooded through me. *He was okay.*

"Yes, please," I told her, nodding my head. Huge mistake. The amount of pressure I felt had me seeing stars from the pain of that small movement.

"Okay, honey. I'll let the doctor know you're awake and go get Mr. Michaels. The doctor should be in shortly."

She placed the remote for the T.V. in my palm before leaving. I sat it down next to my leg, having no interest in the added noise. Shutting my eyes, I regretted not asking her to dim the lights or turn them out completely before she left the room.

Opening my eyes when the door opened, my heart skipped when Cain appeared on the other side. He looked like hell. Dark circles lined his eyes. His hair was a wreck, the elastic that held it in place loose and falling. There was blood on his shirt and jeans, and my heart ached wondering if it was his blood, mine, or someone else's.

For a moment he stood in the doorway, looking at me with emotion heavy in his eyes.

"Hi," I finally said, and that one little word was all it took for him to rush toward me.

When he reached the side of my bed, though, he stopped. I could see the turmoil written all over him, not sure if he should come closer.

But I couldn't stand the distance.

"You won't break me," I encouraged. "Please kiss me, Cain."

I needed him like I needed the air I breathe. Needed him to touch my skin, to kiss me. I needed the reassurance that he was really here, and so was I.

"Fuck, baby, I'm so sorry," he breathed, and then his lips were on mine.

He bent over the bed, pressing his fists on either side of my hips as he leaned in to reach my mouth. His kiss was gentle, too gentle, but I didn't have the energy to deepen it myself.

My head was still leaning back against the bed throbbing,

so even though I craved his closeness, I knew I had to settle for what he was giving me at the moment.

Our foreheads rested against each other and I kept my eyes shut, simply taking a moment to process.

When he pulled away, he went to grab the chair in the corner of the room and moved it to my bedside. He sat, then took my hand, lacing his fingers through mine in that familiar way I loved.

I silently vowed to never take that simple gesture for granted.

"Cain, what happened?" I asked, needing to know. "Who else is here?"

He took a deep breath and studied my face. I hadn't noticed how red his eyes were until now, like he'd been crying. "Nix's cousin Preston, our new prospect, he…he died, Rose."

A lump formed in my throat. Bringing my hand up to my mouth, I choked back a sob. This was so fucked up.

"How's Nixon?"

"Not taking it very well."

I began to tremble. Someone had died. Preston had *died*. Staring at the thin hospital blanket that covered my lower body, I picked at the pilled fibers, processing the information.

"Rose, there's something else you need to know…"

Whipping my head back toward him, I immediately felt nauseous. I couldn't even form a sentence. Cain looked regretful—like whatever he was about to say, he didn't want to.

"Sly took a bullet to the chest. He was brought in, but we haven't gotten an update yet…"

The tears spilled over.

Sly...

"I don't know for sure, Rose, but I think he's the reason why you're not worse off. By the time I made it to you, you were already on the ground, baby, and Sly was on top of you. From how it looked, he shielded your body with his, or at the very least, knocked you out of the way."

I looked away; the tears flowing freely as I replayed Cain's words. I remembered the feeling of someone slamming into me, knocking me down. My hands fluttered up to the bandage on my head again, touching the spot at the base of my skull. I had to have slammed my head when I fell...when Sly shielded me from a bullet.

Had Sly saved my life?

Looking down at my arm again, I remembered the searing pain I'd felt right before I went down.

I had so many questions, and the only person I knew could help me get the answers was currently a giant question mark.

Picking up the bed's remote again, I clicked the nurse's call button over and over.

"Baby, talk to me," Cain urged. His hand squeezed mine, and he reached over to grab the remote out of my hands.

I jerked it away from him. "No, Cain. I need to know he's okay. This is my fault. If he hadn't been trying to protect me, we wouldn't be wondering if he's even *alive* right now."

Cain stood and snatched the remote, throwing it. It dangled off the edge of the bed from its cord. "This is *not* your fault, Rose. It's mine. I'm responsible for The Reaper's Wings retaliating against us. *I* killed their guy. Preston's death is on *my* hands. Your injuries are on *my* hands. Sly's..." But he didn't finish the sentence.

The door of my hospital room opened and a tall man wearing a doctor's coat walked in. He was quite handsome and looked like he'd stepped right off the set of *Grey's Anatomy*.

"Hello, Ms. Adler, I'm Doctor Robinson. How are yo—"

I cut him off, not caring about pleasantries or how *I* was doing. I was alive, and that was more than I knew about Sly at this point. "I need an update on another patient here. Sylvester Lucchetti."

The doctor looked a little taken aback at my outburst, but then, to my surprise, agreed. "I'd be happy to see what I can find out about Mr. Lucchetti, but first we need to discuss your charts, Ms. Adler. May I proceed?"

Cain gave my hand a small squeeze. It did little to comfort my anxiety, but I nodded at the doctor.

"Ms. Adler, we've treated you for two injuries. The first, a gunshot wound to the surface of your arm, was assessed and thoroughly cleaned before we dressed the wound. Changing the dressing and keeping it clean will be the biggest component of the healing process. You should seek care immediately if any symptoms of infection arise. Your second injury was worse as you suffered blunt force trauma to the back of your head, which is why you were unconscious when you arrived. We were concerned about the length of time you were unconscious for, but we've concluded that, along with a concussion, your body went into a state of shock. We monitored you closely and ran some tests, but everything came back as normal. You had a nasty cut to the back of your head, but overall, you're very lucky, Ms. Adler. We expect you to make a full recovery."

"Thank you so much, doctor," Cain told him. "When can we expect her to be discharged?"

"I'd like to keep her hooked up to the monitors for a while longer, but if there are no changes, we'll be able to discharge her within a few hours, pending she has someone who can monitor her condition closely at home."

"I won't leave her side."

"Excellent. Do you have any questions, Ms. Adler?" he asked, bringing the conversation back to me.

"I want to know how Sly is," I rasped. Clearing my throat, I turned to Cain. "Can you get me some water?"

Cain nodded and left the room to find me some. When he was gone, I met the doctor's eyes.

"Sylvester doesn't have any family nearby and I'm the closest thing. Please, I just need him to know he's *not* alone."

He nodded, seeming to understand my urgency. "I'll see if I can find you an update on Mr. Lucchetti. The nurses will be in for their rounds shortly."

"Thank you," I murmured. I felt completely defeated as the doctor walked out of the room and I was left alone.

When Cain returned, ice cold water bottle in hand, he handed it to me with the top already off. Greedily, I chugged it down until it was empty. The cold hurt my already throbbing head, but the way the water took the edge off my thirst was worth it.

"Is Indy okay?" I asked. Last I'd seen her, she was heading inside the bar, but the fear of something happening to her ran through me.

"She's in the waiting room. She's okay, baby."

"Thank God," I breathed, my shoulders relaxing.

"She drove us here. She's been here the entire time."

"Wait, I didn't come in an ambulance?"

Cain shook his head. "No, I wasn't going to wait for one to show up. Indy and I got you here as fast as we could."

Conflicting emotions tugged at my heart. I was so grateful, but also feeling incredibly guilty.

Lifting my hand, I reached for Cain. He sat down in his chair and curled both of hands around mine.

"I'm so glad you're okay, Rose. I've never felt so scared or helpless. If something had happened to you...I never want to live in a world that you're not in." He pressed his lips to the top of my fingers. "I love you so much, baby."

"I love you too."

And I did, with every beat of my heart.

Resting my head back against the bed, I decided I needed to drown my thoughts with something else, and picked up the T.V. remote.

"You should go check on Nixon," I suggested. "Let whoever's in the waiting room know I'm okay. See what you can find out about Sly?"

"I'm not leaving you."

"*Please*, Cain. I need to know my people are alright."

He nodded and stood, leaning over to kiss me on the forehead. "Okay baby, I'll be twenty minutes, max."

I offered him a weak smile, mentally and physically drained. "Take your time."

Once he left, I placed the remote back down and closed my eyes, my mind reeling from everything.

My body ached, my heart ached, and all I wanted was an update on Sly.

No, all I wanted was to go back in time and erase the past —make it so this nightmare never happened in the first place.

But none of this was within my control and the only thing I could do was lie in this hospital bed and pray no one else I cared about got hurt.

CHAPTER TWENTY-SEVEN

Rosie

Hushed voices stirred me from an unrestful nap, and as my eyes focused, I saw Cain speaking with my nurse, his head bobbing animatedly as she quietly read from her clipboard.

Pushing up on my hands, I groaned as I adjusted my body upright. My head was still pounding, but the throbbing had lessened from the intensity it was earlier.

"Oh! You're awake. Wonderful," the nurse exclaimed, walking over to me. "I have news for you, Ms. Adler. We're working on your discharge paperwork now and you'll be able to go home within the hour."

"That's great." My eyes met Cain's from across the room, and he moved toward me.

The nurse went over what she'd been speaking to Cain about, which were the signs and symptoms to watch for with my concussion and potential infection. "If you start feeling any of those, call your regular care physician immediately for further advice and instruction. If need be, you can always come back into the ER for treatment, too."

She turned to Cain, her voice stern. "Mr. Michaels, if she suffers any symptoms from her concussion that we spoke about earlier, seek medical treatment immediately."

"We will," he agreed.

"Alright then, kiddos. Someone will be in shortly with your paperwork and you'll be free to go."

"What about my friend?" I asked as the nurse turned to leave. "Sylvester Lucchetti. We're still waiting for an update."

"Ah, yes. Mr. Lucchetti. Unfortunately, I have no update as of now. He's still in surgery."

"Surgery?" I asked, my stomach sinking.

"Yes, Ms. Adler. Unfortunately, Mr. Lucchetti's injuries were quite extensive, but that's all the information I'm allowed to give as you are not family—"

"I'm the closest thing to family he has out here," I argued.

"I understand." She nodded sympathetically. "But we have been in touch with his immediate family and they haven't given us authorization to disclose his health with anyone who is *physically* here. You understand."

"You have?"

"Yes, Ms. Adler. Mr. Lucchetti kept a contact card in his wallet for emergencies. We reached out to his family immediately to inform them."

Anger prickled into my bloodstream. "So how will I know when he's out of surgery? That he's okay?"

"The best thing to do, Ms. Adler, is to try to get as much rest as you can and to take care of yourself. I'm sorry I can't be of more help." She offered a weak smile before she left the room.

Unshed tears filled my eyes. Cain sat on the edge of my bed and leaned in to kiss my forehead.

"Let's just get you home and relaxed, and see what happens. I'll make some calls, try to reach out to Sly's family. We'll get answers, baby. Try not to worry."

"I don't want to go home. Sly doesn't deserve to wake up in a hospital bed alone, Cain. We're all he has out here."

"I know, but they're not giving us any information right now. We'll get you home and cleaned up first, and I will figure this out, okay? I promise I'll find out what's going on."

Nodding, I took the hair tie off Cain's wrist and put my hair into a messy bun on top of my head. My long, brown locks were tangled in a mess of knots, but without my brush, the best I could do was toss it up and forget about it.

Forty-five minutes later, a male nurse I'd never seen before came in with a stack of paperwork and asked if we had any questions before we left.

Once again, my only question was about Sly's condition, but the nurse hadn't even heard Sly's name before, having just started his shift.

I let Cain push me out of the hospital in a wheelchair and when we went past the automatic doors, the familiar faces of Indy, King, and Damon greeted me.

"Oh, Rosie!" Indy cried, hugging me at an awkward angle because of the wheelchair.

When she'd pried herself away, Cain helped me stand, and I pulled her back in for a proper hug while still holding Cain's arm for leverage.

King and Damon approached next, hugging me carefully and telling me how happy they were that I was okay.

"How's Nixon?" I asked as I looped my arm through Cain's, letting him lead me to King's truck.

"He's holding up," Damon responded, but offered no information other than that.

Cain helped hoist me into the back of the truck and slid in beside me while King hopped into the driver's seat. I reached over Cain and rolled down the window.

"I'll call you later," I told Indy, who was standing on the curb with Damon.

"Go get some rest. Everything is under control at Andromeda, so *please* don't even think about work or trying to come back anytime soon."

"She won't be," Cain interjected. Rolling up the window, he tipped his chin to them and said, "See you guys later."

The drive to my house was quiet, but I was grateful for it. My migraine was starting to subside, but my body felt like a Mack truck hit it. I needed a long nap in my bed.

King dropped us off without coming in, and silently, Cain ushered me to the bathroom. He stripped me out of my clothes, being mindful to not snag the bandages on my arm and head. We were told they could come off for showers, but to make sure we thoroughly dried the wounds before dressing them again.

Once I was naked, Cain turned the shower on to warm and removed his clothing.

The spray of the water felt like both heaven and hell as I stepped under it. Tears flowed down my cheeks, mixing with the water, as the weight and pain of the last twenty-four hours flooded through me.

Cain let me cry, knowing my body needed this release, and gently washed me from head to toe. He scrubbed away the dried blood and dirt, and carefully ran my hairbrush through my hair as it sat with conditioner in it.

He took care of me in a way I hadn't expected, once again proving to me just how deep his love ran.

He'd even sat me down on the closed toilet, and blow dried my hair.

"You've surprised me," I whispered later as we laid in bed facing each other. It was early morning and my eyes were heavy with discomfort. I snuggled into my pillow, ready for sleep to take me.

"How?" he asked, his voice gruff and thick with exhaustion.

"You really *do* love me," I said, yawning a little. I closed my eyes.

"You doubted that?"

"Not doubt, but...I guess I just didn't expect for you to love me this much. You've surprised me, that's all."

He sighed deeply and scooted his body closer so we were pressed together. "You've spent your life with guys who didn't deserve you, Rose. They took you for granted and showed you a watered-down version of love, if it was even that. You protected your heart by being with shitty men after what I did to you. But, Rose, the scars on your heart are mine and I plan to make sure each one is fully healed and that you only experience *real* love for the rest of your life. *My* love. And my love for you is nothing short of unconditional."

Kissing me softly, he ran his fingers down the side of my cheek rhythmically until I fell asleep.

CHAPTER TWENTY-EIGHT

Rosie

The call I'd been waiting for came a little after three in the afternoon. I'd made sure my phone was on the loudest ring setting when I placed it on the charger by my bed, and curled up with Cain. When the ear-splitting ring sounded, I reached over immediately and answered it.

"Hello?" I said, sitting up quickly. My hand flew to the top of my head, the sudden movement causing a ricocheting pain through my skull.

"Hello, is this Ms. Adler I'm speaking with?"

"This is she."

Cain sat up next to me, the call waking him, too. His hand reached to where mine sat on top of my head. Pushing it aside, he started to lightly massage my scalp.

"My name is Marie Bonvie, I'm Sylvester Lucchetti's nurse."

My heart skipped, and I looked at Cain with the first

genuine smile I'd had in days. "Yes, hi! How is Sly? Is he awake? Can we see him?"

She laughed politely. "Yes, Mr. Lucchetti is awake and has asked for you and also a Mr. Michaels. He said you'd be together? You're welcome to come pay him a visit whenever you're available."

"We'll be there as soon as possible. Please tell him we're on our way."

"Will do, sweetheart."

"Thank you! Thank you so much."

I hung up and tossed my phone on the bed, ripping off my covers. "Sly's awake and wants us to come to the hospital. Get dressed."

Standing too fast, I swayed slightly, my head feeling floaty. Cain was out of bed and by my side within a millisecond, grabbing onto me.

"Slow down, Rose. We'll get there, but not at the expense of you hurting yourself."

Ignoring him, I walked over to my dresser and pulled out a pair of leggings and a t-shirt, and got myself dressed.

"Do you have any of my shirts lying around?" Cain asked, tugging yesterday's jeans back on.

My stomach rolled at the dried blood stained on the legs. It wasn't a lot, but it resurfaced things I was trying to push out of my mind, if only for a little while. My gaze transfixed on the little dark red splotches, and I felt my heartbeat spike. My hearing muffled—the noise around me sounded like I was underwater. What I knew was Cain's voice was distorted and distant as memories flew rapid-fire through my brain.

"Baby," Cain's voice cut through the fog as he wrapped his arms around me. "Baby, breathe."

I blew out a breath.

"I'm sorry," I said, snapping out of my daze. "I'm sorry. I just..."

"It's okay, don't apologize. The shit you've been through in the last two days..." He shook his head and looked down. "On our way to the hospital, I'd like to stop by my room and change into clean pants."

"Okay," I whispered, still feeling out of it.

Forcing myself to put one foot in front of the other, I walked into the bathroom and pulled out my makeup bag, applying a few dabs of concealer under my eyes to hide the dark circles, and a quick swipe of mascara to my upper and lower lashes.

It brought me a small semblance of normal.

When I finished, I stared at my reflection, zoning out at the image of the woman looking back at me. In some ways, it felt like I was on the outside of my life looking in.

Things felt so different.

In such a short time, *everything* had changed.

WHEN CAIN and I approached the nurse's station, the nurse who'd been by my side while I was here was sitting at the desk, chatting with two other women. She stopped talking when she saw me, grinning widely.

"Oh, Ms. Adler, you're looking much more well-rested!"

"Thank you." I smiled, appreciating the way she seemed

genuinely happy I'd gotten some sleep. "I'm feeling a little more well-rested. We're here to see Sylvester Lucchetti. His nurse called earlier and said he was awake and asking for us."

"That was me," another nurse interjected. She stood and came around the station. "I'm Nurse Bonvie. Come with me."

We walked together, with Cain trailing behind us. The walk was short—his room was only a couple of doors down from the nurses' station.

She stopped in front of his door, blocking it so she could speak to us before we went in. "Visiting hours end in two hours, but it's possible Mr. Lucchetti will need to rest before that. I also would like to let you know he has given us verbal authorization to inform you both of his medical updates. Now, he's suffered extensive trauma and underwent a lengthy surgery."

"What was the extent of his injuries?" Cain asked prematurely, his arms crossing over his chest as he readied himself to hear what Sly had gone through.

"Mr. Lucchetti came to us with a gunshot wound to the chest. The fragments punctured his lung, which resulted in a tension pneumothorax—or collapsed lung. He's expected to make a full recovery, but it will take time."

"How long can we anticipate him being here?" I questioned. My body was shaking, a small rush of anxiety hitting me.

Sly could have died. Instead of the fragments puncturing his lung, they could have hit his heart.

And then he'd be gone...

Preston was gone...

My vision swam.

Sensing, or maybe seeing, my panic, Cain stepped closer and wrapped his arm around me, keeping me stable.

"I'd say no less than a week, but that'll depend on his recovery and what his doctors decide."

"Thank you. Could we see him now?" Cain asked, stealing the thoughts out of my head.

Inwardly, it felt like my heart would explode at how quickly it was beating. Excitement mixed with fear, the anticipation of seeing Sly, but knowing his condition, had anxiety coiling tightly in my chest.

The nurse opened the door and before we could step into the room, she'd already moved across it to check his machines.

When my eyes met with the beautiful hazel of Sly's, I immediately ran to him, only slowing when I reached his bedside, realizing I couldn't slam into him for a hug like I wanted to.

Up close, my heart shattered as I took in his appearance. The side of his face had several cuts, and bruising that was already shifting colors. A nasal cannula sat in his nose, helping him breathe. He looked exhausted, but despite his battered exterior, he grinned back at me with a smile that covered his entire face.

"Mia preferita," he purred, lifting his hand slightly for me to take. I did without hesitation. "I'm so relieved to see you in front of me. I was worried when I woke—it took two nurses before I learned you'd been discharged. Are you feeling okay?"

"I'm okay," I reassured him. "Minor injuries compared to yours. Are *you* okay, Sly? How are you feeling?"

"I feel stiff, but other than that, I am still here and cannot complain, bella. Just so happy to see you and Cain." Cain closed the distance between them and I shuffled Sly's hand over to his.

"Good to see you, brother," Cain affirmed. He set Sly's hand back down on the bed and came over to me to rub my shoulders. "You saved my girl, Sly. I'll never be able to repay you for that."

Looking up, my gaze met Cain's, and I could see unshed tears in his eyes, emotions hitting him again.

"I would give my life for either one of you, if it meant you two continued to have each other. But I didn't save her, mio amico. If anything, I caused her injury. Rosie, I watched your head slam into the pavement with unwavering force. I am so sorry, bella. I never wanted you to get hurt."

I opened my mouth to argue, but Cain beat me to it.

"Had you not pushed her, the bullet you took could have hit her. You *saved* her. There is no point in you trying to change the narrative, because whichever way you try to spin it, it will always end the same: you saved Rose's life. Don't bother arguing."

He didn't. Instead, Sly gave a nod and looked back at me. "I'm just grateful we are both still here."

"It's more than some can say," I muttered, the heaviness settling in my chest again.

Sly's eyes darkened, and he turned to Cain with a look of anguish. "Who?"

"Preston," Cain said soberly.

"And the rest of the Sinners?"

I stared down at my lap and closed my eyes as I listened to

them discuss the shootout and all the details Sly had missed while in surgery. Their voices became distant and muffled as I sank into my own thoughts.

"What is the plan, mio amico? Will we retaliate?"

Sly's question snapped me back to reality, words flying from my mouth. "NO, you guys will not."

Livid at the thought, I stood from my chair and faced Cain. "That's reckless and dangerous. They already pulled their 'eye for an eye' bullshit, and if you clap back, they'll come at you again harder."

Cain wrapped his strong arms around me, pulling me in close. My face pressed against his chest, and it was then I realized I was shaking.

"Please, Cain," I murmured into his chest. "No one else needs to get hurt."

"I know, baby, I know," he crooned. "King and I are meeting tomorrow to discuss our next steps. Until then, everyone is lying low." He kissed the top of my head, running his hand down the back of my hair softly. I felt his head tilt away from mine, and I knew he was looking at Sly.

After I calmed down, we spent the rest of the night with Sly in his room. Cain went out and grabbed us burgers, having no interest in eating hospital food, and while he was gone, Sly and I watched a mindless game show on the T.V. as we sat in comfortable silence.

Being around him—knowing he was alive and breathing—was all I needed for my heart to feel a little peace.

Around eight, a nurse came in to check on Sly and shoo us out.

"Visiting hours are long past over. You guys are welcome

to come back tomorrow, but Mr. Lucchetti needs some rest, and frankly, Ms. Adler, you look like you could use some, too."

"Then bring me a cot, because we're not leaving," I argued.

My body was screaming, exhaustion plaguing me with force, but I refused to leave Sly again. Not when he'd already been by himself for so long. They never kicked Cain out once they finally let him back to see me, so I knew their rules could be broken.

"Ms. Adler—"

"No," I said with conviction. "Look, either I'm sleeping on this chair or I'm sleeping on a cot you provide, but I'm not leaving. And honestly, I'd prefer a cot. Sharing a chair with that giant man over there doesn't seem like the most comfortable option when I'm still dealing with a concussion."

She looked from me, to Cain, then finally to Sly, who just shrugged at her. Letting out a frustrated sigh, she left, and returned a few minutes later with a small folded cot on wheels, and linens folded over her arms.

"If I get in trouble for this, I'm sending my bosses to you," she promised, shoving the linens into Cain's arms.

Cain laughed as he sat the blankets down and started helping her with the cot. "Sounds fair."

When she walked out the door, she turned to us once again with a scowl on her face. "Get some rest. You all need it," she scolded us like a mother would her children. And we listened.

Cain shut the lights off and got himself comfortable on the chair while I curled onto the cot and closed my eyes.

Sly's eyes were already closed, but I heard his soft laughter. "Whatever *mia preferita* wants, *mia preferita* gets."

THE ROOM WAS dark when I opened my eyes, roused from my sleep by the sound of a commotion in the hallway.

"Where is he?" a feminine voice shouted.

Though I was groggy and her voice was suppressed from the walls, I could hear the fear in her tone. A familiar sinking struck my heart...I knew how she was feeling.

Glancing over at Sly, I saw he was awake and had a dark, confused look on his face. I smiled at him, but he didn't return it.

The nurse's voice had my head turning back toward the door, which I then realized wasn't closed fully.

"Miss, it's past midnight. Visiting hours are between eleven and eight tomorrow if you'd like to come back then, but it's too—"

"I don't care what time it is! I need to see him."

"Vincenza?" I heard Sly mutter under his breath as he adjusted his bed to sit upright. He was staring at the door, his eyebrows creased together.

"Miss, please, if you just come back tomorr—"

"I've been on a plane for six hours. *Please*. Just for a few minutes, at the very least. Just to know he's okay."

There was a moment of silence in the hallway. I sat up a little straighter, hoping to hear what was going on.

"If you won't tell me where he is, I'll find him myself," the woman seethed, and I heard soft footsteps coming down the hallway.

By this point, I was fully awake and sitting up on my cot as I looked toward the door, hoping to catch a glimpse of the woman as she went by.

Only she didn't walk by. Instead, when she snuck a glance through the small window, her piercing gray-blue eyes went round and she threw the door open.

"Sly!" she cried, rushing into the room.

"Vinnie?" he questioned as she crashed herself into him, her hands flying around him as best they could.

He pulled her closer, his hands immediately tangling into her long, dark hair.

She was absolutely stunning. Her dark chocolate hair was long, reaching her waistline, and hung down in loose curls. She wore a black peacoat that ended mid-thigh, with dark wash jeans and black ballet flats.

It was obvious to see that she was the one Sly held so deeply in his heart.

"Vinnie, what are you doing here, amore mio?" he asked, pulling back to look at her. His hands encircled her face, and he brushed the hair away.

"You honestly think I wouldn't hear about you being in the hospital, Sly? As soon as I heard, I got on a plane."

"Vincenza, your family. Do they know you've come?"

She sat on the edge of his bed and softly rested her left hand on his chest. Dim light from the hallway shimmered off the enormous diamond ring on her finger.

She shook her head softly. "If they haven't figured it out already, it won't take long now."

"Do you know the risk you've taken to be here?" he asked, pulling her to him again.

Her head rested on her chest, and from my cot I could see her eyes close. "You've always been worth any risk, Sly."

Tears sprung to my eyes, feeling guilty for witnessing such an intimate moment between these two star-crossed lovers, but also feeling so, so grateful that this woman had gone to such lengths to get here for him.

Sly had been such a beautiful piece of my life since the moment he'd walked into it, but he always kept his past locked up tight. I knew he'd left behind a great love, but until Vinnie walked into the room, I always assumed it was a painful part of him he didn't want to talk about.

Seeing it made me realize not only how hard the pain of leaving her behind must have been, but how raw and real their love truly *still* was.

Cain pulled me from my trance of watching them when he placed his hand on my shoulder, rubbing it in light circles before he took my hand, urging me to stand. Wrapping his arm around my shoulder, he leaned in, his lips brushing against my ear as he said, "Let's give them some space, baby. He's not alone anymore."

CHAPTER TWENTY-NINE

Rosie

"Baby, how many times do I have to ask before you finally say yes?"

Cain was kneeling down in the middle of my office, holding a velvet box open with a gorgeous marquise diamond ring inside.

This was the second time he'd proposed in the six months following the attack on the Sinners. So much for our talk about me never wanting a normal life, but then again, the thought didn't seem so scary these days. Not that I'd admit that to him yet.

"I've told you a million times now, I'm not sure I ever want to get married, Cainy-boo. How many times are you going to propose until you realize that I'm not the barefoot and pregnant marriage material type?"

A low growl rumbled through his chest at my refusal. Standing quickly, he scooped me up and tossed me over his shoulder.

"Put me down, jackass!" I laughed, hitting him in the back with my fists playfully.

Cain brought me to my desk chair and deposited me in it, then dropped to his knees. He had that look in his eyes that made my toes curl without a single touch.

"You wore a dress today, baby. I like it," Cain told me, temporarily distracted. He slid his finger against the triangle of fabric that acted as a barrier between us.

Instinctually, my back arched against the chair.

He rubbed my clit through my underwear, and I spread my legs wider for him. Pulling the fabric aside, he dipped one finger into me, watching the way it slid in and out through my wetness.

"And I told you, I'll never stop trying to put a ring on your finger," he said, picking up where the conversation left off.

His finger curled upward, and he made stroking motions inside me. My ass slid further down in the chair, and he used his free hand to roll me closer to him. Groaning, he undid his belt buckle with one hand while he fucked me with his fingers.

My breathing hitched. "You're insufferable."

"But you love me anyway," he countered, adjusting his hand so he could rub my clit with his thumb.

"You're right," I moaned. "More than I thought possible."

My thoughts floated back to how so quickly everything had changed, and throughout it all, the intensity of my love for him only grew.

It'd been months since the family barbeque from hell, and I still found myself looking over my shoulder constantly. My heart raced in fear every time I heard a motorcycle pass by.

After Sly was discharged from the hospital, we spent the next week helping Nixon plan Preston's funeral, while the Sinners also held Church several times to discuss The Reaper's Wings. Cain didn't fill me in often on what happened in the meetings, knowing how much I was already struggling with the constant worrying. But I knew enough. I knew the important details.

The Sinners were far out of their depth. It was a constant debate in which the vote was split on how to handle it. Some wanted retaliation, while others believed that the 'debt had been paid.' An eye for an eye. Cain killed one of their own, and they killed Preston.

There was no longer a debt to be settled.

Cain had spent many late nights with the club, and in the end, they'd decided to call a meeting with Rifton, their president. They met at a halfway point to discuss their feud.

I'd never been so fucking scared.

The entire time Cain was gone, Noah sat with me at the bar and we tossed back whiskey like it was water. I checked my phone obsessively, anxious to find the text he'd promised to send, and terrified I'd end up with a call from someone saying the meeting had gone sideways.

When I'd picked up my cell phone for the millionth time, Noah finally admitted that I should relax a little. Some officers on the Ridgewood P.D. had posed as Sinners and were with them right that very moment, waiting for The Reaper's Wings to do or say something to incriminate themselves.

The Sinners intended to dismantle The Reaper's Wings entirely, and while the roadside meeting hadn't offered any usable evidence against them, the Sinners continued working with the Ridgewood P.D. and Bridge Point's department to make it happen.

Shortly after the meeting, the Sinners moved out.

As in, out of my bar.

And Cain had moved into my place.

I tried to assure him that it was fine if the Sinners stayed...that *I* was fine if they stayed. We had a contract, but more than that, the Sinners had become family. We'd been through so much together. But he realized the implications of having a motorcycle club living above his girlfriend's business.

Neither of us wanted history to ever repeat itself.

But with the Sinners gone, that space and all those rooms were being wasted. It sat empty for a couple of months before one day, while prepping to open with Indy, an idea struck. After a few days of brainstorming and a meeting with Chief Duquette at the Ridgewood Police Department, I hit the ground running.

Rosie's Refuge opened two weeks ago and already housed three women who needed a safe place to go after being assaulted. The police department connected survivors with us, and we greeted them with open arms, giving them the support they needed. Rosie's Refuge had room for up to ten, or more, if some were willing to share a room with another woman in need. We provided them with meals, shelter, and protection—the Sinners worked in shifts to act as security at the base of the staircase.

Until the women who came to us were comfortable enough to be on their own again, they were welcome as long as they needed. The charity I set up to fund us helped with the cost of food and utilities, but even if it hadn't, I'd never ask these women for a penny.

It was the single most rewarding thing I'd ever done.

Aside from choosing to let go of my fear and allow myself to fully let my guard down with Cain.

Pulling me back to the present, his finger grazed my clit, making my eyes roll to the back of my head. A wanton moan floated past my lips as my hips bucked, desperate for more of his touch.

"*Fuck*, Rose, you're so wet," Cain groaned, another finger inside my pussy. The way he watched his fingers slide in and out of me made my body shudder.

I wrapped my legs around his neck, forcing his mouth closer to my center.

"Eat me," I demanded, lifting my hips to further my request. I *needed* the feel of his tongue against me. *Craved* the way his lips left against my clit.

"Gladly," he said, pulling his fingers from me. Ripping the underwear from my body, he left me bare as he sat back on his heels and simply admired the view.

I squirmed in my seat, aroused and needy, growing increasingly more frustrated, until his tongue connected with my wet flesh.

"Mmmmm," I hummed, rolling my hips to meet the thrusts of his tongue.

He reached around my leg and connected his thumb to my clit again, rolling it around.

"Fuck, you're so good with your mouth," I complimented. It was the truth. Cain was a master at my body, knowing it literally inside and out. Every time he touched me, I turned to putty almost instantly because he knew exactly what I craved.

He lapped at my pussy and brought me closer to my orgasm with every flick of his fingers.

"I want you to fuck me, Cain. Now."

He pulled away and stood up, grabbing my arm and pulling me to stand, too. My dress fell back into place.

Walking over to the couch, he took a seat, leaning back as he draped an arm over the top, looking relaxed. He also looked like he was ready to fuck me into oblivion, if the way his cock poking out of his jeans was any indication.

After things had settled, we'd turned the couch around. I'd made a habit of constantly staring out into the bar and obsessively watching every guy to make sure he wasn't being sketchy, and it wasn't healthy.

Now that it was turned, Cain spent a lot of time watching me work. He kept me company, which I appreciated. It helped keep me from running away with my thoughts.

It also kept me from missing my best friends.

Elle and Ryder just had their baby, a little girl. Zoë had me wrapped around her itty-bitty finger, and as much as I loved going over to see all of them, they needed their time to bond as a new family.

Noah had finally proposed to his girlfriend, Lily, and they were currently undergoing IVF and trying to start their family while simultaneously planning their wedding. Lily and I never grew super close, but Noah held a special place in my heart. The brother I never had. His happiness was my happiness, and I prayed every day IVF would work for them.

And Sly...my wonderful, beautiful, Italian friend, turned

lover, turned friend again. Once discharged from the hospital, he stuck around for a while, but ultimately decided to go back to New York. I suspected he left to be closer to Vinnie—maybe even to try and get her back. Since leaving, our communication had lessened, and even though it broke my heart, I hoped his was full.

He deserved to feel the love that I felt every day with Cain.

Cain Michaels.

Goddamn, did I waste a lot of time finding my way back to him.

Licking his lips, he smirked at me as though my face revealed everything I was thinking. "Rose, Rose, Rose. You're the most independent, headstrong woman I've ever met. I love you so fucking much, but we're both alphas, and when two alphas get together, they have to take turns submitting, otherwise the power share between them will never last. We've done a good job at that so far, but right now, I want you to submit. Can you do that for me, baby?"

Little did he know, I already had. I may have been independent and headstrong, like he'd said, but I *loved* the way he took control, especially when we were both naked.

I nodded.

He smirked again, rubbing his tattooed hand along his jawline. "Good. Now I want you to crawl to me, Rose."

His words surprised me, and I cocked my head. "Crawl? You want me to fucking crawl?"

"Yes. On your hands and knees, ass out, with that pretty little dress of yours hiked so far up your legs that if I were to walk behind you, I'd see your pussy. And you know what, I just might get up and do that, just to see it. It *is* my favorite view, after all."

I shook my head, attitude at the tip of my tongue, but did as he asked. Dropping to my knees, I flipped my dress up onto my hips and slowly crawled toward him. It wasn't far, but the whole time I stared up at him from beneath my lashes and watched as he struggled to maintain his composure at the sight of me.

Tugging down his pants, he pushed them beneath his knees and let them fall to the floor before he kicked them away, just as I made it to him. Kneeling, I placed my hands on his thighs.

"Now what?" I asked, arousal thick in my voice. I practically felt wetness dripping down my thighs, and I was excited to see where he'd take this.

"Climb on, baby."

And I did. I scurried onto his lap and wrapped my hand around his fully erect cock as I lowered myself onto it, taking him inch by inch until he filled me completely. We groaned in unison and I started to move, riding him as he guided my hips, helping my body take him faster.

Over his shoulder, I caught my reflection in the mirror propped against the wall and thought back to the first time I let my walls down with Cain and gave into his temptation.

I'd *always* been his.

One being ripped in two.

Kindred souls always searching for one another.

The other half of my heart.

And when we came, we came together as one, just as we were always meant to.

Cain

One Year Later

When Rose suggested we take a quick weekend trip to Las Vegas, the last thing I expected was to be standing here in my dark jeans and leather jacket in front of Elvis.

Over the course of the last eighteen months, I'd asked Rose to marry me no less than five times. I'd tried every type of proposal from romantic to spontaneous, involving our friends to having it just be the two of us.

Casual.

Extravagant.

I tried everything to get her to say yes.

She said no every single time.

I didn't let it discourage me. I knew she wasn't wanting a traditional life—hell, I hadn't wanted it either until after I had to watch her lie in a hospital bed because of *me*.

Nothing makes a man crave a normal, domestic life with the woman he loves more than having her be involved in a shooting.

But my little firecracker didn't let that deter her, and over these last several months, I'd been by her side watching her accomplish anything she put her mind to.

Her business at the bar was booming. She created a charity and safe haven for survivors of sexual assault, and had many women who needed that solitude come through. I was so proud of her taking the once terrifying situation she'd be put in and spinning it into something not only positive, but necessary for the community.

She was an amazing girlfriend, friend, boss, and aunt to her best friend's kid.

I loved everything about her, but most of all, I admired the woman she was.

But she was a bit of a workaholic, so when she suggested a weekend away, I threw her on a plane with no questions asked. A quickie vacation with my girl is exactly what I needed, in fact, I'd even brought her engagement ring with me in case an opportunity for proposal number six presented itself.

Little did I know, Rose had plans for us.

When she came out of the hotel's bathroom wearing the sexiest black mini dress, I nearly came on the spot. The neckline dipped low between her breasts and hugged her midsection tightly, but flared slightly at her hips. It was short—mid-thigh, and it drove me fucking wild.

"And it has pockets," she told me with excitement, sticking her hands into them. She had a hint of mischief in her eyes when she said it, and I couldn't help but wonder what it was about pockets on a dress that every woman went insane for.

If I thought the dress was sexy though, watching her put on her heels practically killed me. The thin strapped heels wrapped and tied up around her calf. I didn't even know they made heels like that, but now I had plans for her to *only* be wearing them later tonight.

What had really thrown me through a loop though, was when she dragged me through the hotel's casino and out onto the strip where an Uber was waiting for us. When we pulled up to the wedding chapel, my whole world turned upside down as we stepped out of the car and Rose turned to me and said, "You still want to marry me, Cainy-boo?"

I scooped her into my arms so fast and ran her inside before she could change her mind. She laughed the entire time and wrapped her arms around my neck, peppering my face with her kisses.

Now, as the classic bridal march started on the sound system, and the door to the chapel opened, I turned my attention to the spot where the woman of my dreams would walk through.

After a second, Rose stepped into view, holding a single blue dahlia as her wedding bouquet. She looked stunning, but the most gorgeous thing she was wearing was the smile on her face as she walked toward me.

Finally, she was about to become Rose Michaels.

After almost an entire decade of loving her, we stood before each other, Elvis, and the old couple who owned the joint, and I repeated my vows, stepping forward to say a few words that were only meant for her to hear.

When it was time for her vows, she held my gaze and repeated them, while also adding the extra things she wanted to say to me.

So many times I had pictured this moment...sans Elvis. It almost felt surreal to be living it.

"And do you, Rose, take this man to be your husband?" Elvis asked, adding his signature impersonator flair to the words.

She smiled, and with such ease that I almost missed it, Rose dipped her hand inside of her pocket, before bringing it back out.

"I do," she said confidently, her sweet smile transforming into a wicked grin that I knew meant mischief.

Her hand was curled into a fist as she lifted it closer to her face, and sticking out from the bend of her fingers, I could see the glint of the confetti she was holding.

A smile pursed her lips as she tried to hide her laugh, but I didn't hide mine. I knew what she was up to, and I laughed openly as I shook my head at her.

It'd taken her longer than I thought it would, but my time meeting those little holographic dicks had finally come.

It was because I'd *relentlessly* asked her to marry me for the last eighteen months that it was about to happen.

I was about to get dicked by Rose.

With Rose confirming her vows, Elvis began speaking again, concluding our ceremony, but I couldn't concentrate on his words.

Not when my new missus had something up her sleeve.

Rose mouthed *I love you* and lifted her hand to her mouth. Uncurling her fingers, she revealed what she'd been holding inside.

When her red-stained lips parted to blow the confetti at me, I stepped forward and grabbed her hand, letting every last shiny dick fall to the floor as I slammed my lips against hers and kissed my bride.

Thank you for reading Marked By Cain! Your reviews are important, please considering leaving your review of Marked By Cain on Amazon.

Ready for more?

1. Read the Marked By Cain BONUS CHAPTER - Chapter 18 in Sly's Point of View!
2. Read the first book of Sly's duet, Sins of Sorrow!

Still craving more A.R. Rose books?

Wreck Me: New adult, rich girl/poor boy, insta-love, light suspense.

It's never to early to get in the Christmas spirit! Check out I Really Can't Stay: Fake Dating, Found Family, Insta-love

RESOURCES

If you or someone you know is the victim of sexual assault and need resources, please call the National Sexual Assault Hotline at 800-656-4673 or visit www.rainn.org/resources.

The hotline is available 24/7 and has additional options to speak with someone, such as online chat in English and Spanish, and a male survivors online chat.

ACKNOWLEDGMENTS

Dang, I can't believe the Ridgewood Series has come to a close with Rosie & Cain's Story. I hope you loved following their journey as much as I did. Rosie has held a special place in my heart since the first time she appeared in Between the Flames. When I envisioned Rosie and her personality, I saw piece of myself and my two best friends within her character.

When I started writing, I had an idea of what I wanted to do with Rosie's story, but she immediately threw a wrench into it and gave me severe writers block until I listened to what she actually wanted. Crazy, I know, but that's how I roll. My books are character driven, and I let them guide me, which is sometimes a blessing, and other times is a curse. Regardless, I hope you enjoyed Marked By Cain and are excited for future publications.

A very special thank you to my amazing team I have beside me. My alpha and beta readers who really help shape the story: Amanda, DeLynda, Tawny, & Kerri. Thank you to my amazing editor Virginia, and my proofreader Nicole.

To Rana for being my friend, mentor, and honestly, a lot of times, my writing therapist.

To my husband, parents, and my besties Amanda, April,

for always being there for me throughout my writing journey, and for being the best cheerleaders I could ever ask for.

An extra special thank you to the amazing teams of women I have on my promo squad and my ARC team, and the influencers who always show their love and support. And of course to my PA, Cassie, who I truly don't think I could live without! I'm so grateful for you and all that you've helped me accomplish so far.

Lastly, to the amazing readers who have taken a chance on my books. Without you, writing would still just be a dream I was too scared to chase. Your support and willingness to read my words means the world to me.

LOVE YOU ALL.

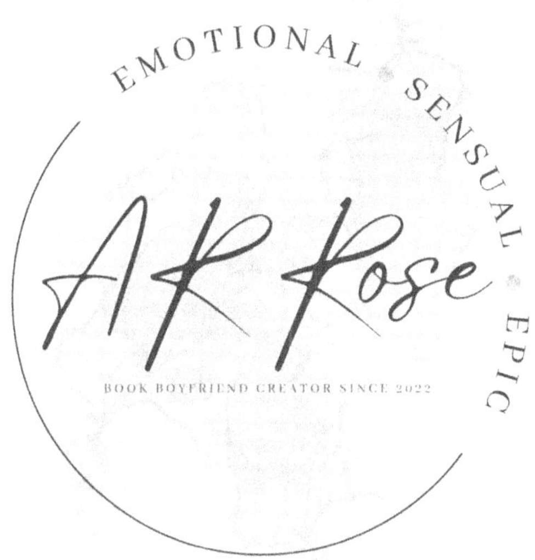

A.R. Rose is a wife, mom, reader, and writer, who lives in sunny California with her family and two dogs. She loves to hang out at home, drink copious amounts of coffee, and eat yummy food

90% of the time you will find her with a book or her Kindle in hand, reading a spicy romance novel, which not so coincidentally is what she has fallen in love with writing.

CONNECT

Join A.R. Rose's newsletter for info & updates
🤍https://www.authorarrose.com/email-subscribe

Website
🤍www.authorarrose.com

Reading Group
🤍https://www.facebook.com/groups/authorarrose

Facebook
🤍https://www.facebook.com/authorarrose

TikTok
🤍https://www.tiktok.com/@authorarrose
🤍https://www.tiktok.com/@alexreadsromance

Instagram
🤍 https://www.instagram.com/authorarrose

Want a sneak peek of Sly's story?

Continue reading for a modern day Romeo & Juliet reimagining that will keep you hooked page after page!

Sins of Sorrow by A.R. Rose

💋High Society
💋Enemies to Lovers
💋Forbidden Romance
💋Biker MMC
💋Pleasure Dom

SLY

CHAPTER ONE

Age 9, Verona, Italy

"Papà! Mamma!"

The shrill sound of my six-year-old brother's laughter rises through the fragrant air as we run around my parents, playing a game of tag in the kitchen while my mother cooks. Mio padre sits at our kitchen table rubbing his temples as we race around him, my brother completely oblivious of the irritation that permeates off our father.

Tossing my hand out, I whip my fingers against his arm, just barely ghosting him as he lunges forward to avoid my touch.

"Ugh, Giulio! Sei un imbroglione!" *You're a cheater.*

He laughs again and keeps running, tripping over Mamma's feet. As he goes flying, skidding across the floor, she wags her finger at him. "I've told you the kitchen is not for playing, Giulio."

My brother stands and starts to run again until Papà stops him in his tracks.

"Enough!" Papà's voice booms as his fists hit the table. "My head is pounding, and your mother is cooking. Find somewhere else to play."

Papà is a doctor. A world-renowned surgeon, I've heard Mamma say. He works at the hospital that my bisnonno founded, and my nonno was a surgeon before my father. Nonno died when I was five, but his picture still hangs in the lobby of the hospital, alongside bisnonnos, and mio padres. Three generations of Lucchettis as doctors. *Surgeons*.

Papà says he looks forward to me becoming one, too.

Turning to my mother, his gaze softens as it lands on her. "Mia mogile, we have staff who can prepare the meals. You should be resting."

His gaze falls to where her hand rests on her stomach, rubbing where my youngest brother grows. "I love to cook, Antonio. You know this."

"Sì, bellissima. And you are so good at it. But your doctor—"

"Shh, shh. I know my body, and I will rest when it tells me to."

"C'mon, Sly, let's go upstairs!" Guilio pulls my attention from our parents as he retreats from the kitchen, his small, chubby hand beckoning for me to follow.

"No, grazie, I want to draw again." Taking the seat opposite my father, I pick up my charcoal and pull my sketch pad toward me, resuming the drawing I was working on before we started our game. I've always loved to sketch, and Mamma says I've been improving greatly.

Our black lab, Polpetta, is the perfect muse for me to practice. Mamma and Papà got her when I was two, and they say my favorite food was meatballs then, so the name stuck. Nowadays, she's old and lazy, looking as round as the food she is named after.

"It's looking well," Papà compliments as he watches me shadow the outline of her nose.

"Grazie, Papà."

A loud, abrupt ringing makes me jump, shifting my charcoal into a harsh line against my page. Frowning, I look at the mistake, my shoulders sagging in defeat.

"Pronto?" my mother singsongs into the telephone. The room falls silent as my father watches with intent while she nods her head, her hand flying over her mouth as she looks at my father. Pulling the phone away from her ear, she holds it out, signaling for him to come take it from her. "It's Gabriele."

My eyes perk up at the mention of Uncle Gabriele. He lives in America, in a city full of skyscrapers and twinkling lights. The photos he brought during his last visit were magnifico, and I long to go see it for myself.

I also wish to see my cousin Lorenzo, who is the same age as I am. It makes me sad that my best friend and playmate is across the ocean, and even though I ask a lot, Mamma and Papà still have not taken me and Giulio to see them.

"Gabriele," my father barks into the phone. "What is it this time?"

My father's expression morphs from irritated to infuriated, his golden-bronze skin turning red from his neck through his face.

"HOW?" he shouts, his eyes darting to Mamma before he lowers his tone. "How could you get yourself into *that* much trouble, Gabriele? I—no. *No*. Absolutely not."

He turns his back, cupping his hand over the place where he speaks as though to shield his words. I don't hear what he says before he slams the phone into where it rests on the wall.

"Sylvester, go to your room, please. Mamma and I need to speak alone." I can hear the anger in his tone, see the quake in his shoulders, but he doesn't look over at me as he commands my instructions. I know better than to argue, so I collect my sketchbook and shuffle out of the kitchen without a word.

For the next two hours, me and Guilio sit at the top of our home's staircase, listening to Mamma and Papà argue. The sounds of heightened yet muffled voices and Mamma's anguished sobs traveling through the polished surfaces of our house.

One of our housemaids tried to shoo us back to our bedrooms an hour ago, but instead, I tucked my younger brother under my arm and stayed put. We can't hear what our parents speak of, but a twisting in my stomach tells me nothing good will come of it.

A gulp of saliva catches in my throat as I tilt my head back and look at the giant stone mansion. Mamma tucks my hand into hers, ushering Guilio and me away from the car that brought us here while it idles against the curb.

"Boys, you are to be on your best behavior. This is a business visit for your Papà and Uncle Gabriele. You are to be seen and not heard—it is of much importance. Do you understand me?"

"Sì, Mamma," I answer for both of us.

It has been one week since we moved to America, and three weeks since the phone call from Uncle Gabriele that changed everything for our family.

That very same night Guilio and I listened to Mamma and Papà argue—they came into our rooms and told us Uncle Gabriele needed his family close and we would be moving to New York.

Eavesdropping on several of Papà's phone calls taught me Uncle Gabriele made some bad decisions and owed someone a lot of money. And if they didn't get it, they would do very bad things to him.

I still don't understand why we had to leave our country to go help him, but at least I get to see Lorenzo more.

The steps leading up to the house make me feel like I am climbing a mountain. The stone clicks beneath Mamma's pointy shoes and I look down at them for distraction. My heart races, and Papà's hand engulfs my shoulder as he comes to stand behind me while we wait for the door to be answered. Uncle Gabriele stands to his right, fidgeting, while Aunt Andrea squats to smooth the front of Lorenzo's jacket.

When the door opens, a tall man wearing a suit greets us with an unfriendly look on his face. Beyond him, I take in the elegance of the house. Shiny marble floors, a grand staircase, sculptures and artwork—this place could be a museum.

"Come in," the man says simply, then steps aside while holding the door.

I hear my uncle clear his throat as Mamma steps forward with me and my brother in tow. Once inside, a line of women in plain dresses stand, and one rushes to my mother.

Once the door closes, the loudness of the city disappears, and a cold silence takes its place.

"May I take your coat, ma'am?"

"Yes, grazie," she says, letting go of our hands to shrug out of her coat. Papà steps forward to help before removing his own and hands both to the lady waiting.

"Gabriele," a man says as he steps out of a nearby room. His hands are in the pockets of his pants as he moves slowly toward us, his eyes glued to my uncle. He walks like a hungry lion stalking a gazelle.

He looks mean. Scary.

Is this the man who is mad at my uncle? If he is, why are we here, at his house?

"Maurizio." My uncle's head dips as though he's bowing. "Thank you for having my family at your lovely home. This is my beautiful wife, Andrea, and son Lorenzo. As well as my brother, Antonio, and his family."

Giulio shuffles sideways until he's hidden behind Mamma's legs, but I stand straighter and move my shoulders back, trying not to seem as small as I feel.

The man my uncle introduced us to looks at us each and hums, scrunching his lips as he rubs his well-groomed beard.

My father clears his throat and takes a step forward, his hand extended. "Pleased to meet you, amico mio. Thank you for having us."

"I wasn't aware there was an *us* attending when I extended the invitation to Gabriele, but alas, our staff has prepared a large meal. We may as well break bread." He never takes Papà's hand.

I watch my father's eyes narrow before he quickly stows the look away and masks it with a smile. "I see. Well, I hope there is no trouble."

"Not at all," Maurizio clips and turns to one of the women standing along the wall. "Please see to it that the kitchen places...seven additional seats at the table."

"Certainly, Mr. Paladino." She practically runs through a set of doors just a few steps away.

The man turns to my mother and aunt, his tone softening as he speaks to them. "My wife, Leighton, should be down with our daughter any minute. You can wait in the sitting room while I take the men to my office. Should you need anything, Capaul can assist you."

"Thank you, Mr. Paladino," Aunt Andrea says as she ushers Lorenzo through the archway in the wall and into the room to our left. Mamma does the same, steering Giulio and me right behind her.

The room is bright from the sun, with plush couches and fluffy pillows, and a small table with a neat pile of children's books and grown-up magazines. It looks fancy, and immediately I am afraid to dirty it and get in trouble.

Lorenzo, on the other hand, takes a running leap onto the light gray sofa across the room, landing with a soft thud face down. His laugh is muffled as his mother scolds him.

"Enzo!" she hisses. "This is not the place for jokes!"

Pulling him up, she pushes his small body until he's sitting on the couch as he should be.

Mamma's hand on my back urges me forward, and I sit on the bigger of the two couches as she and Giulio do the same. Handing us both a book, she passes another to my cousin. "Read these, boys. And keep quiet until we tell you otherwise. *Please*, behave." She shares a look with my aunt before I look down at my book.

The Giving Tree by Shel Silverstein.

I huff out an annoyed breath, not wanting to read this dumb book again but knowing if I don't, Mamma will be angry. The book is made for little kids, and I'm *nine*. But Mamma says the best way to practice my second language is through repetition.

Staring at the pages without reading the words, we wait in the room for what feels like forever. Mamma and Aunt Andrea keep sharing looks. Guilio gets restless, sliding off the couch and onto the floor to crawl under the table. I sneak a peek at Enzo and see that he looks as though he's about to fall asleep with his arm propped up on the side of the couch.

What is taking so long?

More long minutes pass before the sound of footsteps pulls my attention and I glue my eyes to what I can see of the hallway. Moments later, a lady and a girl appear, both with smiles on their faces.

The girl looks to be about my age. She wears a puffy pink dress and her dark brown hair is long. I wonder if she has any brothers for me to play with.

Mamma and Aunt Andrea stand. Should I?

"Hello, ladies. Boys," the lady greets happily, walking over to us.

Sliding off the couch, I stand close to Mamma as the lady approaches and reaches for her hands.

"It's so nice to meet you! I'm Leighton, and this is my daughter, Vincenza. Come here, Vincenza."

The girl bounces over to her mother and waves at mine.

"I wasn't aware Gabriele was bringing his whole family for his meeting with my husband, or I never would have let my father take our boys this week for a hunting trip! They would have loved more little boys to play with."

"That's alright," Mamma affirms. "It seems as though our presence was a bit of a surprise. My name is Valentina, and these are my sons Sylvester and Giulio."

Aunt Andrea steps forward and extends a hand to shake with the lady, Lee-something. "Thank you for having us in your gorgeous home. I'm Andrea, Gabriele's wife. And this is our son Lorenzo."

"Ah, yes. I've met Gabriele a few times now! So nice to finally meet you." She gestures for everyone to sit, so we do, and she takes a seat in the armchair across from us. The girl settles on the floor by her mother's side with a chapter book on her lap.

"How old are your boys?" Aunt Andrea asks as she places her hand on Enzo's knee to keep him from wiggling.

"Luciano, my oldest, is fourteen. Then we have Joseph, who is eleven, Vincenza here, just turned nine, and Samuele, my baby, is four." She sighs. "They just grow so quickly. I can't believe I have a teenager." Looking over at my mother, she squeals, "And you! Look at that baby bump! When are you due?"

"Federico will be arriving in three to four months. Lord never knows with my boys, they come when they please. Sylvester was nearly two weeks late, but Giulio was a month early. I've stopped trying to guess when the Lucchetti boys may arrive." My eyes trace where my mother rubs my baby brother in her stomach, and she smiles warmly at me. "Sly is nine, Giulio is six."

"Oh, I understand that, honey. My kids were all over the place too." She smiles warmly at Enzo. "And you, sir? How old are you?"

Enzo shifts in his seat, sitting up taller as he proudly boasts, "I'm about to turn ten!"

"Such a little man you are!" Lee-whatever says affectionately.

Her sentence is barely finished when a woman wearing the same plain dress as all the other maids comes into the room.

"Your presence is requested in the dining room," she tells us and curtsies low before leaving.

It's very strange.

The grown-ups stand and Mamma pulls Giulio to his feet before we follow the lady out of the room. I watch as the girl bounces on her feet, skipping and twirling the whole way across the hall.

She's odd. So bouncy, and why is her dress so big?

When we enter through the open double doors of the dining room, Papà, Uncle Gabriele, and the scary man are already sitting at the table. They stand when they see us, and I follow Mamma over to the side where Papà sits.

She settles us, and once the room grows still, the scary man stands and clinks a knife against his short glass filled with a dark-golden liquid.

"I find myself to be a reasonable man. A *family* man. Which is why I'd like to welcome you all to my home this evening for dinner. Though unplanned, it seems fitting, as I have recently learned that things don't always go *as planned*. I hope that through this act of breaking bread and sharing time, minds will change before the night is over." His words trail off as he stares at my uncle, who I see gulp, the knob in his throat moving. "Now, please join me in prayer. Dear Heavenly Father, we ask that you bless our food and the guests we have here tonight to share it. May you offer your wisdom and guidance to those who may need it the most, and that you share your light by blessing our families, cultivating our relationships, and nurturing our businesses. In Jesus' name, Amen."

"Amen," I whisper, as everyone joins in.

Mamma and Papà exchange a look right before the sound of a loud snap echoes through the room.

With it, four people in black clothes walk forward and reach between us, pulling the shiny silver tops off the food sitting in the middle of the table.

Immediately, several scents hit me, and my stomach growls. Roasted chicken, steak, capellini pasta with Alfredo sauce, penne marinara, and fresh baked bread. My eyes bounce from dish to dish, skipping quickly over anything green—Mamma will make me eat my vegetables, but that doesn't mean I have to look forward to them.

With the clatter of dishes around us, I hear Mamma

whisper to Papà, "Cosa significa che spera che le menti cambiano?" *What does he mean he hopes minds will change?*

"Shh, shh," Papà whispers, before painting on a smile and turning to the head of the table. "Everything looks delizioso, Maurizio. Grazie."

The scary man, Maurizio, begins to serve himself, and as soon as his wife does, the rest of the adults do the same.

When our plates and our mouths are full, I realize no one is speaking. A rarity for a meal with my family.

Looking around the table, I see the scary man sending mean looks in my uncle's direction, while his wife fusses over the girl, trying to get her to try the food on her plate.

I don't know why she wouldn't want to.

Shoveling my mouth full bite after bite, I clear my plate and lean back in my chair, my stomach protruding.

"That was delizioso!" I exclaim loudly, knowing I was to be seen and not heard tonight, but not liking the silence. We speak at dinner. Why is no one speaking?

The scary man turns his attention to me, and suddenly I wish I had kept quiet. I am surprised when his grumpy look wipes clean. "I am glad, piccolo Lucchetti."

His gaze sweeps along the table, and he turns to his wife. "Leighton, my dear, perhaps now that we have finished, the men can speak once more?"

"Sure, my love," she tells him, then leans over to kiss him —*ew*. "Ladies, kiddos, shall we?"

Standing, she helps her daughter pull out her chair while Mamma and Aunt Andrea help us. Mamma casts another look to Papà, who nods, and Aunt Andrea bends to kiss Uncle Gabriele.

Why is everyone kissing?

As we walk away, I slow my steps to eavesdrop. "Have you thought about my offer, Gabriele?"

"Maurizio, *please*, there must be another way I can—"

"You have stolen from me, Gabriele! I have given more than enough time and patience because at one time I called you my most loyal employee, but *now* I need an answer. Have we come to an understanding?"

I look over my shoulder in time to see my uncle shake his head no, and watch as the scary man stands, forcing my uncle to look up at him. "How disappointing. You abuse my patience, even after I am gracious enough to take in your family for a meal."

My mother turns and sees that I have completely stopped walking, and hurries back to grab my arm. As she pulls me toward the door, the scary man continues yelling at my uncle, without actually raising his voice. "I put my trust in you, Gabriele. It was misguided, and it won't be forgotten. Let this be a warning to you, Antonio, of what happens when you cross Maurizio Paladino." Maurizio's gaze lifts and he watches us as we near the door.

We hardly cross the threshold before their butler pulls both doors closed behind us, slamming them shut. They hardly click into place when the piercing sound of a gunshot rings out behind them.

"NO!" Aunt Andrea screams, charging toward the door, but the man blocking it holds her back.

The girl, Vincenza, whimpers at the sound and curls into her mother, burying her head into the fabric of her dress. Her mother's hand covers her own mouth as though she's surprised.

"I'm so sorry," she cries out, but she's already pushing her daughter down the hall and away from us.

They disappear quickly as Mamma rushes to Aunt Andrea, pulling her into her arms while she sobs louder than I've ever heard anyone cry before.

Seconds later the doorknobs twist loudly, and Papà appears, tossing open the doors and stepping through them. His eyes are wild and fearful as he looks at each one of us. "Come," he says hurriedly. "We must leave. *Now*."

His eyes zero in on mine, speaking what he cannot say aloud. I nod in a silent understanding and grab the hands of my brother and my cousin, and pull them to the front door. Papà's footsteps are heavy behind mine as he guides Mamma and Aunt Andrea, leaning around me to open the front door when we reach it.

Once we're in the town car again, and our driver has made it safely away from the Paladino home, does the reality of what happened sink in.

Everything happened so quickly, and if I thought our lives were turned upside down before, I have a feeling I am sadly mistaken.

Aunt Andrea's loud sobs have turned into breathless hysteria as she cries into Mamma's bosom. Lorenzo is curled up on the seat, folded into himself with his head on his mother's lap. I can't tell if he's crying.

Papà hands Giulio his activity pack he brings with him on car rides to keep him occupied before looking at me.

It's then I see smatters of blood across his white starched shirt. My stomach dips and I look away, out the window.

The city lights are bright, even through the darkened tint of the car, and it's only when the traffic begins to move and the lights begin to blur, do I allow a quiet stream of tears to fall.

There are two things I learned for certain today.

One: My uncle is dead.

And two: Never trust a Paladino.

VINNIE

CHAPTER TWO

Age 13

"Remind me why I have to go to this stupid dinner?" I complain to my nanny, Cecilia, as I look at her through the reflection of my vanity mirror.

Cecilia is less of a nanny and more of an older sister figure. She's twenty-three, and even though she was hired on to care for me, she and I quickly bonded, and the formalities dropped. Cecilia helps me with everything: school, hair, makeup, *boys*. She accompanies me to almost every event I am forced by my parents to attend. She even lives here at the estate, although her room isn't on the same floor as mine.

"Because, it's a charity fundraiser at the mayor's house and anyone worth a damn is invited," she reprimands as she lets a curl loose from the wand, letting the hot strand bounce against her hand as it immediately starts to cool. She passes the handle of the curling wand to me so I can hold it while she sprays my hair with hairspray.

"The Townsends will be there," she continues with a coy smile. "I was talking to Esther today. She said Summer is ecstatic to go tonight."

I roll my eyes at the mention of Summer, and her keeper —I mean nanny—Esther.

Summer is three years younger than I am and tries desperately to act like she's my age. I only tolerate her presence at these dumb events because of her brother. Her brother makes my heart soar. I've had a crush on him since I was five.

I try to act casual as I ask Cecilia, "And Mason? Will he be there?"

She releases another curl and hands the wand back to me. Her lips turn up into a cheeky smile. "Maybe."

"Make sure my hair is perfect," I snap, but a smile plays against my lips as she narrows her eyes at me.

"I may be hired to be your nanny, young lady, but I'm still older than you. It'd behoove you to remember that."

"And it'd behoove *you* to remember that I'm your boss."

We stare at each other through the mirror for several seconds, our expressions hard, before we both burst into laughter.

She pokes my side with her freshly manicured fingernail. "You're a little princess, Vinnie. You're lucky I'm so fond of you."

"Mmmhmm," I hum and bring a tube of pink gloss to my lips. Mom won't let me wear makeup yet, but she lets Cecilia style my hair however I want, and buys me a new lip gloss whenever I ask. This one tastes like cotton candy.

When my hair is done, I stand, and Cecilia grabs my dress from where it hangs nearby. It's beautiful. Ice-blue chiffon with a fitted bodice, and thick straps that tie on the top of my shoulders. It reminds me of a modern-day Cinderella, without the hoop skirt.

Shrugging from my robe, Cecilia slips the dress over my outstretched arms, careful as she brings it over my head, as to not ruin my hair or rub my gloss. Once I'm situated, she zips the back and turns me toward my mirror.

It's lovely. I can't wait for Mason to see me in it, and I wonder if he'll finally notice me as *more* than just a childhood playmate.

***

Mayor Conrad Moser's charity dinner is an absolute snoozefest. Nothing more than a four-course meal in their grand ballroom, packed with round tables for the most elite New York families to pretend like they care what each other has to say.

Mom insisted we attend tonight when Mayor Moser extended the invitation. This is their first social gathering in their new luxury 5th Avenue penthouse, since typically parties were thrown at their main residence, Gracie Mansion. Mom gushed about how close they live to the Met, if only part-time, and how she couldn't wait to see it because it was a tri-level penthouse—a unique rarity at this level of extravagance. So naturally, Father accepted the invitation, and here we are.

The auction was the most entertaining part of the evening, and even that was hardly bearable.

Leaning against my mother's shoulder, my finger traces along the extravagant beadwork on her tight champagne and gold gown. I was underdressed in comparison to her, but as she liked to remind me, "it's not your job to stand out, Vincenza."

Yet.

It's not my job to stand out, *yet*.

But I will, someday soon.

"Mom, can I go find the boys?" I ask, waiting until there is a lull in her conversation with Mayor Moser's wife, Elena. My brothers had slipped from the room ages ago and were probably exploring the grounds or playing with some of the other kids I saw earlier who have also disappeared. Who I really want to find, though, is Mason.

Looking around the ballroom, I realize I'm the only kid still sitting with their parents.

"Sure, sweetheart, but be careful wandering about on your own until you find them."

Smiling tightly, I stand and slightly bow my head as a sign of respect to Mrs. Moser. "Dinner was lovely. Thank you so much, Mrs. Moser."

"What a well-mannered daughter you have, Leighton," she praises. "A little not-so-well-kept secret, my dear. If you go through the main doors and up the staircase to the third floor, you'll find an access door to the roof. Somehow, all the children find a way to sneak into my rooftop hideaway. It's not much, but the view of the city is breathtaking."

"Thank you," I tell her, then spin on my heel and force every bone in my 'well-mannered' body to walk, *not run*, across the ballroom and to the stairs.

My nude sling-back kitten heels echo against the dark wooden staircase as I climb higher, craning my neck to see if anyone is on the second floor. It's quiet up here, so I turn immediately and climb the second staircase leading to the third floor.

Once at the top, I find the door Mrs. Moser mentioned will take me to the roof. For whatever reason though, I hesitate before stepping toward it.

My gaze sweeps over the ostentatious landing of the third floor and catches on a set of glass French doors that are slightly open. A light breeze ruffles the sheer curtains of the window next to it, the sounds of the bustling city pouring in.

I cross the space, drawn to the open doors, and push one just enough for me to slide through the gap.

Pressing my back against the door, it clicks into place, and the moment it does, a boy about my age slips out of the shadow cast by the wall of the balcony.

He wears simple black dress pants and a crisp white buttoned shirt, with a plain maroon tie hanging around his neck. But perhaps the most captivating thing this boy wears is his expression.

He looks sad, and angry, and above all, he looks lonely.

Something about his scowl makes me want to take his sadness away. I want to make him smile.

"Hi," I say shyly, tucking a lock of hair behind my ear.

"Hi," he replies, and takes a seat on the stone bench in the center of the balcony. From there, he stares straight out at the lights of the city.

"What are you doing up here?"

"Probably the same thing you are."

"Oh. Well, I was actually looking for my brothers."

"Haven't seen them," he says with boredom. It makes me deflate a little inside.

"Do you want company?" I ask as I take a step forward.

His head swings toward me, and he looks me up and down before turning back to the city. Nodding once, he says, "Sure, but can we not talk?"

"Okay."

Rounding the bench, I sit down next to him, leaving as much space between us as possible. I follow his line of sight and stare out at the twinkling skyscrapers. A few blocks over, a helicopter lands on the roof of Lenox Hill.

After several minutes, I can't take the silence. "Are you sitting up here alone because something made you sad?"

"I thought we agreed no talking."

My mouth opens, then closes again. There are so many questions on the tip of my tongue. A large part of me thinks it may be wise to go leave and find Mason, or my brothers, after all.

The boy exhales and leans forward with his elbows pressed against his knees. "Sì," he sighs. "I miss my home. I wish to go back."

"I'm sure your family will be leaving soon. The auction has finished and everyone is just talking and dancing."

He laughs as I speak, turning to look at me. With his full attention, it feels like there is a spotlight shining down on me, the warmth of the light stifling. I squirm uncomfortably.

"I did not mean my house, I meant my *home*. Verona."

"As in Italy?"

"Sì. The one and only."

"Wow," I whisper to myself, before asking. "What's it like there? I've always dreamt of visiting. I'm half Italian, possibly a little more. My father is full, and my mother is half, mixed with Irish and French."

"It's very beautiful. A different beauty than New York has to offer." He looks back out to the skyline. His tone is a little more chipper when he eventually turns back to me. "Were you born here? You must have been—your accent is purely American."

"I was. Right here in New York, actually. My mom was born in Virginia and happened to meet my father when he was here for a summer abroad. They fell in love and he moved to the U.S. for her, and they settled here." It's more information than a teenage boy needs, but I love the story of my parents. Their love story gives me hope I'll find my own someday. If they could find their soulmate by chance, after living an ocean apart for so long, certainly destiny has plans for all of us.

"Romantic," he says, scrunching his nose slightly, though his voice holds no sarcasm.

"When did you move her—"

"Vincenza!" My mom stops my sentence, her voice carrying through the closed doors as she looks for me.

His gaze snaps back to mine when he hears my mom, and I swear I see his eyes widen for a moment.

I sigh with annoyance. I want to know more about this boy...hear more about growing up in Italy, and why he's here. How long he's lived here. But instead, I discreetly wipe my sweaty palms on the underside of my dress and stand.

"I have to go. Thank you for keeping me company."

Smiling sweetly, I notice the way he stares blankly at me instead of returning the sentiment. It wipes the smile off my face, and I take steps backward to the door, not taking my eyes off him as he continues to stare at me with a cold look in his.

He glares at me as I twist the handle and step back into the penthouse, wondering where I went wrong.

Boys are so confusing.

"Oh, there you are, sweetheart! I was worried when your brothers showed back up at the table, but you weren't with them. It's time to go—your father's already sent for the car."

"Alright." I follow her to the staircase, and grab onto the railing, turning to glance over my shoulder one more time at where the boy sits alone again, cloaked in the night's darkness. I can just make out his silhouette, and I ignore my inner persuasion that begs for me to go back out there and find out what I did to offend him.

Back on the main floor of the penthouse, Mayor Moser's coat check attendant drapes my black coat over my shoulders. My father and brothers position their own coats, adjusting them while they talk amongst themselves.

When my mother ushers me into the waiting elevator and asks me if I had fun this evening, it's with the *ding* of the doors enclosing our family inside that I realize I never even got the boy's name.

Click here to start reading book one of Sly's duet,
Sins of Sorrow